THE DEBT

INSTALLMENT FIVE

THE DEBT

THE DEBT

INSTALLMENT FIVE

YAMASHITA'S GOLD

PHILLIP GWYNNE

Kane Miller
A DIVISION OF EDC PUBLISHING

First American Edition 2014
Kane Miller, A Division of EDC Publishing

Copyright © Phillip Gwynne 2013
Cover and internal design copyright © Allen & Unwin 2013
Cover and text design by Natalie Winter
Cover photography: (boy) by Alan Richardson Photography,
    model: Nicolai Laptev; (shipwreck) by Zena Holloway / Getty
    Images; (shark) by Shutterstock

For information contact:
Kane Miller, A Division of EDC Publishing
PO Box 470663
Tulsa, OK 74147-0663

www.kanemiller.com
www.edcpub.com
www.usbornebooksandmore.com

Library of Congress Control Number: 2013953414

Printed and bound in the United States of America
1 2 3 4 5 6 7 8 9 10
ISBN: 978-1-61067-307-5

To Angus, Cat and kids

GOLD FEVER

"You moron!" I yelled.

"You cretin!

"You utter piece of utter crap!"

As you can see, I was fast running out of innovative ways to insult the Pacemaster 9650MX Pro treadmill.

"You putrid lump of plastic!

"Yesterday's technology!"

Fast running out.

No matter how much I dissed it, all it could come up with, in that annoying California voice, was the usual mundanities.

"You've reached the programmed goal," and "Great workout! Champ!"

In the end I thumped the stop button and stepped off the crappy CPU-deficient lump of cretinoid plastic.

1

It had once told me to turn off all the lights on the Gold Coast. So why wasn't it doing what I desperately wanted it to do: give me the fifth installment, tell me I had to get out there and find Yamashita's Gold?

It had been almost three months since I'd returned from Rome, and I'd heard nothing at all from The Debt.

The day after I'd gotten back we'd had our usual human barbecue at Gus's house and I'd had another letter *A* branded on the inside of my leg.

Meaning I now had *PAGA* emblazoned there.

Which, in case you don't know, is a small town in northern Ghana, near the Burkina Faso border.

Which was yet another reason why The Debt needed to get a move on, give me the next installment to repay, so I could get another letter to add to *PAGA*, so that it ceased to be a small town on the Burkina Faso border.

As I walked out of the room I ran into Dad coming the other way.

In his ironed shorts and his ironed tank top, ready for one of his workouts.

"You were sure making plenty of noise in there," he said, in that annoyingly bland way he had.

So would you if you had to go through what I'm going through.

But, wait – he had been through what I was going through.

"Was it ever like nothing was happening?" I asked.

It was a pretty generic type of statement, but Dad knew exactly what I was talking about.

"Maybe you need to just make it happen," he said, sounding like an ad for some sort of sports product. But then, in a voice that had lost all its original blandness, he added, "Give yourself a good kick up the bum."

I went upstairs to my bedroom.

ClamTop was sitting on my desk, living up to its name: well and truly clammed shut.

I gave it some major lip as well.

"You useless craptop!"

Why wasn't it talking to me, like it had for the first installment?

Why weren't we out there looking for Yamashita's Gold?

We'd captured the Zolt and, more importantly, we'd found out from him where the treasure was.

We'd decommissioned the Diablo Bay Nuclear Power Station, and the waters adjacent to it, previously off-limits to the public, were now accessible to everyone.

We'd acquired Cerberus, the electronic device that supposedly, once adapted, was perfect for searching for Yamashita's Gold.

E. Lee Marx, the most experienced and successful underwater treasure hunter in the world, had promised to come to Australia to head up the search effort.

And I'd read, and reread, every book I could find about treasure hunting, including all of E. Lee Marx's.

I'd watched, and re-watched, every TV program I could find about treasure hunting, including E. Lee Marx's.

I'd devoured every movie I could find that had anything remotely to do with treasure hunting.

I'd been online, lurking at all the numerous treasure-hunting forums. Never posting, though – I didn't want anybody to get even a sniff of Yamashita's Gold.

And pretty much all my thoughts were thoughts of gold.

And pretty much all my dreams were dreams of gold.

And it had occurred to me that my ancestor had the same dreams, the same thoughts, when he came to Australia looking for gold to pay back The Debt. Before he was killed in the Eureka Stockade in 1854, that is.

Once again I entered *E. Lee Marx* into Google on my desktop. Once again I hit return. Once again I got the same results I always got, the last reference from months ago.

If E. Lee Marx was in Australia, then Google

certainly didn't know about it; and if Google didn't know about it, then forget it, it didn't exist, it hadn't happened.

I entered *E. Lee Marx* into Google on my phone, hit enter and – guess what? – got the same results.

I carelessly tossed my phone onto my bed. And then I carelessly tossed myself onto my bed. Closed my eyes.

Okay, I get the irony, if that's the right word.

The Debt was the worst thing to have come into my life. It had almost killed me about a dozen times in a dozen different ways.

But here I was wanting, willing, it to contact me. To give me the next installment.

There's this play we studied at school – *Waiting for Godot*. Let me tell you, it was pretty excruciating. Just two dudes waiting for somebody to show.

And that's why it was so excruciating, because waiting is excruciating.

Thoughts ricocheting around in my head, my arms and legs twitching – it was like my nerves were on fire.

Usually this would be the cue for a run, but I'd given up running. In fact, the last time I'd done any at all was the final of the 1500 meters at the World Youth Games in Rome.

Where I'd come fourth.

But when I returned home I soon found out that I'd been banned from competitive running for a year because I'd "broken team rules."

Mrs. Jenkins, boss of everybody, boss of everything, had had her revenge.

I figured that if they could ban me for a year, I could ban them forever – I'd quit running.

Okay, the posters of famous runners were still on my walls. All the running books were still on my bookshelves.

But I hadn't been for a run since.

"Maybe a break's not such a bad thing," is all Gus had said.

Coach Sheeds hadn't been so casual about it. "Are you kidding?" she'd thundered. "You ran just about the best time for anybody in the world for your age in that heat."

So what, this wasn't a break: I'd seriously quit running.

And, yes, I still woke up at the same time every morning, but instead of having to get out of bed and put my running gear on, I just lay there as the daylight found its way into my room.

My phone beeped.

Again, a surge of excitement: could this be them?

No, it was a text from Tristan. A single word: *swim.*

Which he had even managed to spell correctly.

Instead of running, I was swimming.

And Tristan and I were training together.

Yes, the same Tristan who only a while ago had kneed me spectacularly in the knurries, turning them into mush.

But I'd forgiven him that particular act of ultra-violence because a) my knurries had gotten better and b) if I was going to hunt for underwater treasure I needed to be swim fit.

As for Tristan, us training together was pretty much the ideal opportunity for him to demonstrate to me how much of a superior swimmer he was.

And I guess it's not such a bad thing always to be striving to keep up with somebody who is much faster than you, even if that somebody is a complete tool.

my pool in ten? I texted back.

☺ was Tristan's reply.

Again he'd spelled it correctly.

I got out of bed, checked my emails once more, gave ClamTop one last dirty look, changed into a Speedo and made for the pool. There were no sounds from downstairs, so I skipped down into the kitchen and out through the back door.

There was loud music coming from the pool area. I recognized it as Rage Against the Machine, Miranda's favorite band.

She must be there, I thought.

I was right. I could see her now, stretched out on a lounge chair. Bikini. Book. Sunglasses. She was in vacation mode.

But then somebody else came into view: Seb.

He was dressed in the khaki of the pool maintenance company and he was scooping leaves from the water with a long-handle net, droplets flying, silver in the sun. Then he stopped scooping and said something to Miranda. She put down her book and said something in reply.

I stopped.

It was the first time I'd seen Seb since Rome, and instantly I felt a mixture of emotions, a licorice allsort of feelings.

I felt resentful because here he was talking to my sister.

I felt distrustful because I was pretty sure he was involved with The Debt.

I felt grateful because without him I doubt whether I could've paid the last installment.

But then something occurred to me, something actually pretty momentous: if the old Sebster was part of The Debt, then why not use him to communicate with them?

There was no need for talking treadmills or recalcitrant computers or relentless googling, because here was a real live leaf-scooping human being.

"Hi, guys!" I said, trying, and failing, to keep the excitement from my voice.

Seb smiled at me and said, "If it ain't Jumpin' Jack Flash!"

"You take a happy pill this morning or something?" said Miranda.

"What do you mean?"

"You haven't exactly been the happiest little Vegemite since you came back from Rome."

"Probably jet lag," I said.

"Months of it?"

She had a point – Miranda always had a point – but I wasn't going to get sidetracked.

"Seb, the pool's looking great," I said.

He gave me a funny look.

"I've been swimming a lot lately," I said. "And the water's been perfect."

Another funny look, but I persevered.

"I've been hassling Mom and Dad to let me do a scuba diving course," I said, which was absolutely the truth. If I was going to go searching for underwater treasure, I needed to know how to dive correctly.

"That'd be cool," he said.

"Then I could go diving anytime *anybody* wanted me to," I said.

"Okay, you're officially being weird," said Miranda. "And look who's arrived just in time to stop you from getting even weirder."

The tall, lean shape of Tristan appeared from around the corner, towel slung around his neck, swimming goggles dangling from his hand.

"Great to see you again," I said to Seb. "You've got my number, right, just in case anything comes up and you need to contact me?"

"Sure," said Seb, but it was a pretty tentative "sure," and not for the first time I wondered if somehow I had this all wrong, if Seb wasn't part of The Debt at all.

I walked over to the end of the pool where Tristan was doing some stretches.

"Ready to eat some bubbles?" he said.

I nodded – I was going to eat his bubbles, why pretend I wasn't?

"Let's start off with thirty laps of freestyle warm-up," he said. "Then twenty forty-meter sprints with a five-second break in between. Then we'll take it from there."

"Fine with me," I said.

We dived in.

Even Tristan's warm-up speed was a challenge for me, and after a couple of laps I was struggling to keep up. Losing rhythm, I was breaking form, throwing in an extra breath every now and then.

But I was determined not to let him get away from me.

Because when The Debt gave me the installment, when they asked me to get Yamashita's Gold, I wanted to be swim fit, I wanted to be ready.

After a hundred lengths of the pool, after two kays, Tristan said it was enough, that we'd only have a light session today.

He left and I flopped onto a lounge chair.

On the other side of the pool Seb and Miranda were still talking, though from where I was I couldn't hear what they were saying.

Somehow, I didn't think I had it wrong about Seb – he had to be part of The Debt. But I guess the question was: how much of a part was he? How connected was he?

I was just about to get up when Mom came into view, making straight for Seb and Miranda.

When I'd first arrived back from Rome, I'd been absolutely determined to confront Mom about San Luca.

Was she Californian or Italian?

But exactly the right moment just hadn't happened, and the days passed, and the weeks passed, and that determination weakened. One day I would confront her. But not until I'd gotten Yamashita's Gold.

She said something to Miranda, and I could tell from the way my sister immediately sat up, the way she snatched off her sunglasses, that it wasn't just, "It's a nice day."

Then Mom walked over to where Seb had recommenced work, the net dipping in and out of the water. They had a conversation, though my impression was that it was Mom who did most of the talking.

After they'd finished, Seb took his net and bucket and walked off. Mom had a few more words with Miranda before she disappeared, too.

I walked over to where Miranda, still sunglass-less, was staring off into the distance.

"What was that about?" I said.

Miranda glared at me.

"Hey, I didn't do anything," I said, my hands up in mock surrender.

"She's such a snob," said Miranda. "Despite all that PC rubbish that comes out of her mouth."

"PC?" I said. "Personal computer?"

"No, PC as in politically correct," said Miranda, giving me one of her trademark why-is-my-brother-so-dumb? looks.

"So what did Mom say?" I said.

Miranda rolled her eyes.

"You don't want to know," she said.

Well, I did actually, so I dug a bit deeper.

"Was it about you and Seb?" I said.

Miranda put her glasses back on. She sighed, and then said, "Yes, it was about me and Seb. Basically she wants me to cool it. She says I'm too young for a serious relationship, especially while my studying is so important."

Which all sounded pretty reasonable to me, but I wasn't going to say so.

"That sucks," I said.

"Sucks it does," said Miranda.

It seemed to be the logical end of our conversation so I went back to my lounge chair.

Then my phone, which was in the pocket of my shorts, beeped. Could Seb have contacted The Debt so quickly?

Excited, I checked the message.

Atque ita semineces partim ferventibus artus mollit aquis, partim subiecto torruit igni

I scrolled back to the other message I'd received, the one in Latin.

Discipule, caro mortua es

Which Dr. Chakrabarty had translated as, "Schoolboy, you are dead meat."

This had to be Latin, too!

I guess, with everything else that had happened to me since, I'd sort of forgotten about that dead-meat message. But now I remembered how scared I'd been when I'd received it at school. How I'd wondered whether it had been The Debt or not.

But what did this one mean?

Still in my Speedo, I hurried back up to my room, sat down at my desk, and copied the phrase into Google Translate.

I selected "From: Latin" and "To: English" and clicked on the "Translate" button. The result: *half frame softens and partly boiling water partly roasted over the fire.*

Lovely work, Google Translate. Don't give up your day job.

But it had to be from The Debt, didn't it, some sort of coded message?

I remembered Gus had told me that sometimes half the battle was working out what the installment actually was.

Surely this was it.

But how to get it translated?

I considered my options.

It didn't take long because, really, I only had one: it started with "Chakra" and ended with "barty." I had to find Dr. Chakrabarty.

I wondered if I was the first schoolkid ever in the history of schools and kids who was desperate to see a teacher during vacation.

Especially given that the teacher in question wasn't even my teacher.

But how to find Dr. Chakrabarty?

I started at the obvious place: Google.

There was a Dr. Paramita Chakrabarty who was an expert on neurodegenerative diseases. There was a Dr. Amit Chakrabarty who was a urologist and the winner of seven patients' choice awards.

And there was Dr. K.V. Chakrabarty who I found on YouTube addressing a keen audience at a conference on Systemic Risk, whatever that was.

But I couldn't find my Dr. Chakrabarty anywhere.

What was my Dr. Chakrabarty's first name anyway?

I couldn't remember having seen it anywhere.

Maybe he didn't have one, like Pink, Prince and Warnie.

I tried the online White Pages. No Chakrabartys in the whole of Queensland, let alone the Gold Coast.

I tried my school's website. Dr. Chakrabarty was mentioned as teacher of classics, but there were no contact details for him, no phone number, no email address.

Again I looked at the text message.

Atque ita semineces partim ferventibus artus mollit aquis, partim subiecto torruit igni

It seemed to mock me, taunt me, like the most annoying kid at your primary school: *nah nah you can't understand me, nah nah you can't understand me.*

Now I was determined to find out what it meant. Although I could've posted it on some nerdy Latin forum on the net something told me that Dr. Chakrabarty was the one I had to ask.

Okay, so what else did I know about the shaggy-eyebrowed teacher of classics?

I thought of the two occasions I'd been to his office, how Spartan it had been.

No obvious clues there.

I remembered the conversations I'd heard him have on the phone.

But when I thought about it, there had only been one conversation, and that had been with a telephone company, with Virgin.

I did some more remembering, some more trawling, but that was the only thing I dredged up.

That was the only thing I had to work with.

Dr. Chakrabarty was with Virgin.

Why not start with the obvious, I asked myself.

I called Virgin.

Well, Virgin's answering service.

After negotiating layer after layer of options, then waiting for half an hour, I finally got to speak to a real live person.

"Hi there," said the real live person. "How can I help you?"

I'd already decided that I was going to go with the truth. Well, a version of the truth.

"I really need to get the number of one of your subscribers," I said.

A big intake of breath from the other end.

"That's not going to happen," said the real live person.

"It's not?" I said.

"Company policy, my friend. Cannot, cannot, cannot give out any numeros."

Even by Virgin's jaunty standards, this person was really out there.

Which was sort of encouraging – surely there was a way around somebody as loose as this – and sort of discouraging – maybe they kept all their looseness on the outside and on the inside they played totally by the rules.

"It's my classics teacher at school," I said. "I need him to translate this text I got that's in Latin."

Silence at the other end, and I thought, *That's it, he thinks I'm mad, or I'm talking crap, and he's going to give me another "cannot cannot cannot give out any numeros" line.*

"Latin?" he said, and I knew now that perhaps I was in with a chance if I played it right.

"You see, I got this other text in Latin a few months ago," I said.

"You did?"

"It said, *Discipule, caro mortua es.*"

A low whistle from the other end, followed by, "And this dude translated it for you?"

"He's about the best there is," I said.

"And what does it mean?" he said.

"It's not that nice," I said.

"Man, I'm up for it. You've got to tell me, what does it mean?"

I dropped my voice an octave and said, "Schoolboy, you are dead meat."

He gave a shivery "Whoa," and added, "that's unconscionable."

I wasn't sure what unconscionable meant, but I agreed with him. "Completely."

"So how you bearing up?" he said, and the concern in his voice sounded genuine to me.

"I was doing okay," I said. "But then I got this latest message."

Another "Whoa," maybe a bit less shivery than the previous one, then he said, "what does it say?"

I read it out to him, even though I'm sure my pronunciation was terrible.

"Whoa," he said yet again. "That sounds even worse than the other one."

"I know," I said, injecting what I hoped was the right amount of fright into my voice.

Actually, I didn't even have to do that much injecting, because I was starting to realize just how spooky all this was.

"So who do you think is sending you this stuff?" he asked.

"I'm not sure," I said. "But I'm hoping Dr. Chakrabarty will be able to help me. He knows all about this kind of thing – you know, secret societies and so on."

More silence at the other end.

"If anybody asks you, you never talked to me, okay?"

"Of course," I said.

"So how do you spell his name?"

I spelled out his name and he gave me Dr. Chakrabarty's number.

"This conversation never happened, right?" he said.

"Right."

"And you be careful, okay, kid? There's some weird stuff going down here."

"Unconscionable," I said.

"You got it."

After I'd hung up I sent a text to the number he had given me: *dr Chakrabarty i received another text in latin, dom.*

It took ten minutes to get a reply. *How did you get this number?*

Sprung!

I got online, on to a website with a lengthy list of Latin sayings. It didn't take me long to find the right one.

I entered *extremis malis extrema remedia* into the iPhone, making sure I got the spelling right.

Desperate times call for desperate measures.

This time the reply came in less than a minute. *Ne puero gladium.*

I guess it was my fault. I'd started it.

I put that into Google Translate and got "not boy sword," so I put it into Google and hit search and found out that it actually meant: Do not give a boy a sword.

It was time to revert to my native tongue.

dr Chakrabarty, i'm afraid that's the extent of my latin, I typed, thumbs dancing. *i received another text message can I send it to you so you can translate it?*

I received the reply, *It's better we meet.*

Which was exactly what I'd hoped.

when and where?

The Seaway at six, came the reply.

Did he mean the place where all the fishermen went? Or was there another Seaway?

I was just about to send a text *which seaway?* when I thought better of it – it had to be that Seaway.

It was a pretty unlikely place to meet a classics teacher, but there again, Dr. Chakrabarty was a pretty unlikely classics teacher.

SEAWAY

The bus I caught to Seaway was crowded and I wondered why so many people seemed to be headed in that direction. But when I got there I could see why: there was some sort of rally.

People were holding signs that said *Save Straddie, Save Wavebreak, Save the Spit, No Cruise Ship Terminal!*

There were at least a couple of hundred protestors, and not the usual rent-a-crowd either: these people seemed to come from all walks of life.

Old people, young people, and all of them pretty angry about the plans.

"Two. Four. Six. Eight. Stick your terminal up your date!" somebody chanted through a loudspeaker.

Was Dr. Chakrabarty among them?

Holding up a sign in Latin, perhaps *Ne puero gladium.*

I couldn't see him, however.

I was just about to move away from the crowd, to search for him further down the Seaway, when somebody behind me clamped their hand on my shoulder.

It was a very big hand, and it obviously belonged to a very big person.

"Youngblood!" said the owner of the hand.

I should've guessed: Hound de Villiers, PI.

But what was he doing here? He certainly wasn't the first person who sprang to mind when I thought of political activism. Then I remembered – he lived on the Spit, and probably didn't want a whole lot of cruise ship passengers staring into his backyard while he sunbaked in his mankini.

I remembered something else: the last time I'd talked to Hound it had been to ask him for a favor. I'd dangled the solid-gold carrot that was Yamashita's Treasure in front of his double-bent nose.

"So how's life been treating you?" he said.

"Can't complain," I replied – I can do mundane conversation as well as the next chump. "How about you, Hound?"

"Work's picking up," he said.

We'd exchanged four banalities and still no hint of General Yamashita or his gold.

"If you wanted some work over vacation, Youngblood, I could use somebody like you," he said.

Was he serious?

Yes, he appeared to be.

"I'll see how it goes," I said. "I've got your number."

"Why don't you drop into the office?" he said. "We could go out for Japanese."

He was obviously alluding to Yamashita's Gold, but why was he talking in code like that? Then it came to me: when a large part of your job is covert surveillance, then you're probably going to think that there's always somebody watching, listening.

"Yes, I really like Japanese food," I said. "The wasabi sure does the trick."

Hound gave me a funny look – *the wasabi does what?*

I left him and his funny look and moved further up the Seaway.

I had a vague recollection of walking up here with Dad. Maybe we'd even gone fishing one day. But it must've been a long time ago, when I was a little kid.

I wondered why we hadn't come back, because it was a pretty cool place, especially for dads and sons.

There were boats out at sea, crisscrossing the water. I watched as a couple of scuba divers entered the water from the rocks, disappearing with a flurry of bubbles.

Again I thought of that scuba course – I had to keep hassling the olds.

And there were fishermen everywhere.

Some looked like they'd just wandered down with a rod. Ready to chance their luck.

Others looked like they were waging piscatorial war. They had rods of varying lengths and thicknesses, hi-tech reels that gleamed in the sun, multiple tackle boxes, and a variety of cunning baits.

And very comfortable chairs.

But none of them was Dr. Chakrabarty.

I was starting to think that he'd stood me up – if that's the right term – and I was going to be left here like a shag on a rock – if that's the right expression.

I was just about to text him when there was a commotion from behind me.

I looked around. A short, slight man with a floppy sun hat was holding a rod, and the rod was bent double, and the reel was screaming.

He'd hooked a monster.

He was getting all sorts of advice from the crowd that had quickly assembled.

"Hold your rod up higher."

"Hold your rod lower."

"Increase the drag."

"Decrease the drag."

Eventually the short man in the floppy sun hat rattled off something in a foreign language. Very foreign, like Latin or Ancient Greek.

Chakra plus Barty equals Chakrabarty! Dr. Chakrabarty!

I'd walked right past him. Immediately I was

reminded of the last time I'd seen him – in Italy, on the train to Calabria. And with that memory came a revelation: Dr. Chakrabarty was The Debt! But that was just too much to get my head around. Way too much. So I right-clicked on that memory and hit delete.

The very foreign language worked, the experts offering no further advice. Besides, it was pretty obvious that Dr. Chakrabarty knew exactly what he was doing.

He acknowledged me with a nod when I joined the crowd.

The fish ran twice again, but Dr. Chakrabarty played it expertly, eliciting murmurs of approval from the assorted onlookers.

"Lovely touch," somebody remarked.

Eventually Dr. Chakrabarty said, "I believe we have color."

I looked into the water: he was right, we had color, a twist of silver down deep.

"Dom, if you could assist me?" he said.

"Sure," I replied. "What do you need me to do?"

"In the top of my tackle box there's some pliers – could you get them for me?"

I did as he asked.

The fish was closer to the surface now – it looked like a kingfish to me, and it was enormous, at least twenty kilos.

An even bigger crowd had gathered, keen to see the fish landed.

"I've got a gaff if you need it," one man said.

"Thank you, old chap, but that won't be necessary," said Dr. Chakrabarty.

I saw a couple of people exchange amused glances – *Old chap?*

"Do you think you could handle this?" Dr. Chakrabarty said, indicating the rod. "All you need to do is keep the tip up."

I wasn't sure I could handle it at all, but this was an ideal opportunity to go one up in the favor bank, Hound-style.

"Sure," I said, taking the rod.

I did exactly – or tried to do exactly – as Dr. Chakrabarty had requested, but it wasn't as easy as it sounded. Even though the kingfish was tired it still moved around.

Dr. Chakrabarty, pliers in hand, stepped carefully over the slippery rocks to the water's edge.

Once he was in position he said, "Bring it over here a bit, Dom."

I tried my best, coaxing the fish towards the doctor.

He reached out and grabbed the line and my job was over.

I hadn't given much consideration to what Dr. Chakrabarty was going to do.

If anything, I'd thought that he was going to use

the pliers to pry the hook out of the fish's mouth and then he was going to hoist his catch up over the rocks.

I was right about the first part.

Dr. Chakrabarty delicately removed the hook from the fish's mouth.

And then he released the fish back to the sea.

The assembled crowd found their voice again.

"You idiot!" somebody called.

But a couple of people applauded as well.

When Dr. Chakrabarty clambered back up the rocks he was wearing an enormous smile.

"What a tremendous beast," he said. "Such a pleasure to dance with it."

Okay, that was pretty weird. In what sort of dance does one of the dancers have a sharpened piece of high tensile metal through its lip? But I sort of got what he meant.

Now that the excitement was over the spectators dispersed, and Dr. Chakrabarty rebaited and cast out his line again.

"I never pegged you for a fisherman," I said.

"No, not many people do," he said.

We sat there in silence for a while, Dr. Chakrabarty on his folding chair and me perched on top of the tackle box.

Eventually Dr. Chakrabarty said, "So, Pheidippides, you received another text?"

"You can probably lose the Pheidippides thing now, Dr. Chakrabarty."

"How so?"

"I've given up running and I've taken up swimming instead."

"Pheidippides no longer," said Dr. Chakrabarty, winding in some line. "Then you are Leander, who swam across the Hellespont every night!"

"He did?" I said, thinking I liked the sound of Leander, even if the idea of swimming at night freaked me out a fair bit. "But what for?"

"To be with the lovely Hero, of course."

I was tempted to ask what happened to Leander, but not for long: my limited knowledge of the classics told me mostly people came to grisly ends. That they were pretty much the world's first action films.

Apparently Pheidippides, my previous incarnation, dropped dead after running forty kilometers from the battlefield at Marathon to Athens to announce a Greek victory.

"The text?" said Dr. Chakrabarty.

I handed him my phone.

He took it and read it, his eyebrows dancing, and a look of great concern appeared on his face. If he had written the texts then it was a very impressive acting performance – worthy of an Oscar, and several lesser awards.

"So you have no idea who is sending you these threats?" he said.

Yes, of course I have an idea: it's The Debt, I thought. *But there's no way I'm going to tell you that.*

I shook my head.

"Surely you must have some inkling," he said, the slightest hint of impatience in his voice.

It's The Debt!

But then something occurred to me, something really obvious: perhaps it wasn't The Debt.

ClamTop. The treadmill. Sure, The Debt communicated in unorthodox ways, but they communicated clearly. Catch the Zolt! Turn off the lights!

Obscure Latin text messages weren't really their style, were they?

But then again, maybe obscure Latin text messages were exactly my style, because they were testing me, making sure I was the right person to send in search of Yamashita's Gold.

Besides, if it wasn't The Debt, who was it?

"So what does it mean?" I said.

"It's from Ovid's *Metamorphoses*," said Dr. Chakrabarty. "The myth of Lycaon."

Typical teacher's response, I thought. One that answered a question, just not the one you'd asked.

"And what exactly is the myth of Lycaon?" I asked.

"Lycaon, who was a king of Arcadia, came up with this idea of testing whether Zeus was truly omniscient by feeding him a dish of his dismembered son."

"Charming," I said.

"As a reward Zeus transformed Lycaon into a wolf and killed his fifty useless sons with lightning bolts. Except Nyctimus, the son he served up, who instead was restored to life."

I couldn't even manage a "Charming" now – this was getting too freaky.

Dr. Chakrabarty handed me the phone and said, with an urgency in his voice I had not heard before, "Just delete the thing and find out who is sending them and demand that they stop!"

"Why do you want me to delete it?" I said, looking at the message again. "What does it mean?"

Dr. Chakrabarty sighed before he declaimed – and declaimed was the right word because there was something theatrical in his delivery – "And thus partly he softened the half-dead limbs in boiling waters, partly he roasted in an open fire."

"Whoa!" I said.

"Whoa, indeed," said Dr. Chakrabarty. "But of course these myths predate Judeo-Christian beliefs. Which is perhaps why they are so powerful. And why it would be in your best interests to delete this and find out who is sending these things."

There was something in both his voice and his face that was making me quite scared.

"And you can't think of anybody who is versed in the classics?" he said.

Of course not, I thought, looking at Dr. Chakrabarty. *The only person I know who takes one of your crazy mad subjects is Peter Eisinger. And he is so not the type to send freaky messages about half-dead limbs in boiling waters.*

Finger hovering over the delete icon, I looked again at the text message.

I hit a button, but it wasn't delete.

Then I looked at my watch and said, "I better get going."

"Of course," said Dr. Chakrabarty.

I thanked him and his shaggy eyebrows and hurried back down the Seaway.

SPY VS SPY

From outside I could see that the spy shop was crowded, that there was at least five bikies in there. In full leathers.

There were a lot of bikies on the Gold Coast – you saw them around all the time, and the local paper loved to publicize their exploits.

Bikie War Erupts in Suburban Shopping Center

That sort of thing.

Okay, every year they did do a stuffed toy run to the children's hospital, but apart from that it was pretty much murder, mayhem and the manufacture of illicit substances.

I hesitated at the door – did I really want to get this close to them?

I could feel the urgency waning, the urgency that

had chewed at me through the night, had propelled me up and into town early that morning.

This wasn't a good thing – I needed to track the sender of that text – so I set my shoulders, pushed open the door and walked in.

Hanley, the Kiwi owner, acknowledged me with a nod, before he turned his attention to his customers.

Now that I was in the small shop with five large bikies in full leathers, I sort of wished I wasn't.

They weren't aggressive, or threatening, but they were still bikies, and that part of my brain, the be-scared-of-bikies part, was firing up big-time.

It wanted me out of there, running down the street.

"So this digital CCTV, what's the difference in picture quality with analog?" asked one of the bikies in his scary bikie voice.

"Sixty, seventy percent," said Hanley. "I can give you a demo if you like."

"But you're paying, what, three times as much?" said another bikie, maybe the organization's financial officer, who sported a spectacular handlebar moustache.

The discussion went on and on while I pretended to be engrossed in a pair of night vision binoculars.

Hanley knew his stuff, but it was pretty obvious that he was no salesman.

In the end I couldn't help myself.

"Do you mind if I say something?" I said.

Instantly five sets of bikie eyes were on me.

"The problem with analog is that it's yesterday's technology. And what happens with yesterday's technology is that it ceases to be supported. I mean, have any of you tried to get a VCR fixed lately?"

There were a couple of murmurs of bikie approval – *the kid's on to something here.*

"So even if you pay a bit more now, you know that in the future you will have full support. And like any new technology, you have to jump in somewhere. It doesn't really make sense to wait until the prices come down, because the prices are always coming down."

More murmurs of bikie approval.

Hanley smiled, "Dom's absolutely right there."

The head bikie said, "So what is this, a setup? How much you paying this kid, bru?"

Hanley shrugged. "Kid knows his stuff."

Again I couldn't help myself. "He actually doesn't like the 'bru' thing that much," I said to the bikie.

He glared at me, and then said, "Fair enough."

Turning back to Hanley, he said, "Let's have us some of this new technology."

Hanley's eyes opened wide. "You want to buy the whole system?"

"It's what you've been selling us, isn't it?" said the bikie, looking at me and winking: *we're together on this now, what a crap salesman Hanley is.*

"So I assume you'd like to put that on a card?" said Hanley.

The bikie pulled out a bulging wallet and extracted a selection of hundred-dollar bills, which he proceeded to count out on the counter.

I figured I'd played my part, so I turned my attention back to the night binoculars while they finalized the transaction.

When the bikies had left Hanley said, "Owe you one, Dom."

Which, funnily enough, was exactly what I'd been thinking too.

"Do you know much about text messages?" I said.

"They were invented in the late eighties by a Finnish engineer named Matti Makkonen," said Hanley. "The very first one was sent in 1992 in the UK from a PC to a mobile phone."

"Okay, so perhaps you do," I said, though I knew Hanley wasn't showing off – he just knew stuff, a heck of a lot of it.

"So if you get a text from an unknown sender, is that the end of it, you can never know what the sender's number is?"

Hanley smiled at this.

"Not necessarily," he said, or the Kiwi version of "Not necessarily."

"As you probably know, a text message has a limit of a hundred and forty characters for users," said Hanley.

"Of course," I said.

"But there are also another twenty characters reserved for more technical information like package heading and routing stuff."

I didn't even bother with an "Of course" because I was sure there was nothing "Of course" about the look of absolute pig-ignorance on my face.

"So even though the sender has requested that their information not end up on your phone, it doesn't mean that it's not somewhere on the system."

That, I got. And that got me excited.

"So you can find the number?"

"Me?" said Hanley, pointing at himself. "I was under the impression that this was a theoretical discussion."

One of the cardinal rules of The Debt was that nobody was supposed to help you, but I'd been wondering about that for a while now.

A lot of people had helped me repay the first four installments. Maybe they hadn't realized it, but surely that didn't matter, they had still helped.

And nothing had happened to me or to them, had it?

So was The Debt omniscient like Dad and Gus seemed to think it was?

I didn't think so. Yes, The Debt was powerful; you didn't mess with The Debt. But omniscient like Google is omniscient?

I took out my phone, scrolled to the text message and showed it to Hanley.

He studied it for a while and said, "It's something about hot water and roasting fire, but that's about all I can get."

"You know Latin?" I said.

"Did it at school, but like most things I did at school, I've forgotten more than I remember," he said. "So let me guess: you want to know who sent you this?"

"Exactly," I said.

"So what we'd have to do is forward this to a VOIP phone, which will let me have a closer look at those twenty characters I was talking about. I doubt the number would be stored there, but the name of the SMS center would."

"The SMS center?" I said.

"Yeah, you know how when you send a text to somebody when their phone is off, they get it when they turn it back on?"

"Sure," I said, thinking how exciting that noise is: the *beep*, *beep*, *beep* of text messages downloading, each one of them a reminder that you are somebody in the world, that you matter. Unless, of course, they are from your service provider.

"Well, that's because the text is stored at an SMS center."

I pictured this SMS center, like one of those battery hen places that Fiends of the Earth hate so much, cages full of squawky SMS messages just dying to get out.

"Can I have your phone?" said Hanley.

I handed it to him.

As Hanley set about his business, swapping between my phone and a laptop, he kept up a running commentary on what he was doing.

I knew exactly when he lost me, however: when he started using terms like "SS7 connectivity" and "international termination models."

My attention wandered, taking in all the other stuff on the counter.

There were bits and pieces of hardware, lots of fine-precision tools, a soldering iron and a few well-thumbed technical papers.

The title of one of them caught my eye: "The Use of Multi-Sensor Data Fusion in Marine Archaeology."

Hanley sure was into a lot of weird stuff.

"Not an easy nut to crack, this one," said Hanley.

"So it can't be done?" I said.

"I didn't say that, I said it wasn't an easy nut to crack."

Hanley was so engrossed in his work that when some customers entered the shop he didn't even seem to notice them.

A woman wanted some sort of hidden device to record the supervisor at the pub where she worked because he had been "hitting on her" and her boss didn't believe her.

I showed her what was available and she ended up choosing a pen recorder with a four-gig memory.

"You'll be very happy with that," I told her before she left.

Two kids also came in but, being a kid myself, I knew they were time-wasters so I didn't encourage them to hang around.

Eventually Hanley said, "I reckon we might be there."

"You have a number?" I said.

"I'm pretty sure this is it," he said, pointing to the screen of his laptop.

Two shivers, one starting at my head, the other starting at my feet, traveled through my body and met with a shudder in my guts.

I had The Debt's number!

I could call them, text them, but I knew that wasn't the way to go about it.

"If only I could get an address," I said, thinking aloud, staring at the number.

"Why didn't you say?" said Hanley.

He tapped at his keyboard. He clicked his mouse. Like Miranda, and Imogen for that matter, he seemed to be able to have a dozen things on the go at the same time.

After a while he pointed at the screen, at Google Maps.

"For some reason it's not being that specific, but the call originated from this general area," he said. "You know anybody from there?"

I followed his finger.

Nimbin!

Suddenly I got it. Well, half got it. It wasn't The Debt, after all. But I had to make sure.

I thanked Hanley for his help. He thanked me for my help. It was pretty much one big thank-fest. But once we'd managed to get away from each other, once I was on the footpath outside, I figured it wasn't far from the spy shop to Coast Grammar so I might as well run it.

It didn't take long before it started to hurt, though.

When I told Coach Sheeds that I'd retired from running, among the many things she'd said was that without constant training I'd get very unfit very quickly.

She was right, even though I didn't think I was that unfit – my swimming had improved dramatically – but I guess it was just a different sort of fitness.

Usually, during school vacations, I gave Coast Grammar the finger when I passed by it.

I'm sure I wasn't the only one.

I reckon they should employ somebody to sit there, at the entrance, one of those clickers in their hand, to see how many fingers it received in one day.

At least a hundred was my guess.

Today, however, as I reached the main gates, my finger remained where it was.

Just because it was vacation didn't mean the school wasn't in use – no way.

Coast Grammar was totally into "brokering cost-effective and proactive resource-utilization strategies via co-payment arrangements."

In other words, they rented the joint out.

This week, according to the sign, it was some sort of seminar.

The security guard at the gate stopped me as I went to go inside.

"Your pass, please?"

"I'm a student here," I said. "I need to look something up in the library."

"What, Internet broken?" he said.

"Look, not everything's available online," I said, feeling very Mirandaesque as I did so.

"I'm sorry, but you need a pass."

"So I can't even come into my own school?"

He folded his arms across his considerable chest – security guard language for "no."

"Then I would like to speak to your manager," I said, channeling my mother.

"The principal, you mean?"

"Yes, if he's available."

"What's your name?" he said.

I told him my name, he looked unimpressed, so I quickly added, "My father is David Silvagni."

"Well, my dad's name is Trevor Jones, and that hasn't gotten me very far," he said.

"Could you please just contact the principal?" I said.

The security guard took a couple of steps away and spoke into his walkie-talkie.

As he talked he shot a couple of looks in my direction.

When he came back he said through gritted teeth, "Okay, you can go on through."

I felt bad now, dropping my dad's name like that.

So as I walked past the security guard and into the school I said, "I'm sorry."

"Why? I wouldn't be," he said.

Now, as I made my way past Hogwarts, I was worried that the library would be closed. I needn't have been, however, as it was being used as a lecture room.

According to the sign, Dr. Patrick Wundita was

talking about "Contextualizing Actuarial Solutions." Obviously a hot topic, because the room was crowded; all the seats were taken and there were many people standing.

I could've waited, I guess, but an hour and a half is a very long time.

So, standing at the door, I plotted a route to the other side of the library to where the reference section was.

One. Two. Three. Go.

As soon as I stepped into the library proper I knew I wasn't going to be as invisible as I hoped.

People smiled at me – *Isn't it wonderful to see a young person interested in contextualizing actuarial solutions!* their faces said. They shuffled aside to let me past.

When one man dropped the pad he was holding Dr. Wundita said, "Maybe I should stop talking while our latecomer finds himself a spot."

Now all eyes, and there were a lot of eyes, were on me.

A man with a bow tie stood up and indicated his now-empty seat.

I didn't feel as if I had a choice: I sat down.

The talk went for an hour – it made *Waiting for Godot* seem like a Tarantino movie. When at last, finally, eventually, it ended and people started leaving, I was stuck to my seat, shell shocked.

How could life possibly be this boring?

How did these people let that happen?

It was only when I heard somebody say, "Look, sir, droids!" that I snapped out of it.

It could only be one person – Mr. Kotzur, the head librarian, vice president of the Gold Coast Star Wars Society.

"Don't you have vacation too?" I asked.

"No rest for the wicked," he said.

I wondered what his definition of wicked would actually be: somebody who watched the *Star Wars* movies out of order?

"To what do we owe the pleasure of your extracurricular visit?" he said.

"Could you tell me where we keep the yearbooks?" I said.

"Certainly, walk this way," he said and then started to walk with an exaggerated limp.

If not the oldest joke in the book, it was pretty close to it, but I thought *whatever*, and I copied Mr. Kotzur's limp.

But when we'd reached the reference section he said, "I don't think it's particularly funny mocking somebody who's had a bike accident."

"You fell off your recumbent?" I said.

"I didn't fall off, I was knocked off!" Mr. Kotzur waved his hand at some books. "There they are."

"Great," I said, and I wished my knowledge of

Star Wars trivia was better so I could hit him with some appropriate quote.

Nice tomes, stormtrooper – something like that.

"By the way, they're all digitized, you know."

"They're online?"

"Of course."

D'oh!

But I figured that since I was here I might as well do it the old way.

I guessed that Thor was in his mid to late thirties, that he'd been at this school around twenty years ago. The 1994 and 1993 yearbooks yielded nothing, but with the next book I struck gold.

In fact, they should've renamed the Grammar 1992 yearbook "The Many and Various Accomplishments of the Student Formerly Known as Byron Farr-Jones."

The classics prize. Math prize. Physics prize. Essay award. Dux of the school. You name it, he won it. Not only that, he was a champion rugby player and a rower. He didn't have dreadlocks in the photo, but it was him all right: it was Thor, eco-ninja extraordinaire.

I was actually feeling quite pleased with myself; it had only been the smallest of clues: Thor asking me if Dr. Chakrabarty still taught at the school, Hanley finding that the message had come from that one area of Nimbin, but it had led me here.

Now I had another decision to make: what to do about it?

On the one hand they were only text messages, they couldn't hurt me; but on the other hand I recalled the urgency in Dr. Chakrabarty's voice when he said, "Find out who is sending them and demand that they stop!"

Besides, and maybe this was the real reason: anything was better than waiting for Godot, than waiting for The Debt.

TO NIMBIN, AGAIN

The first time I'd gone to Nimbin it hadn't been a whole lot of fun.

Getting there hadn't been a whole lot of fun.

Being there hadn't been a whole lot of fun.

And getting home hadn't been a whole lot of fun either.

So this time I figured, why make it hard on myself, why not go there in some style? No scuzzy public buses, no taking my life in my hands by hitchhiking – none of that.

I called Luiz Antonio instead.

He answered straightaway.

"Can you drive me to Nimbin?" I said.

"Nimbin is a long way," he said.

"I'm well aware of that. Can you take me or not?"

"At least two hundred dollars."

Yes, I know that generally taxi drivers require money for their services, but because I couldn't remember ever having paid Luiz Antonio for his, this mention of money came as a shock.

"Two hundred dollars?" I said.

"At least."

"You take cards?" I said.

"Of course," said Luiz Antonio in a weary voice.

He picked me up fifteen minutes later from outside Cozzi's and even the black coffee I handed him didn't seem to cheer him up.

"Coffee in this country," he said after taking a sip, "it's not like at home."

"It's not good?" I said.

"I didn't say that – of course it's good. Especially from Cozzi's. It's just not like it is at home."

Now I wished that I had caught the bus, scuzzy or not, because this wasn't much fun either.

"How about some samba?" I said. "Bad feet and a sick head."

"The other way around," he said.

"Yeah, that's right – bad head and sick feet."

Luiz Antonio fiddled with the stereo and the samba came on.

But that didn't seem to work either so I thought, *bugger it, why not ask him right now*?

"Can I ask you a question?" I said.

"You're going to anyway, aren't you?" he said.

"Not if you don't want me to."

"Just ask the question," he said.

"Why are you watching my back?"

"Because you're a stupid dumb kid, and if I don't you're going to end up *morto*," he said.

"Dead?"

"*Morto*."

"But why me?" I said. "Isn't the world full of stupid dumb kids?"

"Not so stupid. Not so dumb."

Enough with the random insults already. Really, was I that stupid, that dumb? Hadn't I managed to pay four installments, a small town in northern Ghana branded on the inside of my thigh as the proof?

"Whatever," I said, and I leaned back into the seat and looked out the window at the rain forest that crept up almost onto the road.

Just as we neared Nimbin Luiz Antonio said, "I am not that man of that night."

"You mean the man who dropped those thugs – you were awesome," I said.

"That is not who I am," he said. "Not anymore."

There were a lot of things I wasn't getting here.

I picked one out.

"But you are, like, totally into UFC. You love that stuff."

"I watch it," said Luiz Antonio. "But I don't do it."

I thought about this for a while.

"So what are you asking me?"

"Please don't put me in the situation where I have to become that man again."

"So don't ask you to take me places? To pick me up?"

"That's not what I said."

I didn't push it any further.

When we reached the center of Nimbin Luiz Antonio said, "Where to?"

"Right here will do," I said. "In front of the police station."

Luiz Antonio pulled up and I took my credit card from my wallet and went to hand it to him.

He waved it away.

"Later," he said. "I wait here for you."

"No, it's okay." I said, opening the door. "You can go back if you like."

He wouldn't go back; he never did. It was just this game we played.

"Okay, I go back," he said.

I got out and he took off and left me in Nimbin.

So what, I thought. *It's about time I started standing on my own two feet.*

Ω   Ω   Ω

It seemed ages since I'd been here last, but it didn't seem to have changed much. Again I got offered several different sorts of drugs from several different pushers as I walked down the main street. The woman in the short skirt and low-cut blouse wasn't on the corner, though, and I wondered if her life had gotten better, whether she was now manning a counter at Centerlink or something. Something told me that wouldn't be the case, however.

I walked past Coast Home Loans, the office I'd seen Dad come out of that day with Rocco Taverniti and Ron Gatto and another man I didn't know, speaking Calabrian like a 'Ndranghetista.

I thought of what Mr. Jazy had said about the housing boom in the Gold Coast, about it being one big Ponzi scheme.

I'm not sure why this had found what seemed like a permanent place in my brain – housing booms and Ponzi schemes weren't exactly major fields of interest to me – but it had.

But I didn't have time to explore any of that further because – big wheels rolling – Mandy was coming towards me in her wheelchair.

I'd met some seriously scary people since The Debt had come into my life.

Hound de Villiers was major-league scary. So were the Lazarus brothers. The Mattners. Not to forget the two Warnies with their liking for testicular electrocution.

But none of them scared me as much as the handi-capable Mandy.

I quickly looked at my watch, smacked my head as if – der-brain! – I'd forgotten something, and spun around and walked back in the direction I'd come.

As far as acting performances went, it wasn't brilliant, but it seemed to serve its purpose because Mandy rolled off in the opposite direction, having given absolutely no indication that she'd recognized me. I watched her disappear around the corner before I retraced my steps.

The café where I'd drunk all the chai that day had closed down and there was an enormous *For Rent* sign on the front of it, graffiti scrawled all over it.

A quick read told me that the residents of Nimbin, those with spray cans anyway, weren't great fans of the local police. Not only that, they had many suggestions as to what they should do with their spare time. And a lot of it seemed anatomically implausible.

Now that I'd made it to the front of the Fiends of the Earth office, I seriously had to ask myself if it was as good an idea as it had seemed a couple of hours ago.

Because it was pretty obvious that I was walking into a big old trap.

The text message had been the bait and I'd followed it all the way here.

As soon as I walked through the door – *snap!* I'd be like one of those mice, legs twitching, head twitching, unable to move, my guts squashed by that steel wire.

Still, I pushed the door to the Fiends of the Earth office – it creaked open.

Wider. And wider.

Alpha and Thor, the two eco-ninjas, were sitting on either side of a desk. Bigger, more imposing than I remembered them. And they were playing Scrabble.

"Bez? No way!" said Alpha.

"The second tine of a deer's horn," said Thor, former dux of Coast Grammar.

They didn't even look up, both sets of eyes on the board.

"That's fifty-two and the game, I believe," said Thor. "Care for another one?"

They still didn't look up – I cleared my throat.

It half worked – while Alpha kept interrogating the board, wondering, no doubt, how he'd been beaten by the second tine of a deer's horn, Thor looked up at me.

His reaction?

Not what I'd expected, which was *Nah-ha-ha, our cunning plan has worked.* I could see surprise, and perhaps anger, and then even friendliness, like I was an old pal who had just dropped in.

"Alph, look who's just dropped in," he said.

See, told you!

Alpha looked up at me, but there was definitely a lot more hostility in his face.

"That second tine of the deer's horn will get you every time," I said.

Even more anger.

"Alpha?" prompted Thor.

The two eco-ninjas exchanged looks, and the anger disappeared.

"Dominic Silvagni, long time no see," said Thor, standing up, offering his hand for me to shake.

Now I was totally confused.

"Aren't you, like, mad at me?" I asked.

Again Thor and Alpha exchanged looks.

"Why don't you sit down," said Thor. "Can I get you a drink or something?"

"Just a water," I said.

Thor got me the water, and I sat down, and so did Thor and Alpha and they explained why they weren't angry with me.

It was all about the planet, you see. Not people and their puny egos.

And my achievement – the decommissioning of Diablo Bay – was a far greater outcome than they had ever hoped for.

In fact, it was a major win in the campaign against nuclear energy.

What they didn't understand, however, was why I hadn't included them in my plans, why we couldn't have all worked together, given that we had the same ideals.

"I'm a bit of a lone wolf like that," I said.

As I sat there, opposite Thor and Alpha, I had a sort of – I'm not sure what you would call it – a revelation.

Maybe we didn't have exactly the same ideals, but I sure shared more stuff with these crazy eco-ninjas than I did with people who were about Contextualizing Actuarial Solutions.

I hadn't set out to decommission Diablo Bay, but that had been the result, and I couldn't help but feel pretty chuffed about it.

When The Debt was repaid, maybe we actually could all work together one day. Free some chickens, or something. But in the meantime there were those text messages to deal with.

"So Dom, to what do we owe the pleasure of your visit today?" said Alpha.

They'd been straight with me, so I thought I'd repay the favor.

"I'd appreciate it if you stopped sending me text messages," I said.

"Text messages?" said Thor, the surprise in his voice surprisingly authentic.

I wasn't about to be deterred.

"Yes, text messages," I said.

A woman came into the office then, and our conversation was interrupted while Alpha dealt with her.

She wanted information about dolphins kept in captivity.

Alpha gave her some brochures, and told her the name of a couple of websites she could go to for more detail.

After she had gone I said, "Is it really that bad for the dolphins?"

"Dolphins are free-ranging, social and highly intelligent animals with extraordinarily sensitive hearing," said Thor. "Do you think being stuck in an enclosure and bombarded with techno music is good for them?"

Actually, I didn't think being bombarded with techno music was good for anybody.

"But the ones in Sealands always look so happy," I said.

"Don't be fooled," said Alpha. "They perform because they're hungry."

"Anyway, let's get back to these text messages," said Thor.

I took out my phone, read out the text.

"No offense, Dom, but that is probably the most appalling pronunciation I have ever heard," he said. "May I have a look?"

I handed him the phone.

"Ah, yes. I remember this well, the myth of Lycaon from Ovid's *Metamorphoses*. I had to do an assignment on it in Year 12. Let me remember. *And thus partly he softened the half-dead limbs in boiling waters, partly he roasted in an open fire*."

I knew it was Thor who had sent the text!

He continued, "Chakra couldn't get enough of *Metamorphoses*, could he?" Thor then went into a really good imitation of Dr. Chakrabarty's theatrical way of talking: "Ovid shows us that it is only through art that we can be released from the suffering we are born into, only art can change us, transform us, meta-mor-phose us."

Thor had been very civil so far and I thought there was no reason not to repay the favor.

"So could I ask you to please stop sending me these messages?" I said. "They're sort of scary."

Thor looked taken aback.

"But I didn't send this," he said.

Was he really that good a liar?

"Yeah, right," I said.

"I can assure you I didn't send this."

Then it occurred to me how I could totally spring him.

I took my phone, went to the number Hanley had found, and hit dial.

The phone on the other end rang, and I smiled.

Soon Thor's phone would start singing, jumping around in his pocket or wherever he kept it.

Except it didn't.

The phone kept ringing until it rang out – no voice mail, none of that.

Thor shrugged his shoulders, as if to say, *Have it your own way, but you'll find out.*

Suddenly there was a noise from outside, the door swung open, and Mandy rolled into the room. When she saw me, her eyes grew wide and angry, and she kept rolling.

I tried to get out of her way, but I wasn't quick enough; Mandy and her wheelchair smashed into me, knocking me to the ground.

I scrambled to my feet.

Mandy had swung around and was about to launch another attack.

"Amanda, stop that!" said Thor, grabbing the back of her wheelchair.

"Let me at him!" she yelled, trying to pry his hands free.

"Just calm down!" he said.

"You can be as Gandhi as you like," she said. "But he put you in jail!"

"Amanda, we are not important!" said Thor. "Think of Gaia."

"Gaia?" I said.

"The Earth Goddess," said Thor.

The Earth Goddess didn't seem to work for Mandy, because she came at me again. I managed to get out of her way. Managed to get out of the building.

As I hurried back along the mall, past the Coast Home Loans office I had a thought: according to Hanley the text had been sent from this area.

But if Thor hadn't sent it, who had?

I called Hanley's number and he answered straightaway.

"How'd you do?" he said.

"Pretty good," I replied. "You know when you said you couldn't be sure exactly where the text was sent from, what sort of distance are we talking about?"

"A hundred meters radius," he said.

Because I am – or was – a runner, I guess I still had a better-than-average appreciation as to what it actually felt like to cover a hundred meters.

My estimate was that the distance from the Coast Home Loans office to the Fiends of the Earth office was seventy, eighty meters at the most.

Why Rent When You Can Buy? Loan Approval within the Hour! yelled the sign outside.

I pushed open the door and a woman on the other side of the counter was talking to a couple.

"So what you're telling us," said the man, "is that we don't need that much of deposit."

"Of course not," said the woman. "We can structure our loans to cater for any income stream."

In her bright-yellow uniform, with her high chirpy voice, she reminded me of a budgie.

I pretended to be interested in a brochure, but I was actually clocking something else: how easy would this place be to bust into?

The answer to that was "not easy at all," especially as I had none of my customary tools with me. No ClamTop, no lock picks.

I'd already noted that the doors were sturdy, the locks high quality and the CCTV more than adequate.

I'd also noted something else, a set of keys tossed carelessly – for my purposes, anyway – on the edge of the desk.

Now all I had to do was get them.

I approached the counter.

The couple were pretty much spinning their wheels.

"So what you're telling us is that we can still get a loan without a huge deposit."

The budgie gave the same answer as before, but I guess budgies are famous for that, saying the same thing over and over.

"Excuse me," I said, putting on my best Coast Boys Grammar voice. "Do you think I could possibly use your bathroom?"

"It's not that sort of place," said Budgie. "There's a public bathroom just down the road."

Just as I'd feared: despite my Coast Grammar

accent, she'd pegged me as the sort of kid who leaves more skid marks on the porcelain than a Formula One driver.

I had one more card to play, and it was a doozy, but for obvious reasons I was reluctant to use it.

"So you're definitely not looking for some crazy deposit?" said the man.

Before Budgie could give the same answer yet again I butted in, "I'm sure my dad wouldn't mind."

"Your dad?"

"David Silvagni."

"Oh, yes, I can see the resemblance now. It's just through that door, love, then to your right."

As I passed the desk, I grabbed the keys, holding tight so they didn't jangle, and continued out back.

I went to the bathroom without going to the bathroom, if you get my drift, and then returned the way I'd come.

"Thanks so much," I said.

"My pleasure," said Budgie, before she turned back to the couple. "That's right, any income stream."

There were eight keys on the ring so I got them copied in three different places – one locksmith and two hardware shops – so as not to raise any suspicions.

Now to get the original keys back to Budgie.

When I returned, the office was empty, and I wondered if the couple had found the right loan for their income stream.

As I walked in Budgie appeared.

"Dom!" she said.

How did she know who I was? Had she already been talking to my dad?

"You know my name?" I said.

"Sure, David often talks about you. You're the runner, right?"

I nodded.

"He's such a proud father."

He is?

"I'm sorry to bother you, but I'm having some tummy trouble and your bathroom was so, you know, comfortable."

"Of course, Dom. Feel at home."

As I walked past the desk, I put the keys where I'd found them. Again I went to the bathroom without going to the bathroom. After what seemed like a respectable tummy-trouble time span, I came out, thanked Budgie, and got out of there.

But now there was another three hours until it was dark, and I could risk going back into Coast Home Loans.

I found the public library, and perused the shelves for the right book. When I'd found it, I set myself up in a beanbag. The book was perfect: wide enough, and tall enough, to hide the fact that I was actually asleep.

When I woke again, it was already dark. Time to

get to work. I headed off towards the Coast Home Loans office.

As I turned into the main street a kid popped out of the shadows; he didn't look much older than me.

"You want some Smoky A?" he said.

I didn't have a clue what that was – not even our drug education programs at school had mentioned Smoky A – and I was sort of intrigued.

"What's that?" I said.

"The best time you ever had," he said.

"What, even better than Disneyland?" I said.

A voice came from behind him, from the shadows.

"Luke, what are you doing?"

I knew that voice.

I want a Cerberus. I want one.

"Anna?" I said.

The shadow seemed to bulge, and then she was there.

Anna.

Gaunt. Eyes sunk right back in her head.

Her sixteenth birthday had been, what, four months ago?

It was like she'd had about fifty since.

"Dominic," she said. I wondered how she knew my name; I couldn't remember ever introducing myself.

Luke looked at me and then at her.

"You know this smart guy?" he said.

Anna said nothing, but stepped towards me.

I noticed the tattoo on the inside of her wrist – I was sure that hadn't been there before.

"You doing okay?" she said.

I nodded.

She smiled – her teeth seemed so white, so clean, when compared to the rest of her.

"You're going to make it," she said. "You have to."

What is she talking about?

Luke had her by the elbow. "We're out of here."

"Let go of her," I said, grabbing Luke by his arm.

"It's okay," said Anna. "He's my bud."

Luke glared at me and shrugged his arm free.

"Anna, what's your number?" I said as they hurried off, but she didn't answer.

I stood there for a couple of seconds. *What to do?* The answer didn't take long in coming. *Do what you set out to do.*

ENTER ONLY

It was break and enter, without the break.

A total five-star burglary experience.

However, I hadn't come to steal anything except, perhaps, the answers to some questions.

I kept expecting it to get ugly.

An alarm system that needed a code? Um, no.

Some sort of motion-detector alarm? Um, no.

Would it prove impossibly difficult to hack into the CCTV system and edit out my presence? Again, um, no.

With my eight cloned keys it was obviously access all areas. None of the seven I accessed, however, proved to be particularly interesting.

I had one key left, but as far as I could see there were no more doors.

I tried to convince myself that it didn't matter, that key rings all over the world had keys that no longer fitted doors. Locks are changed, doors are demolished, but people don't remove the orphaned keys from their rings.

I wasn't convinced, however.

If the text message hadn't come from the Fiends of the Earth, and I was ninety-nine point nine percent sure that it hadn't, then it must've come from here.

It was the only place, within the hundred-meter radius, that I had any connection to.

Maybe there's a door outside somewhere?

I retraced my steps.

I'd finished relocking the front door, when, suddenly, there was a flashlight beam in my face.

It wasn't just any ordinary beam, either; it was one of those lightsabers made by a Maglite. Dazzled, I managed to lock the door, to slip the keys into my pocket.

I could see my assailant now.

A security guard who, according to his uniform, was from NNS Security. He ticked the usual security guard boxes.

Big. Tick.

Burly. Tick.

Really, really dumb. Tick.

"What do you think you're up to?" he said.

I knew I could play the same trump card I played with Budgie – the Dad of Diamonds. But something told me that this was a last resort.

"I was just checking the place out," I said, and I made to walk off.

He did his lightsaber thing, however, and I was blinded again.

"Hey, watch it with that thing!" I said.

"Empty your pockets out," he said. "Nice and slow."

Once again, I quickly regained my sight. Not only that, I was getting pretty irate. Who in the blazes did he think he was?

"Just because you're wearing some Kmart uniform and have got yourself a big black Maglite doesn't mean you've got any special powers," I said.

I could see the anger starting to cloud his features. I couldn't help myself, however.

"This is public property," I said, waving my hand at the footpath I was standing on. "And I've got all the right in the world to be standing on it." I took out my iPhone. "If you don't get out of my way right now I will call the police who, by the way, do have special powers."

The knuckles on the hand that held the flashlight were white.

Again, I couldn't help myself. "Because, unlike people like you, the police actually have to do some actual training."

He brought his arm back slightly, and for a second I thought I'd gone too far, that a Maglite was going to come crashing down on my skull. But the arm returned to its former position, and I knew I'd won this particular battle. I began walking.

As I passed him, he said, "You're going to regret this, Dom."

I hesitated – how did he know my name?

But again my intuition told me to keep moving, to get out of that place. So that's what I did, and as soon as I was around the corner and out of his sight I broke into a jog. Okay, it was more of a run. Okay, it was pretty much a sprint.

Now I had another problem: how to get home.

But I should've known better. As I reached the main street, a taxi glided up behind me. Luiz Antonio had waited for me, after all.

If I was a man of my words, I would've told him to that I didn't need him and his help, that I could stand on my own two feet.

I wasn't that man. My words were as phony as a Double Eagle without the black eye.

I got into the taxi.

And I let Luiz Antonio drive me all the way.

SEALANDS

The next day, when I went downstairs for lunch, Miranda and Toby were already there, already eating.

"Samsoni found this in the mailbox," said Mom, holding up a plain envelope with my name written on it in neat blocky handwriting.

No stamp, no postmark, just my name.

"Analog," said Miranda, looking up from her pasta. "How very quaint."

I took the envelope and opened it to find a single piece of unlined paper, folded into a square.

As I unfolded the paper, I realized that three sets of eyes were on me.

I turned my back, making sure none of my family could read what was written on the paper.

I KNEW YOU COULDN'T BE TRUSTED DOMINIC SILVAGNI, it said in the same handwriting as the envelope.

Immediately I knew who it was from – Salacia, Goddess of the Sea.

Because I could clearly remember the conversation we'd had in Italy.

What's the problem, are you angry with me? I'd asked, after she'd grunted at me.

No, not angry, she'd said. *It's just that I don't really trust you that much.*

There's excited and there's excited! and there's probably even EXCITED, but these were pretty inadequate representations of how I was feeling right then.

You can't text an envelope.

You can't email one, either.

The only way the envelope, as quaint and as analog as it is, had gotten to Halcyon Grove without a stamp or postmark, was if somebody had brought it.

And that somebody had to be Salacia, didn't it?

"So Samsoni didn't see who delivered this?" I asked Mom.

"I'm not sure, you'd have to ask him," she said.

Which is exactly what I did, dialing him up on the intercom.

"No," said Samsoni. "I found it in the mailbox."

It just had to be her.

And if Salacia was in Australia, then surely her father was too. And if he was in Australia it was for one reason and one reason only: to start searching for Yamashita's Gold.

But if that was the case, why hadn't I been given my fifth installment?

Why hadn't I been told about it?

Why?

I was already on the move, my brain telling me to go one place, my legs taking me to another.

Quick, outside.

Quick, into my bedroom.

Quick!

Quick!

I ended up tripping up on my own feet and falling flat on my face.

And if you think there's anything funnier in the whole world than a bit of sibling slapstick, then, sorry, but you've probably got that really wrong.

Miranda laughed so much she almost cried.

Toby laughed so much he did cry.

And I learned the same lesson I'd already learned a million times: don't rush it!

I picked myself up and I took myself to my bedroom. What I had to do now was work out how I was going to get into contact with Salacia, Goddess of the Sea.

I took out the piece of paper, read it again: *I KNEW YOU COULDN'T BE TRUSTED DOMINIC SILVAGNI.*

Why wasn't I to be trusted?

How had I let her down?

But more importantly: how to contact her?

The paper was high quality, the sort they supply in hotel rooms, the sort nobody actually uses anymore. Why would you when you have texts and emails and Facebook?

But it was a clue: she was staying in a hotel, a pretty posh one by the looks of it.

Mom was still in the kitchen, sitting at the table, travel brochures spread out in front of her; Beijing, Beijing and more Beijing.

I started the conversation off in the customary manner, asking her when she was going to China.

"Very soon," she said.

But then I hit her with the real purpose of my visit.

"Mom, what are, like, the ten poshest hotels you can stay at in the Gold Coast?"

She gave me a funny look.

"I'm probably not the right person to ask," she said, and my spirits did an instant nosedive. "Why don't you ask your brother?"

Of course! Why hadn't I thought of that straight off?

Toby was watching some cooking show, and the mere sight of me set him off again.

"Man, that was the funniest thing I ever saw," he said. "My bro, Mr. Bean."

When he'd calmed down sufficiently, I hit

him with the same question I'd asked Mom. This time the answer was pretty much instant and comprehensive – I got a list of twelve hotels.

Back in my room, I googled the first hotel on the list, got their number and called it. After the receptionist had answered I said, "I'd like to be put through to Mr. Marx."

"Do you have a room number for me?" she said.

"No, I'm afraid not."

"Give me a second."

I gave her a second.

"We don't appear to have anybody by that name staying in our hotel," she said.

There were two ways to look at this: either she was telling the truth, or she wasn't allowed to let anybody know that somebody as famous as E. Lee Marx was staying in her hotel.

If the second option was true, then I was wasting my time. But what else did I have? I called the second hotel. Then the third ...

When I got to the seventh hotel, I could hardly believe my ears when the receptionist said, "Is that Mr. Lee Marx you're after?"

"That's him," I said, trying to keep the excitement from my voice.

"I'll just pop you through, then."

The phone rang, and E. Lee Marx himself answered, "Yes, hello?"

I hung up.

I called a taxi.

And I ran downstairs and to the main gate. When the taxi pulled up a few minutes later, I couldn't get into it quick enough.

"The Pacific Regency," I said.

The driver was one of those drivers who thinks you're paying them to talk, not to drive; that the meter is counting the number of words coming out of their mouths, not the distance you've covered. He talked about a lot of things, but he really only had one theme: in his day, everything was much, much better.

We pulled up outside the Pacific Regency and I paid him and was just about to get out when something flashed in the corner of my eye.

Somebody was walking away from the hotel: messy blond hair, tank top and shorts, barefoot.

Salacia!

Driver, follow that Goddess of the Sea! I didn't say.

Out of the taxi, I took off after her on foot.

During my limited time working for Hound de Villiers PI the on-the-job training hadn't been great. I really didn't know much about tailing somebody except for the pretty obvious: you should keep them in sight, while trying to remain out of sight yourself.

Luckily for me, this was a busy part of the Gold

Coast and there were plenty of people to keep between me and her.

When she halted at a bus stop, I started to panic a bit.

Okay, Hound – what did a professional do in this situation? Get on the same bus, and risk being seen?

But when I saw the bus's destination – Sealands – I relaxed a bit. It made sense that she was headed there, Goddess of the Sea and all that. So I waited until she'd boarded a bus, and I hailed a taxi.

"Sealands, please," I said, to the driver.

"Where?" he said.

"You don't know where Sealands is?" I said.

"I'm new to the job."

So I had to direct him to one of the most well-known landmarks on the whole coast. When we arrived, I paid him. Got out. And hoped like crazy that I had this right, that this had been her destination.

Ω   Ω   Ω

"Are you kidding?" I said to the man at the ticket booth.

I hadn't been to Sealands for ages, and my parents had always paid, so the entrance fee was a bit of a shock.

Especially as it was more than I had in my wallet.

"No, I'm not kidding," said the man. "In fact,

I have this medical condition called Nokiddingitis, which renders me unable to kid no matter what the situation."

The ticket man, obviously, was some sort of stand-up comedian, who had to pay his bills by working at Sealands because the world wasn't quite ready for his comic genius.

"Is there, like, a discount available?" I asked.

"What sort of discount where you referring to?" he asked, eyebrows slightly raised.

"Coast Boys Grammar?" I suggested.

"You've got to be joking."

"Miami State High?" I said.

He rolled his eyes.

"Discount for somebody who just loves their dolphins to bits?" I said.

He brought two fingers to his mouth – *you're making me sick* – but then he lowered his voice and said, "Okay, so how much of the folding do you have?"

"Twenty bucks," I said.

The misunderstood comic genius snorted and said, "Who comes to Sealands with only a lobster in their pocket?"

"A lobster?" I said.

"Yeah, a redback, a ruskie, what's the matter with you kids?"

I wasn't sure how to answer this, so I said nothing.

Misunderstood Comic Genius said, "Give it to me."

I gave him the money, and watched as the lobster, the redback, the ruskie, disappeared under the counter and, I assumed, into his misunderstood comic genius pocket.

"You can scoot through that gate over there," he said, pressing a button.

Which is exactly what I did.

The dolphin show started in five minutes and I figured that was as good a place as any to look for Salacia. Everybody, it seemed, wanted a piece of Putih, the first white dolphin to be born in captivity, and the only empty seat I could find was in the midst of a tour group of senior citizens from Yamba.

I scanned the other seats, row after row of faces, but couldn't see Salacia.

Had I gotten this totally wrong?

Would I have been better off just sitting in the hotel lobby until she returned?

I'd been to Sealands quite a few times – what Gold Coast kid hadn't? – and seen the dolphin show quite a few times – what Gold Coast kid hadn't? – and it was pretty much the same as it had always been: there were dolphins going backwards on their tails, dolphins hurtling through the air, dolphins doing the things that dolphins do, or had been taught to do.

Look, I'm not anti-dolphin or anything. I mean, if I had to make a choice between a world with dolphins and a world without dolphins of course I'd choose the former. It's just that I think they're a teeny weeny bit overrated.

So when Miss Saffrron, the trainer, stood at the side of the pool and yelled out, "Putih! Putih! Putih!" and a little white dolphin poked its little white head out of the water I didn't exactly join everybody else there and go ape; my applause was more modest. I didn't even feel the need to record this momentous event on my smartphone, either.

Saffrron then told us how she'd been there when Putih was born, how it'd been the most extraordinary experience of her life. How after that she'd changed her name from Saffron to Saffrron, the extra letter symbolizing the extra dimension that Putih had brought to her being.

More applause. None of it mine. More smartphone filming. Not mine, either.

"And now who in the audience would like the opportunity to get up close to our star?" she said into the mike.

Various hands shot up, including quite a few that belonged to elderly Yamba residents.

But I guess they were never going to choose somebody with a walker.

"The boy with the green cap in the front row,"

said Saffrron, pointing.

There was applause as he made his way poolside, and you could see he was the type of kid who doesn't mind a bit of the old applause. Who always hammed it up during the school play.

"So where are you from?" Saffrron asked.

Green Cap couldn't wait to get his hands on that mike, but just as he took it, somebody ran out from the audience – messy blond hair, tank top and shorts, barefoot – and snatched it from his hands.

The words in my head just had to find a way out. "It's Salacia, the Goddess of the Sea!" I said, in a very loud voice.

"You don't say?" said the lady with the walker.

"Wild animals should not be kept in captivity," Sal yelled into the mike in that mongrel accent of hers.

When Saffrron tried to grab it from her, Sal easily evaded her grasp. Green Cap tried to regain the spotlight by trying to lay a tackle on her, but she skipped out of the way and he ended up hitting the concrete hard.

Chanting, "Wild animals should not be kept in captivity," Salacia ran around the perimeter of the pool.

A lot of the people in the audience were booing but a few other, mostly younger kids, were clapping; maybe they thought it was part of the act.

"Somebody put a bullet in her scone," said walker lady thoughtfully.

It took five security guards to corner Sal, turn off the mike, and cart her kicking and screaming away.

That seemed to be the end of the show because a prerecorded voice, all honey-dipped, came on. "And ladies and gentlemen, boys and girls, we have the full range of Putih merchandise available on your way out. And don't forget our cheeky new range of Putih lingerie."

As I jumped out of my seat people were already scrambling out of theirs, keen to get their hands on a Putih T-shirt, a Putih thong. I pushed through them, managing to just catch sight of the rapidly disappearing security guards. My hope was that they were just going to boot Sal out, but they didn't seem to be making for the entrance.

In fact, they were headed in the opposite direction.

As I followed them past the shark enclosure it was shark feeding time; I could see a huge isosceles triangle slicing ominously across the water's surface.

"That's Cedric," said the trainer to the onlookers. Okay, Cedric's a pretty amusing name. Like Basil. Or Baldrick.

But when the trainer threw a tuna into the water and Cedric lifted his enormous head, showing jaws crammed full of teeth, it wasn't so amusing anymore.

"Ohmigod!" somebody said.

Shocked, appalled and poo-your-pants-scared ohmigod.

The trainer just raised her eyebrows as if Cedric was some sort of try hard show-off and said, "He's the biggest great white shark in captivity in the world."

After the shark enclosure I hit a dead end – a CCTV-ed steel-gated multi-locked dead end.

I knew Salacia was on the other side, but how to get to her?

I looked at the CCTV.

The CCTV looked at me.

I waved at the CCTV.

The CCTV looked at me.

I made various other hand signals at the CCTV.

You guessed it – the CCTV looked at me.

But a female voice came over a speaker, "Yes, can we help you?"

"That girl you have inside there," I said. "She's a friend of mine."

I could hear some sort of conversation going on and then another voice came over the speaker, a male voice.

"Well, that girl is in serious trouble," he said, his voice half-headmaster half-policeman.

If it had been months ago, if it had been before The Debt, I would've probably backed down then. But something happens to you when you've come that close to being sashimi-ed by an oil tanker, when you've climbed over the wall of the Colosseum, when you've been shot at several times.

"Hey, mister," I said, drawing myself to my full height, looking the CCTV firmly in its electronic eye. "My friend did nothing wrong except to say something she believes in. Which, if I'm not wrong, is pretty much a right in this country. So if you don't let her go right now, I'll exercise another right, which is to call the police and tell them you've kidnapped her."

The CCTV kept looking.

A plane flew overhead.

The speaker crackled.

And three figures appeared on the other side of the gate – Salacia and two members of that de-evolved species *Guardias securitas*.

From a distance one of them looked disturbingly familiar. When they got closer, I could see why. It was him, the Buzz Lightyear look-alike, the security guard from the Diablo Bay Nuclear Power Station. Clearly, after it had been decommissioned, he'd gotten himself a job here. If he recognized me, he gave no indication of it.

The gate was opened; Salacia walked through, and straight past me.

"A 'thank you' would've been nice," I said, catching up to her.

"Have you been stalking me or something?" she said.

A kid walked past, clutching a Putih stuffed toy.

"Wild animals should not be kept in captivity," said Salacia to the kid.

"Why did you leave that letter at my place?" I said.

Salacia stopped and glared at me, hands on her hips.

For a second I thought I was going to get a bit of the old "wild animals should not be kept in captivity" myself.

Instead she glared at me some more and said, "If it wasn't for you we wouldn't have come all the way to this stupid country and spent weeks searching for some stupid treasure that doesn't exist and my mom wouldn't have gotten sick and had to go to the stupid hospital."

Okay, there was a fair bit to unpack here – like when my mom came back from her weekly supermarket trip with bags and bags of stuff.

I know I should've asked about her sick mum, I know that's what a normal decent human being would do, but it's not what came out of my abnormal indecent mouth.

"You've been searching for weeks?"

"All because of you!"

"Where?"

"Diabolical Bay!"

It's like in primary school, where they're picking teams, and nobody picks you, except it was about a billion times worse than that.

They'd left me out!

They'd started without me!

After all I'd done for them!

"Sorry, is your mum okay?" I eventually said.

"No thanks to you," she said, and then she added, "but at least we're going home now."

"You're going home? But when?"

"As soon as possible, I hope," she said, and then she took off, running quickly away.

For a second I thought about chasing after her, and explaining everything to her. But I knew that in order to do that I would have to explain everything to myself first.

TO THE ISLAND

When I got back home the whole family was sitting around the kitchen table.

Mom and Dad on one side, Miranda and Toby on the other.

It looked suspiciously like a family meeting to me, one that I hadn't been told about.

Like I said once before, we weren't the sort of family that was big on family meetings, not like the Silversteins, who were always having family meetings. Somebody didn't replace the toilet paper? Call a family meeting. Light left on? Family meeting. No, a family meeting was a big deal for us.

"We've been waiting for you," said Dad but there was nothing you're-in-big-trouble about his voice. "Sit down."

But where? Yes, there were spare chairs next to Toby and Mom, but if I sat in one of them it would make the whole thing uneven.

Suddenly I had this feeling of being excluded, and it was a horrible feeling, like someone had hollowed out my guts.

Excluded from my own family.

And why? Because of The Debt, of course.

And though I certainly didn't think so at the time, I was grateful that Mr. McFarlane, my English teacher, had spent a whole double lesson explaining irony.

"This text," he'd said, "is replete with irony."

Well, Mr. Mac, my life is replete with irony.

And here was the latest example: The Debt was about paying a family debt, but by paying it I was losing touch with my family.

Miranda pulled out the chair next to her, indicating it with a nod of her head.

I hesitated.

"Sit down, Dom," said Mom. "I'll get you a coffee."

I sat down. Mom got me a coffee. The world was a better place. For now.

Once we were all settled again, Dad said, "We have some great news."

He looked over at Mom, did some of that wordless communication that parents are so good at.

She responded by saying, "It really is great news." Though there was plenty of enthusiasm in her voice, there wasn't much in her face, and I wondered how "great" she really thought this particular news was.

I looked over at Miranda.

She shrugged. She obviously had as much idea as I did what this great news was. Or maybe she was still angry at Mom for being a "snob."

I did the same with Toby. Same result.

So they were as out of the loop as I was, which made me feel sort of okay.

"We're going on a family trip!" said Dad.

"All of us together?" said Miranda, glaring at Mom.

That I got – she probably thought Mom was getting her away from Seb. And it didn't seem such a bad theory, because there was something weird about this sudden trip. And then I remembered something else.

"But Mom, weren't you supposed to be going to Beijing?"

"We've postponed," she said, and there was something in her voice that told me that she wasn't entirely happy with this.

"I'm taking a whole week off work!" said Dad.

This hadn't happened in such a long time, since we were little kids.

Yes, we went on trips, and Dad would join us for maybe a day or two, but then he always had to go back to work, so a whole week was something special.

Yes, it was a family trip.

Yes, there was definitely something weird.

But the next question was where?

Toby was already ahead of me. "Please tell me we're going to Paris," he said. "Please."

"Tokyo," said Miranda. "Or Seoul."

"Disneyland?" I offered, displaying a pretty breathtaking lack of imagination.

"We're going to keep it domestic," said Dad, looking over to Mom for some support.

It took a while to come. "Very domestic."

"So we're going to the beach house?" said Miranda, not bothering to disguise the disgust in her voice.

Beach was so her kryptonite.

"No," said Dad.

"Sydney?" said Toby.

Another response of the "no" variety.

"Melbourne?" I ventured.

Yet another.

"Not the outback?" said Miranda.

If beach was her kryptonite, then the outback was her bubonic plague.

"No, we're going to fly to Reverie Island!" said Dad, looking directly at me. "We're swapping beach houses with the Jazys."

To say that the collective response from the Silvagni children was underwhelming is a bit like saying that poo smells.

The Silvagni children were so underwhelmed

that they said nothing. Just sat there, mute, in their underwhelmedness.

"Isn't that just great?" said Dad, and again his focus was on me.

"Isn't it?" said Mom.

I just knew by the amount of energy she was putting into this that she didn't think it was great either.

What was going on here?

Why were we going somewhere where none of us except Dad wanted to go? And why did he want to go there, anyway?

I thought of what he'd said about giving yourself a kick up the bum.

"I'm not going," said Miranda.

"Neither am I," said Toby.

At last, some sibling solidarity.

Reverie Island, miles and miles from Diablo Bay, from where E. Lee Marx was currently searching for Yamashita's Gold, was the last place I needed to be.

Count me out too, I was about to say, but I bit my tongue.

Reverie Island was where I'd learned all about Yamashita's Gold.

Dad took out a piece of paper, slid it along the table towards me.

I caught the word at the top – PADI – and immediately got excited.

"I've booked you into a diving course," said Dad.

Suddenly Reverie Island and Diablo Bay moved even closer together.

Dad pulled out a box and slid it along the table to Miranda.

"We thought this might keep you busy."

Miranda looked at the contents, a tablet.

I could see Mom and Dad exchange glances – had they misjudged this?

But then Miranda smiled and said, "It just might work."

Which left Toby.

I had a feeling that a new, even more improved egg whisk or the latest cookbook just wasn't going to do the trick – they needed to come up with something pretty spectacular to clinch the three-kid deal.

Toby sat there, arms folded over his belly, with a show-me-what-you've-got look on his face.

Mom took out a brand-new Kindle Fire and put it on the table.

"It's got five hundred classic cookbooks loaded on it," said Dad.

"Elizabeth David?" said Toby, looking at it dubiously.

Dad look at Mom.

"Yes, Elizabeth David, and Claudia Roden and …" said Mom, reeling off the names of a whole lot of people I'd never heard of.

"Okay," said Toby.

That was it, the clincher. We were going to Reverie Island.

I have to admit, it was some pretty stunning work from the parental units, especially the male one.

"Oh, and we're going to have some visitors," he added.

Nobody said anything, but our faces must've all been asking the same question, because Dad said, "Yes, it seems like Imogen and her mum might come and stay for a couple of days."

Not possible, I thought. *Imogen's mother never went anywhere to stay for a couple of days.* But hard on its heels was another thought: *Imogen is going to be there! Imogen!*

This was already the weirdest trip we'd been on, anybody had been on, and we hadn't even packed our bags yet.

GIRLY SWOT FROM HADES

Two days later, we'd touched down at the tiny airport at Reverie, the same airport that the Zolt and I had taken off from at the end of the very first installment. As soon as I'd stepped outside, I could feel it in the air, this electric sense of expectation. That devastating nobody-wants-me-on-their-team feeling I'd had after the conversation with Sal had gone. They needed me, they just didn't know it. But the first step to them needing me was for me to learn to dive.

When we'd arrived at the Jazy house Miranda had gone straight to her room, the Bali room, to do stuff on her tablet. Toby had gone straight to his room, the Goa room, to do stuff on his Kindle Fire. Mom had gone straight to the entertainment room, and put her DVD on, the first season of the TV show *Homeland*. I'd previously decided to keep a low profile, so I reread a couple of E. Lee Marx's books.

The next day Dad drove me into town.

"You want me to hang around?" he said as we pulled up outside Reverie Diving.

"No, I'll be fine," I said.

I saw a flicker of disappointment on Dad's face.

"Hey, maybe you should do the course with me?" I said, perhaps overcompensating a bit.

"I could, couldn't I?" said Dad.

I'm not sure why, but I really didn't want him to do the course with me. "Yeah, you could," I said. "It's a pretty intensive course, though."

"Three days, right?" said Dad.

I nodded.

Was he really considering it?

"And the final day is out on the boat?"

"That's right," I said.

He was actually going to do it!

How dumb had I been encouraging him?

Dad's phone rang, and for perhaps the first time in my life I was grateful that it had.

"Rocco," said Dad. "I'll get back to you in five."

Dad wished me luck, gave me a quick hug, and I was able to walk into Reverie Diving by myself.

It was housed in an old wooden building, one of the few on the island that hadn't been turned into a café.

Not that it wouldn't have made a good café.

Because even though it was pretty run-down, and pretty ramshackle, it was run-down and ramshackle in a very cool, very salty, sort of way.

Helping People Go Under Since 1965, said the faded sign at the front.

As I made my way in I noticed a broken window to the right, shards of glass glinting on the ground.

I pushed open the door and the smell hit me straightaway. It wasn't unpleasant, just smelly: a salty, weedy smell. If the shop had been pretty run-down and pretty ramshackle from the outside, it was even more so on the inside.

This place obviously had a lot of history, history that was all over the walls – photos, newspaper clippings – and history that was hanging from the ceiling – pieces of old diving equipment, a set of enormous shark jaws.

There didn't appear to be anybody about, so I took a look around.

Dive Shop Opens on Island, read the heading from a yellowed newspaper clipping.

I didn't bother reading the rest, because it was the photo that immediately had my attention: two long-haired, suntanned men were standing beside some old-fashioned scuba equipment, smiling at the camera.

Partners Cameron Jamison and Dane Zolton show

off some of their new equipment, read the caption underneath.

Now I was interested in what the article said. Really interested.

Childhood friends Cameron Jamison and Dane Zolton have turned their hobby into their profession by opening the first dive shop on Reverie Island and only the second in the whole of Queensland.

"Plenty of history there," came a voice from behind me.

I turned around to see that the voice belonged to a woman, maybe mid-twenties, with shoulder length red hair. She was wearing a wet suit rolled down to her waist and a bikini top.

"So this is the Zolt's father?" I said.

She gave me a blank look.

"Otto Zolton-Bander? The Zolt? The Facebook Bandit?"

"Oh, yes. I hadn't made the connection," she said, in a way that struck me as being a bit phony.

I noticed her accent now – American, but not very.

"Are you Canadian?" I said.

"Originally," she said, stepping forward, holding out her hand. "I'm Maxine, and you must be Dominic."

"People just call me Dom," I said, shaking her hand.

"Well, Dom, we're going to have a great three days together," she said, the enthusiasm bubbling in her voice.

"I'm sure we will," I said.

A police car pulled up outside, and two police, one male, one female, got out.

As they made their way inside I wanted to run like the wind, and not just any old wind, either – one that was very, very quick.

Because one of the police officers I recognized from the day the Zolt and I stole the plane and flew to Preacher's Forest.

I'd seen his face as he drove the car, using the loudspeaker to tell us to stop. But had he seen my face?

"Boss reported a break-in last night," Maxine said to me. "You'll have to excuse me."

I turned my attention back to the wall.

I didn't want the police to have the opportunity to see too much of my face, but I also wanted to eavesdrop on their conversation.

Who would want to break into a beat-up old dive shop?

As they began talking it soon became obvious who would want to break into a beat-up old dive shop: somebody who wanted to help themselves to a whole lot of diving equipment.

"You're not the only dive shop that's been hit," said the female officer. "So could you tell me exactly what was taken?"

"Well, there was definitely a BCD."

"Buoyancy control device?" queried the female officer.

"That's it," said Maxine. "And it was the largest size we had – an extra-large."

"So we're looking for a big thief," said the policeman. As he wrote, the policeman shot a glance in my direction: perhaps literally sizing me up as the potential thief. I figured it was time to get out of there, so I walked through the back door and into the training area. As I did something occurred to me: the Zolt would definitely need an extra-large. What? Was he planning on joining The Debt in Diablo Bay? Unlikely.

A waft of chlorine rose up from the pool. Beyond that, on the wall, a mural depicting underwater life had been painted. Nothing really surprising about that, except for the number of sharks there were.

Maybe the artist liked sharks – and I have to admit they did seem to be more professionally done than some of the other sea life – or maybe they had a sick sense of humor, but pretty much everywhere you looked there was a shark, sleek, streamlined, its mouth crammed with teeth.

I remembered reading somewhere that sharks have remained the same for thousands of years – no need to change when you've got it so right.

As I was contemplating this, and other questions, a woman joined me.

She looked familiar, somehow – where did I know her from?

"So you're here to do the diving course, are you?"

Of course, it was joyless Joy Wheeler from the Australian Labor Party office.

The woman who had showed me the archives that day.

Who had corresponded with Imogen about her missing father.

If she recognized me, she didn't say so, and I was happy enough with that. I wondered if it was just a coincidence, however. Had Ron Gatto, one of the Nimbin Four, sent her to spy on me? Or was I turning into one of those conspiracy theorists who sees a pattern, and a purpose, in everything?

We talked a bit about diving: she'd always wanted to but hadn't gotten around to it, then a friend had given her this course as a birthday present.

She was still apprehensive, however.

I noticed her giving the sharky mural a couple of nervous glances.

We were then joined by the other students: two male Swiss backpackers.

Except they weren't backpackers.

"We are travelers, not backpackers!" one of them snapped at me after I suggested that backpacking must be great fun.

There was the sound of the police car leaving, and Maxine joined us.

"You can all stop looking at the water," she said. "We won't be hitting that till tomorrow."

Groans – backpackers, Joyless, but not mine.

I understood that before you did the practical you had to do the theory.

"Let's hit the classroom," she said.

"Let's!" I said, doing a very good impression of a girly swot from hades.

As you may have gathered, generally the classroom is not my favorite place in the world.

And a quick perusal of any of my report cards would back that up: *Dominic really needs to apply himself more; Dominic is yet to reach his full potential.*

But this was different, this was learning how to dive, and I could so see the use of that: when The Debt came a-knocking I, Girly Swot from Hades, would be so ready.

As we watched the videos, as Maxine went through the theory, I hung on every word.

I pretty much wrote them down as well.

And whenever Maxine asked if there were any questions, I always had a few ready to go.

At the end of the day, my brain was mush; it was just not used to such full-on concentration.

But when the other students had gone, I did what all girly swots from hades do: I pestered the teacher even more.

"So oxygen poisoning happens when you dive deeper than sixty-five meters?" I pestered.

Maxine answered my question patiently, but then she gave her watch a big old look and said, "Well, look at that, I better be getting home. We've got a big day tomorrow."

"So do we have any homework?" I said.

"Just brush up on what we went over today," she said.

Her phone rang. She looked at the number, and walked away before she answered.

But I did catch a bit of what she said: "Well, Bones will have to wait for a while longer."

I'd been so engrossed in the course, I hadn't even thought about how I was getting home, but when I saw the Jazys' Mercedes sitting outside I figured Mom had come to pick me up.

But as I got closer and heard the Rolling Stones pumping from the stereo I knew it was Dad.

"How'd it go?" he said, sunglasses pushed up high on his head.

"Awesome," I said.

I was almost going to add, "One of the best days of my life," but didn't, because I thought it sounded a bit OTT.

"Really awesome?" said Dad.

"One of the best days of my life," I said, completely OTT.

IMOGEN, OH IMOGEN

The next day we hit the pool.

First was the swimming requirement – two hundred meters, any stroke, no time limit.

All the training I'd done with Tristan meant that I was pretty slick and I thrashed out the laps in a few minutes. Then I had to wait for the others to finish.

The Swiss were pretty strong swimmers, but Joy Wheeler seemed to take forever.

She did it all in old-fashioned breaststroke, head high of the water, as if she was scared to get her hair wet.

Still, she did it, so we were all clear to go on to the next stage. To actually put on our BCD and our mask and our fins and go underwater.

Again, the Girly Swot from Hades aced everything: clearing your mask, changing regulators, taking your weight belt on and off.

I did it all.

And that feeling, the first breath I took underwater, was one of the most magical feelings I'd ever had in my life.

Suddenly, I was no longer a slave to the surface.

By the time we finished the day's course, it was just past three. After the others had gone home, I helped Maxine wash the equipment in fresh water and hang it up on pegs.

"Are you this enthusiastic about everything?" she said.

"Perhaps running," I said. "Before I retired."

"Well, it's obvious you're an athlete. But why did you give up? Was it because of an injury?"

"No, I just had a fight with an official," I said, thinking of that particular official, the loathsome Mrs. Jenkins.

As I said this, for the first time since I'd retired, I felt a pang of longing.

Did I miss running?

Of course not, I had scuba diving now.

"It's the real thing tomorrow," Maxine said. "Open water dive."

"I can't wait," I said, as I put the last dripping BCD on its peg.

Again Dad was waiting for me outside.

I got inside the car, we took off, and I told Dad all about how great, how magical, it had felt to breathe underwater.

"You're making me jealous," he said, laughing. "I wish you hadn't talked me out of doing the course, now!"

Had I talked him out of it? Yeah, maybe. Okay, probably.

When we got back to the Jazys' there was another car parked in the driveway.

I hadn't really believed it when Dad had said the Havillands were coming to visit; Mrs. Havilland never went anywhere.

But I walked inside and, indeed, there she was, sitting at the kitchen table, drinking what looked like a gin and tonic. Yes, she was perched on the very edge of her chair, as though any second she would have to get up and go. And she kept taking these nervous glances, her head darting here and there like a sparrow's. But she *was* here.

But where was Imogen?

The last time we'd been together, we'd kissed. But then, as usual, The Debt had gotten in the way, and I'd gotten distracted, and she'd stormed, like really stormed, out on me. Come to think of it, she'd been more like a cyclone, but I don't think you can say somebody "cycloned out on me."

We hadn't talked since, though I have to admit I had done some cyber-spying on her. Which even creeped me out a bit when I thought of it now.

Great, she's not here, I thought. So I wouldn't have to deal with whatever needed to be dealt with.

But then footsteps, and she was there.

She was overdressed, in a dress and jewelry and makeup, but she was still Imogen.

My heart skipped several thousand beats, and I knew exactly what it was telling me: despite all that had happened, she was still *uh uh uh* the one that I wanted.

But, and it was a major but, I had so much other stuff going on.

The scuba course.

And the scent of Yamashita's Gold.

"Hi, Dom," she said.

"Hi, Im," I said.

It wasn't much, an exchange of names, but it was enough for me to know that the storm/cyclone had passed and we were friends again.

I'm not sure if it was my idea, or Imogen's idea, or maybe even one of our parents had come up with it, but suddenly I was taking Imogen for a spin in the speedboat.

Of course, she had to get changed.

Of course, this took forever.

And when she eventually did appear I actually couldn't see how her new clothes differed that much from what she'd been wearing before.

So by the time we got aboard it was quite late; there was maybe only an hour of daylight left.

The key to the speedboat was in the same spot as before.

And I felt really grown-up as I turned the key in the ignition and the monstrous outboards burbled into life.

"Wow!" said Imogen as I backed the boat away from the pier. "Where did you learn how to do this stuff?"

From Tristan, I didn't say.

"Did Tristan show you?" said Imogen.

"Not really," I said.

I wondered what Imogen would say if I told her that Tristan had pushed me off the boat and that he probably would've run me over if he hadn't been, fortunately for me, shot at.

"So where do you want to go?" I said. "It's a great big ocean out there."

"I'd love to see where the Zolt holed up," she said.

I'd probably forgotten, or had chosen to ignore, how much Imogen had bought into the whole Zolt thing. But it all came rushing back: the day the three of us – Imogen, Tristan, me – had gone to Town Hall Square to celebrate the Zolt's escape. I remembered how comprehensively de-triangled I'd been. Well, there was only the two of us today. A straight line between me and Imogen.

"Gunbolt Bay?" I said.

"Yes, that's the name of it, isn't it?"

It was a pretty outrageous suggestion: Gunbolt Bay was a long way away; Gunbolt Bay was a dangerous place; it was the end of the day.

Imogen didn't know that, though; all she knew was that it was where the Zolt, her hero, had holed up for two years.

And even though the sensible part of me said we shouldn't go, the less sensible part of me was really excited by the idea.

Gunbolt Bay – yeah!

"Ride like the wind, Bullseye?" I said to Imogen.

"Ride like the wind, Bullseye!" she said, all smiles.

If I was going to do the me-all-grown-up routine I was going to do it right.

And it was an ideal time for it: what breeze there had been had died away and the water was mirror calm.

"Ready?" I said.

"Ready," said Imogen.

I gunned it, the outboards growled, the boat reared up and for a terrible second I thought I'd overdone it and we were going to flip over and we were going to die.

But the propellers bit into the water, the boat surged forward and we were off, riding like the wind, Bullseye.

Yes, I know I do bang on a bit about how beautiful Imogen is.

Yes, I know beauty is only skin deep and all that stuff.

But every now and then, when I looked behind and saw her sitting in the stern of the boat, the wind tangling her hair, a this-is-exciting smile adorning her face, the monstrous outboards in my heart starting revving too.

"So your mum seems heaps better," I said, yelling to make myself heard over the roar of the motors.

"I finally got her to see somebody," she said, yelling back at me.

By somebody I guessed she meant a psychiatrist, or a psychologist, a psych-somebody.

"How did you manage that?" I said.

"I told her that if she didn't, that if she kept on drinking like she was, I'd leave home."

I knew Mrs. Havilland was a drinker – a few times I'd been around there I could smell the alcohol on her – but Imogen had never said this outright before.

I looked at her, trying not to let all that beauty get in the way.

And it occurred to me that something had happened to her, that while I'd been dealing with The Debt, she'd been dealing with her own version of teenage misery.

The Imogen of the day of my fifteenth birthday, the day I learned about The Debt, was not this Imogen.

But I knew I wasn't the same Dominic, either.

"You really would've left her?" I said, though I was already pretty sure of the answer.

"Idle threats don't really work that well," she said.

"It's still pretty amazing that she's come all the way here," I said. "Is she taking medication or something?"

"Pills galore," said Imogen. "But so is just about every adult on the Gold Coast. That's not the reason she left the house, though."

"It isn't?" I said.

"First, I promised her I would find out what happened to Daddy."

Guiltily I thought of all that information I had on ClamTop, information I'd downloaded illegally from the Labor Party's computer, information that could help Imogen find out what happened to her missing father.

"And that worked?" I said.

"Absolutely not," said Imogen. "Mum totally freaked. She said that there was absolutely no way I was to get involved. She said it was way too dangerous. She said those drug people would come and get me."

Mrs. Havilland had a pretty valid point, I thought.

"So I went the other way: I told her that if she accepted your dad's invitation to come here I would definitely not try to find out what happened to Daddy."

"So you lied?" I said.

"More or less," said Imogen, with the smallest of smiles.

"So how's it going with that?"

"Slowly," she said. "The Labor Party are definitely hiding something."

I was just about to say, "Guess what, amazing coincidence – Joy Wheeler is on my diving course," before I realized how dumb that would be.

The only reason I knew about Joyless Joy Wheeler was because creepy me had snooped around Imogen's emails!

"Watch out!" yelled Imogen.

I looked up to see that there was a boat right in front of us.

I wrenched the wheel and we swerved away from it.

As we passed I saw a stocky figure on the deck, binoculars to his face.

So he was checking us out. Nothing wrong with that, people were always checking each other out at sea.

But even though I couldn't see his face, there was something familiar about him.

"Is it much further?" said Imogen.

"No." I pointed to the dent in the coastline ahead. "That's it there."

As we got closer, I decreased the revs until I was able to kill the motors completely.

Outboards up, we glided into the shore, bump-bump-bumping along the sand.

I stepped out and pulled the boat in even further so Imogen was able to jump from the bow onto dry sand. I tied the rope off on a tree.

"We better hurry up," I said. "It's going to get dark soon."

I helped Imogen up the rock face and then through the rain forest, along the path that followed the escarpment.

As we neared the Zolt's hideout, I couldn't help but feel scared – last time I'd been here some seriously dangerous stuff had happened. But I felt excited, too. The actual Yamashita's Gold may have been in Diablo Bay, but its trail started right here.

There were no sounds except for the occasional bird call from beyond the escarpment.

"It's over here," I told Imogen.

We scrambled over the rise, and there we were: in the Zolt's hideout.

"This is sooooooooooo exciting," said Imogen, taking out her iPhone, snapping iPhoto after iPhoto. "I can hardly breathe."

As we followed the track down towards the cave I noticed several fresh footprints.

How fresh? Were we walking into some sort of trap?

Once inside the cave I recalled how organized it had been the last time I was here. Now it was trashed – obviously it had been ransacked, torn apart in the search for … I'm not sure what. All the homemade – or cave-made – furniture had been smashed. Papers were strewn everywhere. The books ripped apart.

"To think that he lived here, in this very place, for such a long time!" gushed Imogen. "And all this stuff is his!"

Otto Zolton-Bander was actually a bit of a dill, I wanted to tell her. A dill with a squeaky voice. But of course I couldn't.

I noticed the title of the torn book at my feet: *Principles of Helicopter Flight*.

I guess somebody else, somebody more commercially minded, would've collected all this stuff and flogged it off on eBay.

Even though the Zolt was gone – dead or otherwise – his myth persisted. He still accrued Facebook fans, people still posted stuff about him and girls like Imogen still gushed about him. You could still buy mugs and T-shirts, and download songs written about him.

"We should probably get going," I said, noticing the fading light.

"Just a few minutes more," said Imogen as she moved towards the back of the cave, still snapping iPhotos.

I sat down on a rock.

Closed my eyes.

I had this strange feeling, almost like nostalgia – Catch the Zolt had been my first installment, and now it had this distant, slightly unreal, quality about it, like a movie you saw last year.

From the makers of various other blockbusters comes Catch the Zolt, *the thrilling story of two teenage boys, Otto Zolton-Bander and Dominic Silvagni, the lead roles played by Otto Zolton-Bander and Dominic Silvagni.*

I really wished that I could get my hands on the screenplay, because there was still a lot of stuff I just didn't get.

Like that film *Inception* we all saw one Friday night – it had taken hours for Miranda to explain that sucker to me. And even then I didn't really get it.

I remembered thinking at the time of the first installment that catching the Zolt had been about doing society a favor by apprehending a dangerous criminal.

Yeah, right.

Like I said before, I was a different kid back then.

The Debt is a test of your skill, your mettle, your determination, both Dad and Gus would've said. In Chakrabartian terms: *The Debt is Herculean.*

Yeah, right.

I could hear Imogen pottering around at the back of the cave.

I remembered, in Rome, how liberating that revelation had been: *The Debt wasn't some semi-mythical semi-mystical organization; they were like pretty much everybody else in the world; they were just plain old money-grubbers.*

So how much of this screenplay, exactly, did I know?

The Zolt knew where Yamashita's Gold was; he'd had Kwek Leng Hong's coin to prove it.

So The Debt's plan had been to capture the Zolt and force him – by offering a share, by using torture? – to give up this information.

But – and a rather large but – the only people who had actually captured the Zolt were Hound de Villiers and then Cameron Jamison. And it was obvious from the way they were both still pursuing him that he hadn't divulged where the treasure was.

The Debt had had The Zolt for a maximum of two minutes. And even those were on the back of a very noisy motorbike.

So why were they so certain that Yamashita's Gold was in Diablo Bay? And certain they must've been, because the whole of the second installment was based on that, on getting the power station decommissioned.

It seemed to me that the answer to that question was somewhere here. Again I looked down at my feet, at *Principles of Helicopter Flight*.

Suddenly I realized that Imogen was standing by my side.

"Shouldn't we get going?" she said.

"Yes, we better," I said, surprised at how quickly the light had faded.

I was starting to get this panicky feeling – why had I ever brought Imogen to such a dangerous place?

We hurried back along the path, back down the incline and onto the beach.

JET SKIS AHOY!

Imogen sat up front with me.

The sun was setting behind us in an exuberance of splashy color, like some crazy kid's finger painting. And the water before us had a soft golden glow.

"It's so beautiful," said Imogen.

It was, and that panicky feeling had passed – there was nothing to be worried about. And all that crazy stuff that had been going on in my head had been replaced by one simple fact: it was just me and Imogen, the one that I wanted.

Occasionally a strand of her hair would brush across my bare arm, sending sparks of electricity through my body.

"You want to steer?" I said.

"Sure, why not."

We changed positions and she took the wheel.

"Aim for that spot over there," I said, pointing to the distant shore.

"How do you know where to go?" she asked.

It was a pretty good question: how did I know where to go? I guess I just had a very good sense of direction, because I didn't often get lost. Maybe it had to do with the running I did – or used to do. My internal GPS was finely calibrated.

"This is the best afternoon I've had in ages," said Imogen.

"Me, too," I said.

Again a stray tendril of her hair brushed my arm. Again that flurry of sparks.

"Hey, you're going off course," I said, putting my hand on the steering wheel to adjust it.

But just as I did this Imogen changed the position of her hands, and my hand ended up on top of hers.

"Sorry," I said, and I took it off.

"It's okay," said Imogen. "It felt nice."

So I put my hand back over her hand, and together we steered the boat.

The sparks of electricity had now become one continuous current coursing through me.

I wished the boat wasn't going so fast, because I wanted this to last for hours, days even.

"What's that noise?" said Imogen.

I hadn't heard anything, except perhaps the *boom-boom-boom* of my heart, but now that I listened I could hear what she meant.

A higher-pitched sound, maybe two of them.

"Over there," said Imogen.

A Jet Ski. And then another one.

And they were headed for us.

"They might be friends of your family," said Imogen. "Maybe they got a bit worried about us."

Maybe, but something told me it wasn't likely.

"Do you mind if I steer?" I said.

"No, of course not," said Imogen.

I took the wheel, bumped the throttle up to full and headed away from them.

Except I didn't, because they were catching us, and then they were behind us, and then they were alongside us, two bulky figures in full-length wet suits.

The Mattners.

Stop, they signaled.

I looked over at Imogen; she seemed more intrigued than scared.

Maybe it was a good idea to just stop and see what they wanted. Because if I tried to get away from them it would probably get ugly: from what I knew of the Mattners, they didn't like to go anywhere unarmed.

I cut the motor.

The Mattners pulled up at the stern of the boat and stepped aboard, tying off their Jet Skis on our ski pole.

"Long time no see," said the bigger one.

"What's your pretty girlfriend's name?" said the other one.

"My name's Imogen, what's yours?" said Imogen.

I couldn't help but notice that she hadn't said she wasn't my girlfriend.

"Charles," he said. "But mostly people just call me Roo."

"So what do you want?" I said.

"What were you doing at Gunbolt Bay?"

"Imogen wanted to have a look around – she's a big fan of the Zolt," I said.

The truth, the whole truth and nothing but the truth.

"You expect me to believe that?" he said.

"Yes, I do, actually."

"What do you want?" said Imogen. "You can't just pull people up like this."

The two Mattners exchanged looks – obviously she didn't know the way things were done on the island.

The bigger, non-marsupial Mattner picked up an oar and smashed me on the side of the head.

It was unexpected, but not that unexpected, so even though I fell I managed to break my fall.

"Dominic!" yelled Imogen.

Roo now had a gun in his hand; he must've had it tucked into a waterproof pouch in his wet suit.

And the gun was pointed at Imogen.

I managed to get to my feet, hand feeling the side of my head.

Liquid, warm and gooey.

And very, very red.

"Dom, are you okay?" said Imogen, moving towards me. As she did the boat rocked, and she grabbed hold of the ski pole for balance.

"I'm okay," I said.

"So what were you doing at Gunbolt Bay, what did you get there?" said Roo, waving his gun at me.

What was going on in his little marsupial brain?

The obvious answer was not that much, but thinking like that wasn't going to do me – do us – any good.

He thought we went there to get something, but what?

Again, it seemed to me that it had to do with Yamashita's Gold.

"I went to get a map, but it wasn't there," I said.

A smile from Mattner. This was more like it, this was what he wanted to hear: maps and sunken treasure and riches way beyond his inadequate imagination.

"Empty your pockets out," he demanded.

I emptied them out – nothing.

"He could've hidden it somewhere," said Roo. "Hit him again."

"No!" screamed Imogen.

But he hit me again.

This time it was on the other side of the head, knocking me the other way. More pain, but there was no blood, not on that side of my face anyway.

"We don't know anything," said Imogen. "Can't you get that into your thick head?"

Bad move, Imogen. No moron likes to be reminded that he is one.

"She didn't mean that, did you, Imogen?"

Imogen glared defiantly.

I shook my head – *Don't!*

"I take it back," she eventually said.

"Good move, Princess," said the Mattner.

There was the sound of an engine – a boat was headed in our general direction.

"Okay, we're all going to sit down and pretend we're having a good time. No yelling, no signaling, or Princess ain't going to be so pretty anymore."

We did as Roo instructed – who's going to argue with a moron with a gun? – and the boat quickly passed us; the Mattners both kept careful watch on it as it disappeared.

I caught Imogen's eye.

She gave only the slightest inclination of her head, but it was enough.

She had surreptitiously untied the rope to one of the Jet Skis and it was drifting away; something neither Mattner had noticed.

Another inclination of her head, this time indicating behind me, and I totally got her plan.

She wanted us to go over at the same time, for us both to swim to the now-free Jet Ski and then make our escape.

As far as plans went, it was pretty much in the outrageous category; there were so many things that could go wrong. But it was better than anything I'd come up with.

If I'd had the time, I would've been mega-impressed.

The slightest nod of my head – *Okay*. I slipped the key out of the ignition and into my pocket.

"I'm going to give you a minute to give me something worthwhile. But this time, if you don't, I ain't going to belt you."

He turned his gaze to Imogen.

"It'll be your girlfriend who gets her face rearranged. And let me give you a tip, she won't be appearing on *Australia's Next Top Model* once I get through with her."

I looked at Imogen – she was the one with the gun pointed at her, she had to give the signal.

I rehearsed what I needed to do in my mind – basically I had to fall out of the boat, go deep and come up as close as possible to the Jet Ski.

We waited.

A flock of seagulls flew past, the air full of their raucous squawking.

It wasn't much, but it was enough: the Mattners were momentarily distracted.

Imogen nodded.

And I heaved myself backwards as hard as I could.

My bum hit the side of the boat, I threw my legs up high, and I was in the water. One problem: I'd forgotten to take a big enough breath.

I did that now, and then I went under, just catching sight of Imogen hitting the water.

The first part of the plan had worked beautifully – we were out of the boat, we were in the water, but now for the next stage.

Again, all that training had benefits; my lungs felt as big as bellows as I dived down deep.

Imogen was an okay swimmer, but not a great swimmer. Fortunately she didn't have as far to go as I did.

As I pushed through the water, I kept a lookout for both her and the untethered Jet Ski.

A white shape ahead – Imogen.

Her eyes wide, she pointed to her throat. She was running out of breath – she had to come up.

I thought of the Mattner waiting there with his gun.

I put my hand around the back of Imogen's neck, brought her face to mine, her lips to mine, and gave her some of my breath.

Grabbing her hand, I pulled her along.

Now I could see the Jet Ski, but we had to come up on the other side, so that it would provide cover for us.

Now it was me who was running out of breath, whose lungs were afire.

A few kicks more and we were there. We burst to the surface together, gulping air.

Zing.

A bullet went whizzing overhead.

How to climb aboard the Jet Ski without getting shot?

Steadying myself with one hand, I reached out with the other hand.

Zing.

Another bullet, this one thudding into the Jet Ski.

Fingers were now touching the metal of the ignition key.

Just a little more.

I hoisted myself further out of the water.

Another bullet.

Zing.

This one hit the water with a *hssssss* sound.

I had my fingers around the key, and I twisted it, and the motor started.

"Hold me tight!" I told Imogen.

She wrapped her arms around my midriff.

"Tighter!"

She did as I asked.

Even with the motor in idle the Jet Ski was moving.

Reaching up, I grabbed the handlebars, straightening them so that we were moving slowly away from them.

But then the other Jet Ski's motor started up.

They were coming after us!

"Okay, it's time to get aboard," I said, figuring that a Jet Ski wasn't as stable a platform from which to fire a gun. Our chances of getting shot had just decreased.

"One. Two. Three. Go!" I said.

I scrambled on board. Somehow Imogen got on behind me.

I twisted the throttle and we were away, Imogen hugging me tightly.

There was no way they'd catch us now, I thought.

But when I looked behind, they seemed to be gaining.

How could that be? Surely we must weigh less than they did, and the Jet Skis were the same, with the same power.

But were they the same?

Again, I looked behind, they'd gained on us even more.

No, of course they weren't the same: their Jet Ski was a Polaris 650, ours was a Polaris 500. Theirs was obviously a more powerful model. Inevitably they would catch up with us. Do stuff to us. Face rearranging.

"Hold on!" I said. "We're going to drop a U-ey."

Imogen hugged tighter.

I slowed down, let the Mattners catch up even more.

And then, twisting the throttle to the max, I swung the handlebars hard to one side.

The effect was almost instantaneous – we were now headed straight for the Mattners, them for us.

I kept the revs to maximum.

Us for them. Them for us.

An old-fashioned game of chicken.

Getting closer and closer.

Twenty meters.

Fifteen meters.

Imogen was hugging so tight my ribs were cracking.

Ten meters.

Five meters.

Imogen had found a handful of flesh and was squeezing it hard.

Us for them. Them for us.

I could see the grins on their faces.

An old-fashioned game of chicken.

Every survival instinct I had was telling me to get out of the way.

My knuckles were white, elbows set.

Two meters.

Grins on their faces.

I'm not sure who deviated, but instead of colliding full on, our handlebars clashed.

Jet Skis, riders, sent in all directions.

I came up to the surface, and Imogen was right next to me.

"Imogen, you alright?"

She nodded.

"You okay to take this Jet Ski?" I said, pointing; it was only a meter or so away.

Another nod.

I looked at the other Jet Ski, the nearest Mattner to it, did some instant Pythagoras' theorem.

He was definitely closer to it, maybe five meters closer, but he hadn't moved yet.

And maybe he was a competitive swimmer, the Thorpie of Reverie Bay.

But sometimes you've just got to back yourself, don't you?

Without a wall to kick off, getting up momentum was difficult. I got my bearings, took one deep breath, put my head down and swam, pumping my legs and thrashing my arms as hard as I could.

As I did, Tristan's advice scrolled through my head: *Dude, you've got to roll. Dude, elbows up higher. Dude, you got to push that water behind you.*

I knew I had never, in my entire life, swum as fast as this.

I was surfing a wave that I had made myself.

I could see the white shape bobbing ahead.

I could see a black wet suit making for it.

It would be touch and go who got there first.

Dude, I was rolling. Elbows up high. Pushing water behind me.

Hand touched metal – I'd gotten there.

A hand touched my foot – the Mattner was just behind me. Roo.

I pulled myself onto the Jet Ski, managing to stand up, and an enormous hand gripped my ankle.

I spread my legs, found my balance. I turned the ignition, twisted the throttle.

Roo still had hold of me.

The other Mattner was making for us.

The Jet Ski wobbled this way and that.

With relief I could see Imogen ahead, managing her Jet Ski fine.

I pointed down at the Mattner.

She understood, changing direction until she was alongside.

There is really no other way to describe it – she just gunned it and ran her Jet Ski into the trailing Mattner.

Immediately he let go of my ankle and dropped off.

I pointed to the ski boat.

Imogen understood.

We swapped the Jet Skis for the ski boat, figuring that the Mattners were in for a bit of swim, but it would give us enough time to get home.

Neither of us said anything as we headed back, until we pulled into the jetty.

"I'm so sorry," I said. "Are you okay?"

"I'm fine," said Imogen. "But what was that all about?"

"I'm not sure," I said.

Imogen's eyes searched mine and they kept on searching even when I didn't want them to.

"What is going on with you?"

"One day I will tell you, okay? But right now you just have to trust me."

Imogen considered this for what seemed like ages.

"So I guess we need to come up with some cock-and-bull story to tell the olds."

"I guess," I said.

Which is exactly what we did.

We'd hit the shore and I'd fallen forward and smashed my head.

I could tell that Dad definitely didn't buy it. Mom probably didn't, either. But they didn't say anything, and I guess Imogen thought that we'd pulled a pretty major swiftie. But what she didn't know – how could she? – was that it was all part of the game us

Silvagnis liked to play, called Messing with The Debt.

Ω Ω Ω

That night I couldn't sleep.

It was a familiar feeling now, the aftermath of a major adrenaline hit, a lingering buzz.

I was tired and I was sore but I just couldn't find those z's.

Thoughts were whizzing around in my head like bumper cars, smashing into the rails, smashing into each other.

I felt guilty because I'd involved Imogen, because she could've been killed. Or had her "face rearranged." But it had also felt good to share with her just a little of what my life had become. And I kept thinking of that kiss-of-breath I'd given her underwater.

The Mattners probably weren't the most formidable opponents around out there, but we – well, Imogen – had outsmarted them and that felt good, too.

And the biggest bumper car of them all – I felt so close to Yamashita's Gold here; I could almost see its gleaming bars of gold, and I just knew that soon I would be given my fifth installment, soon I would be joining E. Lee Marx.

A few times the bumper cars stopped and I thought, *Here we go, it's off to z-land.*

But then another car would start up and that would get them all going again.

There was a knock on my door.

"Who is it?"

"I can't sleep, can you?"

I got out of bed, put on some shorts and a T-shirt, and opened the door.

Imogen was wearing a T-shirt and men's pajama bottoms.

"You want to watch a movie or something?" she said. "A really, really bad one?"

"Sure," I said. "Can't think of anything better."

I flicked through the channels until I found a movie that seemed to suit our purposes perfectly. It was a kung fu movie called *One-Armed Hero* because – surprise, surprise – the hero had only one arm.

"This looks perfect," said Imogen, stretching out on the bed, face down, pillow under her chin.

"How about some supplies?" I suggested.

"You really are an ideas man, Dominic Silvagni."

I made a guerilla raid on the kitchen, returning with quite an impressive haul of cashews and M&M's.

"He really is amazingly good for somebody with one arm," said Imogen. "They just had this fight where he wiped out about twenty baddies."

We lay side by side, working our way through the supplies, making silly remarks about the movie.

Not that difficult, given that the whole movie was basically one long, silly remark.

When that movie had finished, I found an even worse one called *Monster a Go Go*.

"This really is terrible," I said after a while.

But there was no reply.

When I looked over at Imogen I could see why – her eyes were closed, she was asleep. I removed a fragment of chocolate from her bottom lip.

Made sure the blanket was over her.

And then I, too, went to sleep.

THE HISPANIOLA

When I woke up, Imogen was gone.

I checked my watch.

Nine thirty-five!

The boat for my open water dive left at ten.

Why had my parents let me sleep in like that?

I cycloned downstairs.

Everybody, including Imogen, was sitting around the table, which was laden with croissants and Danish pastries and all those other things parents feel obliged to buy while they're on vacation.

"It's my open water, why didn't you wake me up?"

Mom looked at Dad.

"After your fall, we thought maybe it was better if you didn't go. I already called the dive school."

"Well, un-call them," I said. "I'm diving."

"Dominic," said Mom. "Have you seen your face?"

"I don't care about my face, I'm going diving," I said.

I looked over at Dad.

The croissant he was holding, which his mouth was half open to receive, was poised midair, as if he wasn't quite sure what to do with it.

"Maybe I can go too, just as a passenger," said Imogen. "Just to make sure he's okay."

Dad looked at Mom, then me, and finally the croissant, before he put it back on his plate.

"Okay, if you feel you're up for it, and the divemaster is okay with it, then I guess I better take you."

He looked over at Imogen. "You too, if your mum's okay with it."

Mrs. Havilland took a gulp of coffee.

"It's okay," she said, her voice uncharacteristically forthright, but then it faltered as she added, "but you're not going underwater or anything, are you, darling?"

"No, Mummy," Imogen assured her. "I'm just going along for the ride."

Right then, I wondered how Mrs. Havilland would react if I told her that last night her one and only daughter had been held up at gunpoint, had made an underwater escape and had then driven a Jet Ski at high speed.

"I'm not sure," said Mrs. Havilland, who seemed to be spiraling now into uncertainty.

"For Pete's sake, Beth!" said Dad, his voice full of aggression.

Startled, Mrs. Havilland looked at Dad, and seemed to shrink right back into her chair.

Was she scared of him?

"Maybe you just need to give the kid some space," said Dad, his tone softer.

Something really complex was going on between Dad and Mrs. Havilland, because now she was glaring defiantly at him.

"Of course you can go," she said to Imogen.

Immediately, I called Maxine.

No, of course they wouldn't leave without me, their "star pupil" as she put it.

Yes, of course Imogen could come along.

We said our good-byes, we got in the Jazys' Merc, and Dad got us to the wharf in no time at all.

"Are we going on that thing?" said Imogen, pointing to the steel boat tied up at the wharf.

I could understand her concern. The *Hispaniola*, as it was called, looked pretty old and pretty decrepit, streaks of rust down its steel sides.

Not the sort of thing to get into when you're wearing white linen pants, suede loafers and a silk Hermès scarf?

But Maxine had seen us by then, and was beckoning from the wharf.

"I'm sure it's okay," I said to Imogen.

She smiled, wrapped the scarf tighter around her neck and said, "I'm sure it is, too."

After asking all the obvious questions about my face and me giving the now well-practiced lies, Maxine helped us on board what she told us was a "converted trawler." We were soon on our way, the *Hispaniola* rocking this way and that as it smacked against the waves; it was obviously a tough old vessel.

The two Swiss backpackers – sorry, travelers – thought it was pretty funny; they kept making I'm-going-to-chunder jokes.

Joy Wheeler wasn't finding it quite as amusing, however.

She was pretty green and really did look like she was going to indulge in a bit of the old chunderama.

As for Imogen, she seemed to be in an almost dreamlike state, entranced by the sea, the ends of her Hermès scarf trailing in the wind.

It was only when I introduced her to my fellow pupils that I remembered Imogen and Joyless Joy actually knew each other through email.

I wasn't about to tell them this, however.

Bag. Cat. Out.

"We'll be sheltered once we get around that point," said Maxine, pointing to a rocky outcrop painted with bird poop in front of us.

She was right – we rounded a headland and the water was instantly calmer.

The Swiss looked almost disappointed.

"Where are we?" I asked Maxine, because there was something familiar about this area.

"Not sure," she answered. "We don't usually come here, but Skipper thought it would work with this wind blowing the way it is."

"Maybe I can ask him?" I said.

"Sure, go ahead."

We'd been given a brief introduction to the skipper when we'd boarded the boat, but that had been pretty much the extent of my interaction with him.

I'd noted how much like an archetypal skipper, a seafarer, he looked – like he could've stepped off any sort of boat anywhere in the world in the last few hundred years: a pirate boat creating havoc in the Caribbean, a clipper racing to the fabled Spice Islands, an aircraft carrier dodging torpedoes during World War II.

All wind-beaten and salty and, well, skippery.

Now he was standing, one hand on the steering wheel, eyes on the echo sounder as it transcribed the seafloor.

I was surprised at how jagged the line was – the seafloor was obviously very irregular.

The skipper was concentrating intently, so I didn't say anything.

When the seabed leveled out he said, "Can I help you, son?"

"Was that Gunbolt Bay we passed before?" I said.

"Sure was," he said.

I considered saying something about the Zolt, but decided against it.

"It's where young Otto was holed up," he said.

"The Zolt?" I said.

The skipper smiled, obviously amused by this nickname. "Yes, the Zolt."

"So you knew him?"

"Sure I knew him," he said, eyes back on the echo sounder. "His old man and me, we grew up together."

The skipper eased back the throttle. "It was a different world back then. This whole island was our playground, if you know what I mean. We'd be on our bikes pedaling from one end of the island to the other. Fishing. Shooting. This place was an absolute paradise."

"It sure must've been," I said.

"The hippies moved in, then came the yuppies, and that pretty much stuffed it up."

In the absence of any meaningful response I just went with, "Yeah, right."

"Now look at us, eh? Bones is out of the picture, and CJ practically owns the island."

"CJ?" I said. "Cameron Jamison?"

The skipper nodded.

"And Bones, is that what you called Mr. Zolton?"

137

"Always been Bones as long as I've known him," he said. "Let's be honest, Dane is no name for a bloke."

I thought of that map, *Dane G. Zolton* written on the back of it.

My brain was whirring, trying to put the other pieces together.

"So were you in business with them?"

The skipper gave a wry smile. "I was in the beginning, but you didn't want to get into bed with those two. Top blokes to have a drink with, but that was about it."

The skipper bellowed, "Chuck the pick!" to the deckhand.

We'd arrived, we'd be diving soon, but I had so many questions bouncing around in my head. I picked one at random.

"You said Bones is out of the picture. Does that mean that you don't think he's dead?"

The skipper narrowed his eyes.

"What did you say your name was?" he said.

"Dom Silvagni," I said, but I knew I had to give him something else, something that would explain all these questions.

But what?

"I'm interested in Yamashita's Gold," I blurted. "It's, like, this hobby of mine."

Something passed across the skipper's face and

for a second I thought I'd really done it, that like his seafaring ancestors he would make me walk the plank or perhaps even keelhaul me. I could almost feel the coral ripping the flesh from my body.

But that look passed and he gave me a friendly slap on the back and said, "Another one, eh?"

"Another what?"

"No offense, young man, but another sucker. Do you really think Yamashita's Gold could've ended up in these waters?"

"A lot of people seem to," I said.

"Look, Bones was a mate of mine, probably my best mate. But he was a con man, a snake oil merchant. He invented this Yamashita's Gold at Reverie story, thought he'd make his fortune out of it. And do you know what, it wasn't such a bad idea."

"The pick's down, Skip," yelled the deckhand.

The skipper killed the motor.

"Time to get you fellows into the drink, eh?" he said.

CINATIT

The four of us – the two Swiss, Joy and me – sat at the stern of the boat while Maxine described the dive we would be taking, our first open water dive.

Imogen was inside the wheelhouse somewhere.

I'd asked her if it was boring for her and she had seemed almost shocked by the question.

"Of course not," she'd answered. "I love it out here."

Maxine told us how we would be going all the way to the bottom, which was ten meters.

"Any questions?" she asked.

Instead of girly swot me, it was Joy who had about a thousand of them. All of which Maxine patiently answered. Eventually even Joy ran out of questions and we could get ready.

I'd been keeping a lid on it, but now I could feel the excitement bubbling up – really, my very first open water dive. I felt a great flush of love for Mom and Dad – what a great present, the best ever.

And with this, when the fifth installment eventually arrived, I would be totally prepared to dive on Yamashita's Gold.

I put on the wet suit, slipped into the BCD. Fins.

Went through the safety checklist.

Weight belt.

Regulator.

Mask.

"I'd like Roger to buddy up with Stefan for this dive," said Maxine.

The two Swisspackers high-fived each other.

"And Dom and Joy, you two can buddy up."

Joy looked at me, and there was something in her eyes.

Not sure what it was, but it was definitely there.

Did she think I was too young?

Joy, I wanted to say, *maybe you should check out the exam results. Or do you remember that I'd already swum my two hundred meters while you were still on your second lap?*

Maxine went through the dive yet again. Okay, it was starting to get a bit boring now, and I was zoning out. But I knew she was just doing her job, that she was an amazing teacher. And I was so glad that she'd be in the water with us.

"Any last questions?" she said.

Again, Joy had some.

As Maxine finished answering them I could see that even she was getting a bit exasperated with Joy.

"Joy," she said. "You probably need to stop thinking so much."

Joy gave her half a smile, if that.

"Okay, let's hit the water."

"Just one last thing?" said Joy.

I'm pretty sure Maxine rolled her eyes.

"Sharks?" said Joy.

"I'm afraid if you're going to think about sharks every time you dive then you're probably better off not diving," said Maxine.

Joy thought about this for a while and then said, "Let's go."

The Swiss went over first, and then it was Joy's turn, and then my turn.

Even with all those exercises in the pool I hadn't gotten used to the wonder of diving, of being able to actually breathe underwater.

And here, in the open water, it was especially magical.

Again that flush of gratitude for Dad and Mom, especially Dad, because it was pretty obvious that he had driven this trip – this was a whole new world they'd given me the password to.

I gave Joy the okay sign. She gave me one in return.

I pointed my thumb downward. *Let's go down.*

I got one in return.

So far so good, but it was pretty obvious who was the senior diver here. Me! The whole fifteen years of me.

I felt both proud and worried.

Joy started descending, her legs and arms, strangely uncoordinated; they seemed to be working against each other.

Still, she was moving, and that was the main thing.

I followed, keeping my distance from her thrashing fins.

I checked my meter – we were four meters down. Only six to go.

Then two to go.

When I looked at the bottom below, the patches of sand, the coral-encrusted reefs, fish flitting about, I had this thought that was both very strange and very seductive: Yamashita's Treasure could be here!

It couldn't be, of course – Yamashita's Treasure was somewhere near Diablo Bay, but I still couldn't lose this feeling of excitement and expectation.

But what was Joy doing?

Instead of going down she was swimming parallel to the bottom, towards one of the reefs.

And she was swimming quite quickly – suddenly she seemed to be amazingly well coordinated.

I looked around for Maxine, but she was with the two Swisspackers.

The visibility, which had been quite good before, had decreased a lot.

I didn't have any choice; I took off after Joy, catching up to her just as she reached the reef.

Now I could see what she'd been chasing: an enormous turtle.

It really was pretty incredible – it was just floating there, looking at us, with what looked like a smile on its face.

Okay, I know turtles really only smile when they're cast in a Disney animated movie, but it did look like it was pretty happy to see us humans.

Joy looked over at me and gave me a huge thumbs-up.

It wasn't really the right signal – a thumbs-up means to ascend – but I knew what she meant.

I looked behind – the Swiss and Maxine were out of sight now.

I indicated to Joy that we should be getting back, but she seemed to be totally mesmerized by Disney the turtle.

I gave her arm a tug.

She pulled her arm away and made a *shoo!* gesture that definitely wasn't in the PADI dive manual.

But then the turtle was gone.

Just like that – one second it was there, all turtle-like, and the next second there was nothing but cloudy water where it had been.

I noticed now that we'd drifted to the other side of the reef, and the other side of the reef was a whole lot scarier because on this side of the reef there was a serious drop-off.

Where the water seemed to plunge deeper and deeper.

I remembered the echo sounder, how scarily jagged the bottom had looked.

Again I tugged at Joy's arm – *Let's get out of here!*

Joy turned her face to me, her eyes huge behind her mask.

What had she seen?

It didn't take long for me to see the answer to this question.

The answer to this question was gray, and it had fins, and a mouth full of teeth.

The answer to this question was a shark, and it swam past.

The answer to this question wasn't big, though.

Less than two meters long.

Still, it was a shark, and that part of my brain that dealt with sharks and crocodiles and all potential life-terminating animals acted appropriately.

Get out of there, it said, and I could feel the adrenaline pouring into my bloodstream.

But Joy seemed stunned.

Again I tugged at her arm.

Come on, let's get out of here.

I'm not exactly sure what happened next, it all happened so quickly.

But Joy grabbed me, and she was pushing me down, like she was trying to climb on top of me.

And she knocked my mask askew and the regulator out of my mouth.

I couldn't see.

I couldn't breathe.

I tried pushing her away, but she was holding me tight.

So I unzipped my BCD, and I unclipped my weight belt, so grateful that I'd practiced this in the pool, and let them drop to the bottom.

Without any weight, I immediately started ascending.

And I remembered the training: the CESA, the controlled emergency swimming ascent.

I had to expel air continuously or my lungs would burst.

It seemed to take no time at all before I was at the surface.

The boat was a surprisingly long way away.

Joy broke the surface a couple of seconds after I did.

"Thank God you're okay," I said.

She looked at me. She screamed. And her mask filled with blood.

I thought she was dead, thought she'd done

exactly what we'd been told about a thousand times not to do: when you ascend, don't under any circumstances hold your breath.

Because if you do, your lungs will burst.

I grabbed her mask and slipped it off her face. I could see now that the blood was coming from her nose.

I remembered Maxine telling us that nosebleeds weren't uncommon when you first started diving.

"Are you okay?" I said.

It took Joy a while to answer, during which time I guessed she was doing some sort of inventory.

"I blew it," she said, which probably wasn't the best analogy to use when diving.

I nodded – how could I not, she really had blown it. She'd broken just about every rule in the PADI manual and had almost gotten us both killed.

"There is no way Maxine's going to pass me," she said.

With good reason, I thought.

But then I had another thought, one not so straightforward as the first.

It went something like this: Maxine would only know that Joy had mucked up if I told her. If I didn't tell her that Joy had mucked up, then Joy owed me big-time.

"Not necessarily," I said.

A gleam came into Joy's eyes; I guess you don't hang around the political scene and not develop a retriever's nose for a shonky deal.

"Are you saying we could come to some sort of mutually beneficial arrangement?" she said as she bobbed up and down on the waves.

"That's exactly what I'm saying."

"But what do you want from me?" she said.

I considered waiting to tell her, but then it occurred to me that the best time was right now, when Joy's shameful behavior was still fresh in Joy's mind.

"That girl on the boat, do you know who she is?"

"Imogen?" said Joy.

"Imogen Havilland," I said. "And I believe she's been asking for some information which your organization has been reluctant to give her."

The look on Joy's face said it all: *What in the blazes is going on here?*

"It's a coincidence," I said. "Don't get yourself too hung up on it. All you have to think about is the deal: yes or no?"

Joy took about a nanosecond to reply. "Yes."

"And you promise to give Imogen the information she asks for?"

"I promise."

"Okay," I said. "I'll be back in a couple of minutes."

I took an enormous breath, and I went down.

The fins I was wearing were hi-tech silicon graphite, and the resulting propulsion was incredible, but ten meters was ten meters – a long way under.

As the pressure increased, I made sure to equalize, pinching my nose.

I could see the BCD, the weight belt next to it.

No air left, my lungs were saying.

My brain was telling me that it was time to go up for some.

But I kept kicking.

My hand reaching out, I grabbed the regulator.

I sucked greedily at the air.

Again I was thankful for all the training we'd done in the pool as I put on my weight belt and then slipped into the BCD.

I then made a slow, effortless ascent.

Joy was still there, still bobbing around. Her nose, thank God, had stopped bleeding.

"I think they've seen us," she said. "The boat's coming here."

She was right – the boat was headed in our direction.

We only had a couple of minutes before they arrived.

"Okay, this is what we tell Maxine," I said, launching into a story about following the turtle.

"No mention of the shark?"

"Absolutely not."

Maxine wasn't happy, and who could blame her?

"A turtle?" she said.

"That's right, a turtle."

"Maybe you two need some more time in the pool," she said.

The Swisspackers didn't high-five each other, but they may as well have.

My guts felt as empty as my tank – I should've let Joyless Joy drown!

The skipper, who I hadn't noticed standing outside the door to the wheelhouse, said, "Max, a word if I could."

Maxine disappeared inside with him, returning five or so minutes later.

"I've decided that we'll all go ahead as planned," she said.

"Awesome!" I said.

The next two dives went flawlessly, Maxine diving with Joy and me, not letting us out of her sight.

At the end Maxine said, "Well, congratulations, you've all graduated."

I looked over at Joy. For once she was living up to her name: she really did seem bursting with joy. The look she gave me was of one hundred percent gratitude, and I knew there was no way she would renege on her part of the deal. I felt a bit guilty – I certainly wouldn't want to be Joy's dive buddy if she ever saw a shark again – but that didn't last for long.

But as we headed back to port, Imogen and I sitting together at the stern, I started to question whether I had actually done the right thing. Mrs. Havilland had told her daughter not to get involved; who was I to question her judgment? She must've known just how ruthless the men her husband had been campaigning against were. And, remembering that Joy Wheeler had said that the Silvagnis were once members of the Labor Party, I wondered what Imogen would actually uncover. Could my own father have somehow been involved in his best friend's disappearance?

But these concerns didn't last long.

Firstly Maxine approached, and said, "Dominic, this is between you and me, but we're diving on a wreck tomorrow, and I reckon you'd love it."

I looked over at the Swiss, the Swiss she hadn't asked. Now it was my turn to gloat.

"I would love it," I said.

"Meet here at seven," she said.

And then Imogen seemed to move in closer, the tendrils of her hair touching my arm, generating more electricity than the Diablo Bay Nuclear Power Station, with all its nuclear fission, ever did.

"I'm feeling a bit cold," said Imogen.

"Do you want to go inside?"

Imogen laughed, and said, "Wrong answer," and leaned into me.

Now I got it – I put my arm around her shoulder.

"It's just like in *Titanic*," said Imogen, looking at the boat's rippling wake. "But backward."

"Cinatit?" I said.

"Cinatit," she replied.

And I really wished Cinatit would go on forever, but all too soon we were pulling into the wharf where Dad was waiting for us. He looked a bit wound-up, not as loose as he had for the last few days.

"You guys have a good time?" he asked, as we got into the car.

"Great time," I said.

"Great time," Imogen concurred.

"And tomorrow's going to be even better!" I said. "I've been asked –"

But Dad didn't let me finish my sentence. "Got some bad news, sport."

Sport?

Dad never called me that; I got ready for the baddest of bad news.

"We're heading back to the Goldie first thing in the morning," he said.

"But why?"

"I've been outvoted," he sighed, as if this was some sort of inevitability. "There's nothing I can do about it."

I hated Toby. I hated Miranda. I hated Mom. All

those stinking outvoters. But only for a second or so – that was something else The Debt had taught me: no use wasting energy on stuff that can't be changed.

"That's okay," I said. "I can stay here with Mrs. Havilland."

"They're going back tonight," he said.

"We are?" said Imogen.

"You are," said Dad, and once again I wondered about the relationship between Dad and Mrs. Havilland.

"I'll be fine by myself," I said, even though I knew how desperately ridiculous those words sounded; no sane parent is going to let a fifteen-year-old kid stay on an island by himself, Debt or no Debt.

"We're heading back to the Goldie tomorrow morning," said Dad, the stamp of finality in his voice.

"Okay," I said, but already my mind was shifting up through the gears, coming up with ways to return to Reverie, to get on one of Maxine's real open water shipwreck dives.

As we left the town something occurred to me. "When's Mom going to Beijing?"

"In a couple of days," answered Dad.

"So Gus is looking after us?" I said.

"Gus will be in charge," said Dad, throwing me a look, and a sort of half wink.

Okay, I got it now – tomorrow we'd go back home, but as soon as Mom had gone Gus and I could return to Reverie.

By this time we were driving through what I liked to think of as Zolton-Bander Land, with its scrubby landscape and prefab houses on blocks and rusted out vehicles everywhere.

The day on the water had obviously taken it out of Imogen, because she'd fallen asleep in the backseat.

I remembered what Tristan had said the first time I'd driven through here: *Somebody should drop a bomb on them.*

Suddenly I had an idea.

"Dad, can you drop me off here?" I said.

He looked around, obviously not impressed by what he saw. When he opened his mouth I was sure he was going to say something like, "What do you want to do here?" or "I don't think that's a great idea."

But instead he said, "Of course, if that's what you need to do."

I nodded – that's what I needed to do.

"So you'll be fine to get home?" he said.

"I'll be fine," I said. "And can you tell Imogen I just wanted to go for a run?"

I watched him take off, and then walked towards the Banders' trailer.

Ever since the crazy visit to Gunbolt Bay yesterday, something had been flitting about at the edge of my consciousness.

Every now and then I would almost catch a glimpse of it, and I would think *got you!* But then it would disappear out of view again.

It was something about the Zolt, about Yamashita's Gold, some connection I hadn't made, and it was driving me crazy.

So why not come here, I'd reasoned. To the Zolt's other home.

As I passed the old mud brick community center, I remembered the first time I'd been here. How it had been Hound de Villiers's idea. And then all that happened after fast-forwarded through my head.

But then something occurred to me. I'd been less than welcome that time; what made me think anything was going to change this time?

Zoe and I hadn't exactly parted on the best terms when I'd last seen her.

I'd pretty much stolen Mrs. Bander's son from her.

And what about the Mattners?

Was I crazy walking into a place like this unarmed, unannounced? Just because I suddenly had this mad hunch?

An unseen dog growled. And then another one.

Brain wave: *I'll give Zoe a call! Tell her that I'm here.*

But as I went to take the phone out of my pocket, it rang.

Zoe calling …

What the?

I answered it.

"Don't go one step further!" she said.

"But how do you know where I am?" I said, looking around.

Just as I'd suspected, there was a CCTV camera on a nearby lamppost.

Paranoid, much? I thought.

But it occurred to me that a much better question was *Paranoid, why?*

What, or who, were they hiding?

"I'll be there in a minute," said Zoe.

The urgency in her voice and the thought of two angry Mattners, marsupial and non-marsupial, was enough to keep me rooted to the spot.

True to her word, she arrived a minute later.

She looked a whole lot taller than the last time I'd seen her. And she'd lost the Heidi braids; her hair now hung loose over her shoulders. She had also acquired a more stylish pair of glasses. And she had what looked suspiciously like a tan – had Zoe been spending time outdoors?

"Wow, makeover," I said.

"Shut up," she said, with a nervous glance behind her. "Follow me!"

I was in no position to argue, so I did as she said. Initially we retraced my steps down the path, but when we reached the ruined community hall she diverged to the right.

The path wound through what looked like a series of old flower beds until we reached a wooden building.

Circular, with a domed roof, it looked like something a nomad would live in.

"Wow," I said. "What's this place?"

"It's the yurt," said Zoe.

I couldn't help laughing.

"What's so funny?"

"Yurt – it sounds like low-fat yogurt or something."

"No, it doesn't," said Zoe. "It sounds like yurt."

For the first time I realized something: Zoe actually had no sense of humor. Zero. Zilch. She and Salacia could form a comedy duo, except there would be no comedy. The audience could sit there, not laughing.

"Anyway," she said, "let's go inside."

I followed her as she pushed open the creaky door and we entered the yurt.

It was pretty scungy – broken floorboards and rat poo everywhere – but I could see how once it might've been a cool place.

"This used to be the meditation center," she said. "Back when everybody was a hippie."

"Everybody?" I said, trying to imagine Mrs.

Bander in beads and a tie-dyed T-shirt spreading a bit of peace, love and understanding.

"You know what I mean," she said. "Anyway, how's the scuba diving course going?"

What, was I suddenly on *Big Brother*? Were there people all over Australia betting as to when I would get voted out of the house … sorry, the yurt?

"How do you know all this stuff?"

"Reverie's a small island," said Zoe, but then her tone suddenly changed, became less combative. "So why are you doing a course here, anyway?"

"My dad arranged it," I said.

It was my turn to do some digging.

"Who would've thought that your dad and Cameron Jamison were once in business together?"

"Not my dad," said Zoe.

"He wasn't your dad?" I said, feeling like a bit of an idiot – all the research I'd done on the Zolt, and I hadn't known this.

Zoe shook her head.

"But your name's Zolton-Bander," I said.

"So what?" she said. "I could call myself Beyoncé if I wanted to."

"Otto's your half brother, then?"

"Yes, logically that would follow."

"But who's your father?" I said.

"None of your business," said Zoe, but again that change of tone. "No offense."

There was a question that had been bugging me for a while, but I'd been too polite – if that's the right word – to ask it. Now that I knew that Zoe wasn't actually Dane Zolton's daughter, I had no such qualms, however.

"So what actually happened to Otto's dad?" I said.

"He died," said Zoe.

"But how?" I persevered. "I couldn't find much info on it."

"You're like a dog with a bone, you are," she said. "He disappeared, okay? While he was out diving."

"Disappeared?" I repeated. "So there was never any body found?"

Zoe nodded.

"No bones," she said.

"Bones?"

"Bones. Body. You know what I mean," she said, and again that tone change. "So what was Italy like?"

How in the blazes did she know that I'd been to Italy?

"It was pretty cool," I said. "Very Italian."

Zoe opened and closed her mouth a few times, as if she was going to say something, but thought better of it.

Finally she said, with a wave of her hand, "I suppose you've heard that E. Lee Marx fellow is out there, somewhere, searching for treasure."

"Yeah, I heard that," I said.

What game was Zoe playing here?

"He must have a pretty good idea where it is, then?" she said.

Suddenly that something that had been flitting about at the edge of my consciousness came into focus.

It was that movie again, *Catch the Zolt.*

Our hero Dominic Silvagni is in the Zolt's lair, and in his hands is a map, or a chart, because it's of the ocean not the land.

It's covered in pencil marks; some of these marks are numbers, but others are weird hieroglyphics.

"This is like a diary or something," says the bad guy Tristan Jazy (played by bad guy Tristan Jazy) from nearby.

Dom looks up to see that Tristan is reading from a small notebook.

Dom folds the map back up and puts it on the top of a pile. As he does, he notices that it has a name written on it in faint pen: Dane G. Zolton.

Soon after that – gunshots! – and the boys make their Indiana-Jones-like escape from the cave, the cave that is subsequently ransacked by … The Debt?

I looked over at Zoe; her mouth was moving, she was obviously talking, but none of her words had made it to my neocortex.

"Sorry, did you say something?" I said.

"Look, Dom, I don't think you're such a bad person," said Zoe.

Shucks, thanks, Zoe.

"But there are quite a few people on the island who hate your guts."

"Like who?" I said. Nobody likes to be hated, especially when it's your guts that are involved. "Give me names."

"My uncle, the one whose car you bulldozed."

"You bulldozed it, not me."

"Whatever, he pretty much wants to kill you. Come to think of it, my mum's not keen on you either."

"No offense, but I'm not exactly president of her fan club, myself," I said.

"And let's not forget the Mattners," she said.

It was a small island – for sure she would know about yesterday's Jet Ski tango.

"I suggest you lie real low," she said. "Do your scuba classes, go back home and do what you rich people do when you're home."

Makeover or what? New hair, new glasses, and new 'tude; now she was handing out advice to people several years older than her.

"And if I don't?" I said.

Zoe shook her head, took out her phone, put it on speaker and dialed a number.

"Hi, Roo," she said.

"What do you want?" he barked.

"You know that kid in the speedboat?"

"Dominic freaking Silvagni," said the Mattner, and the sound of *my* name coming from *his* mouth sent a wobble through me. "You know where he is?"

Zoe hung up then.

She'd made her point, and she'd made it really well.

"Actually, it doesn't really matter anyway," I said. "We're leaving tomorrow morning."

"You are?" she said, and for pretty much the first time in our conversation I had the sense that at last I knew something that she didn't. "But I thought you were going to be here for a week?"

"Tomorrow. Leave. Us." I said.

Something told me that now was also the time to depart Zolton-Bander Land, while I still had all my teeth, and the upper hand as far as who-knows-what goes.

I took out my iPhone. "Is that the time?" I said, "I really need to get home."

Outside, Zoe pointed to a path and said, "That'll lead you back to the main road."

I was just about to take it when I had a thought.

"So how's your brother?" I said, my eyes searching her face.

"My brother's dead," she said, throwing me a pathetically mournful look. "Don't you watch the news?"

"No, he's not!" I said. "You told me that yourself, that day in the hospital."

"Well, he's dead to me!" she said, as she took off down the path.

No, Otto Zolton Bander wasn't dead. In fact, I had this feeling that he was on this very island. And not so far away, either. I thought of the CCTV on the lamppost. Blazing bells and buckets of blood – maybe he'd even been watching me!

By the time I got back to the main road, it was getting dark.

Suddenly I realized how vulnerable I was, standing here by myself.

If a Mattner came along, or any of the islanders who, supposedly, hated my guts ...

I was taking out my phone to call my dad, to ask him if he could pick me up, when a Ferrari came out of nowhere, Ferrari-ing past me in a flash of red.

I looked around for a suitable hiding place, but the Ferrari had done exactly what I'd hoped it wouldn't: it had braked, it had reversed, and it was now next to me.

The passenger window whizzed down, revealing the only occupant of the car, the driver. My dad's age. Designer shades. Rolex on wrist. Confident hair. Cameron Jamison.

The testicular torturer.

"Dominic," he said. "What you doing stuck out here like a shag on a rock?"

It was a good question.

I didn't have a good answer.

"Get in," he said. "I'll give you a ride home."

"My dad's going to pick me up," I lied.

"Well, give him a call and save him the trip," said Cameron Jamison. "Trust me, this is no place to be on your Pat Malone."

This all sounded very reasonable; I didn't feel as if I could say no. Besides, he was right: this was no place to be on my Pat Malone.

So I sent a text to my dad: *home soon*, and I got into the Ferrari.

As I did I made a quick inventory of its contents.

No Warnie masks, no instruments of testicular torture, but the same book on the floor as last time I got a ride. *Gold Warriors: America's Secret Recovery of Yamashita's Gold.*

Cameron Jamison was soon hammering the Ferrari through the turns.

I picked the book up, turned it around in my hands.

My phone beeped a return text from Dad: *great*.

"Dad says thanks," I said.

"No problem," said Cameron Jamison.

Feeling much more confident now – surely he

wouldn't try anything? – I said, "Last time you gave me a ride, you said this book was rubbish."

"That's because it is rubbish," he said, and like last time, the way he spat out "rubbish" was as if the book itself was a pile of festering putridness.

"Why?" I said.

"Because the authors have it totally wrong," he said, his voice getting more and more emotional. "The Yanks never got their hands on Yamashita's Gold, and they certainly didn't use it to finance some anticommunist organization called the Black Eagle Trust."

Wow!

There was an obvious question to be asked, but I felt a bit wary about asking it.

As the Ferrari came out of the turns, and hit the straight, Cameron Jamison put his foot down.

The speedometer needle was now touching two hundred kilometers per hour.

I'm not sure if this was how Cameron Jamison always drove, or if my question about the book had riled him, or if he was just trying to scare the bejesus out of me.

If it was the last, then he'd succeeded, so I thought whatever, there isn't much difference between being really scared and really, really scared.

"So why, exactly, is the book rubbish?" I ventured.

By this time we were approaching the Jazys' house and the needle had started dropping.

"Because the gold is out there," said Cameron Jamison, waving his hand in the general direction of the ocean. "It's out there!"

Did he mean out there, as in out there in the ocean somewhere? Or out there, as in near Reverie Island?

But could The Debt really have gotten it so wrong?

Had they been sold a pup by the Zolt? A fake map, perhaps?

Could Yamashita's Gold be nowhere near Diablo Bay, where the world's foremost treasure hunter was now searching?

The Ferrari pulled up outside the Jazys' house.

"Thanks for the ride," I said.

"My pleasure," said Cameron Jamison, who seemed to have reverted to his confident-hair self.

As I went to get out of the car, he said, "One more thing, Dom."

"Yes, Mr. Jamison?" I said.

"I want you to do something for me."

"Okay," I said.

"I want you to open the glove compartment for me."

"Sure," I said, wondering what I would find in there.

I opened it – there was a large manila envelope.

"There are some photos inside, which I'd like you to take a look at."

I took the envelope. It wasn't sealed. I slid out the black-and-white photos; there were three of them. It took me a while to work out what it was I was looking at but when I did, I immediately looked away.

They were photos of bodies.

They were immolated, mutilated, dismembered. And they were young.

I let them drop out of my hands.

"If you're not off my island by tomorrow," said Cameron Jamison, his voice guttural, "this is what's going to happen to you and your big sister, Miranda, and your little brother, Toby."

For the briefest of seconds I thought this was some sort of sick practical joke, but when I looked at his face, his dark, dark eyes, I knew that it wasn't.

"Sure," I said, my hand on the door handle.

I got out of there, away from those photos.

The Ferrari took off.

And hands on my knees, I opened my mouth, and let the vomit come pouring out of me.

RETURN TO REVERIE

Gus is a very slow driver.

And today, he was driving extra slowly.

Take a slow driver and have him drive slowly and what's the result? *Waiting for Godot* on wheels.

"Geez, Gus," I said, "if you go any slower I reckon we'll enter another time-space continuum."

The irony wasn't lost on me: three days ago I'd been pretty happy to fly out of Reverie, to leave Cameron Jamison and his evil photos behind.

But here I was, anxious as anything to get back there.

"Maybe you'd like to drive," he said.

Maybe I would, I thought. I wasn't too bad on the Jet Ski. The motorbike. The speedboat. The bulldozer. The car seemed like a pretty logical progression.

But just as I was going to point this out, Gus

applied slightly more pressure to the accelerator and the speedometer needle crept up ever so slightly.

"Remind me when the diving's on, again?"

"Tomorrow," I conceded.

"So what's the big rush?"

He had a point, but that's only because he didn't know that now the diving – as amazing as it sounded – was just an alibi, a reason for me to be in Reverie if anybody started asking. The police. Or any of the thousands of people who supposedly hated me and my guts.

The sooner I got there the sooner I could start snooping around. And find out what I needed to find out.

Because during the last few days I'd become more and more certain that there was something going on.

The break-ins at the dive shops.

Zoe's weirder-than-usual behavior.

Cameron Jamison's over-the-top warning.

"So why don't we talk about your running," said Gus.

I'd known he was going to bring this up, that it was probably the reason he let me volunteer him to drive me to Reverie in the first place. Get me in the front seat, snap me in my seat belt, and ear-bash the crap out of me.

"I'm retired," I said.

"Dominic, you ran the fastest time for your age in the world in Rome!"

"Quit while you're on top," I said, though I must admit I did feel another pang of loss; running had been such a big part of my life, running had been almost my best friend.

We had just entered that sleepy little town we'd stopped in with Mr. Jazy that day, the one he said "just had to go," and I couldn't help but noticing that there were *For Sale* signs everywhere.

"Look, I'm not going to be around forever. It would be a shame never to see you race again."

The old I'm-not-going-to-be-around-forever card. An oldie but a definite goldie, guaranteed to make most underachieving teenagers feel like total crap.

But a card that Gus didn't usually play.

"What are you talking about?" I said. "What's your bench press lately? Eighty?"

"Seventy-five," said Gus. "Yet to crack the eighty."

"People who bench press seventy-five don't pop their clogs. That just doesn't happen."

Gus laughed his great rumbly laugh. And everything felt nice and normal again.

But he wasn't about to give up on the running thing.

He tried another tack.

"'To give anything less than your best is to sacrifice the gift.'"

"Steve Prefontaine," I said.

"'A runner must run with dreams in his heart.'"

"Emil Zátopec."

I loved this game, even though I knew I was playing straight into Gus's hands.

"See, you can't escape it. It's in your blood. It's in your DNA," he said.

"Anyway, I'm swimming now," I said.

"Okay, give me one killer swimming quote," said Gus.

He had me, but I wasn't going to give up without a fight.

"'No longer conscious of my movement, I discovered a new unity with nature. I had found a new source of power and beauty, a source I never dreamt existed,'" I said.

"Of course, that great swimmer Sir Roger Bannister," said Gus, laughing. "The man who broke the four-minute aquatic mile."

I guess you'd have to be a running nerd to find any of this amusing, but we happily played the quote game all the way to where the ferry left the mainland for Reverie.

I considered staying in the car for the crossing, remaining as inconspicuous as possible.

Maybe a Zoe-style disguise wouldn't be such a bad idea once we got to the island, I told myself.

But Gus – well, one of his old man's farts – forced us out onto the deck.

The sea was choppy; out further, whitecaps were racing.

"Well, hello there."

Immediately I recognized the tough-sounding voice, but I was hoping against hope that this greeting wasn't directed at me.

No such luck.

"Dominic, isn't it?" said Mrs. Bander, who, according to her daughter Zoe, was one of my guts haters.

She looked pretty much the same as the last time I'd seen her: streaky bottle-blond hair, huge rectangular-framed sunglasses, and a cat's bum of a mouth.

"That's me," I said.

"And this would be ...?"

"My grandfather, Gus," I said.

She stared at Gus for a while before she said, "So what brings you to Reverie?"

"Diving," said Gus. "Clever boy did his PADI here last week and was just backing it up with a couple more open water dives."

"Long way to come to get wet," said Mrs. Bander.

And that, it seemed, was the end of the conversation, because she moved away from us then.

"I'm getting back into the car," I said.

As we rolled off the ferry and headed towards the village I noticed a Subaru WRX with tinted windows keeping some distance behind us.

Maybe it was all innocent – there weren't many places to go on an island, many roads to follow – but after our meeting with Mrs. Cat's Bum Bander there was definitely something ominous about it.

"Gus, I don't want you to freak out, but I think there might be somebody following us."

Gus's eyes immediately shifted to the rearview mirror.

"That's no bloody good," he said, moving on at the same sedate pace.

We continued on towards town.

Once in town, Gus took a left and then a right and then a left again.

The WRX was still there.

Obviously, we couldn't go to our motel, or they would find out where were staying. And there was no way we could outgun a WRX. So I had this mental image of us just driving all night long, the WRX snapping at our heels.

Up ahead was the Reverie Motel. Gus pulled into the driveway.

"But we're not staying –" I started.

He parked the car. "Grab your bag."

We both got out, walked over to the office and went inside.

There were already a couple of people ahead of us, which was perfect. Because after waiting a few minutes, I followed Gus outside.

"Okay, let's go find our room," he said.

We walked along the length of the building, and then took a gravel path to our left.

If the occupants in the WRX had been watching us, which I assumed they had, then we were now out of view.

"Now we just need to find a back exit," said Gus.

"But what about the truck?" I said.

"No rush," said Gus. "I'll come and get it when there's less heat."

Less heat? Not only was my gramps walking the walk, he was talking the talk, too. The back exit involved scrambling over a fence, something Gus did with surprising ease for a mono-pedal septuagenarian.

"Now all we have to do is find our motel," said Gus.

Okay, so this is where being several hundred years old was actually a disadvantage.

I took out my iPhone and checked the signal – no problem, lots of lovely 3G – and went to Google Maps.

I waited until it had GPS-ed where we were, then put in our destination.

"Okay, I'm all over it," I said. "We go to the end of this street, and then take a right and then the second on the left and it's about fifty meters down."

"White man's magic," said Gus, shaking his head.

"Your phone can do it, too," I said. "I'll show you later."

When we walked into the driveway of the HarbourView Motel, Gus's only comment was "Hmmm."

It was one of those hmmms that was layered, that was complex; Mr. McFarlane might even be tempted to say that it was "narrative-like."

"So this is where we're staying," he said, somewhat redundantly after the eloquence of his hmmm.

I'd chosen the night's accommodation, found it on Wotif.com. As in Wotif it actually looked anything like the photos on the Internet?

"I'll book us in," I said, and Gus was happy to stay outside.

I walked past the pool, though "pool" was probably too grand a word for what looked more like a dog's drinking bowl.

A small dog. Or one that wasn't thirsty. Anyway, you get the picture.

The office certainly bore little resemblance to those in the sort of establishments I stayed in with my parents.

It was dingy and shabby and didn't smell that tremendous. On the wall was a list of rules. It was a very long list: no guests after ten, no gutting fish in the bathroom sink, no glassware in the pool area.

You would be lucky to fit a glass in the pool area!

A man was sitting at the desk, peering at a computer screen.

He was pretty old, maybe Gus's age, and like Gus was wearing a tank top that showed off sinewy arms. But his arms, unlike Gus's, had faded, old-style tattoos.

He didn't look up when I entered, so I cleared my throat.

He clocked me now, giving me a forced smile.

"What can I do for you?" he said.

Okay, he looked nothing like the creepy guy in that old black-and-white movie *Psycho*, but he had the same creepy stab-you-in-the-shower vibe.

"I booked two rooms on Wotif," I said. "In the name of Silvagni."

He peered at the screen, pecked at the keyboard for a bit, then looked back at me, not bothering to disguise the fact that he wasn't at all impressed with what he was seeing.

"I'll need to sight an adult," he said. "Driver's license, that sort of thing."

"Okay, I'll get my grandfather," I said.

When I came back in with Gus, a remarkable transformation came over the man's face. "Frankie!"

Frankie? Obviously he was mistaken.

But Gus said, "Bob, long time no see."

"You can say that again," said Bob. "Last time I saw you, you were –"

"It was a long time ago," said Gus, talking over Bob. "And perhaps this is not the time and place for reminiscing."

He was standing behind me and I couldn't see what he'd done, but I was pretty sure he'd indicated to me, as in *not in front of the kid*.

"Righto, we can have a chat over a beer later," said Bob, with what looked suspiciously like an old-fashioned wink.

After Gus had registered and Bob had told us a few more rules, we went to check out our adjoining rooms.

"Hmmmm, I've slept in worse," said Gus.

"I haven't," I said.

"Meet you in half an hour and we'll go get something to eat," said Gus.

I did a further inspection of the room. The carpet looked like it belonged in one of those walk-into-a-bar jokes.

As in *A carpet walks into a bar*.

Why do you look so frayed?

Not funny, but you get the picture.

The sheet on the bed had so many stains it resembled something from Google Maps. The TV wasn't plasma, or LCD; it was so old it probably ran on coal, or steam. I checked out the bathroom. The showerhead was drooping like a flower in the sun. And when I snuck a look at the bathroom bowl, there was a turd in there.

177

No, it can't be, I told myself.

I snuck another look. It hadn't moved.

I dialed reception on the phone.

No answer.

I dialed again.

This time Bob answered. "What is it?"

"There's something in the bathroom," I said.

"Water, perhaps?"

"Yes, water. But something else, a turd."

"And what do you expect me to do? Call in the fire brigade? An ambulance? It's got a flush button, hasn't it? Push the blasted thing!" He hung up.

I considered my options.

Channel my mother and escalate, demand to see the manager? My horrible suspicion was that Bob was the manager.

Threaten to trash him and his turd-ridden motel on TripAdvisor?

But my other horrible suspicion was that Bob couldn't care less about TripAdvisor.

Book into another motel, one that had turd-free bathrooms but wasn't as close to the harbor?

No, not with the WRX lurking out there.

Or, and this is exactly what I did, push the blasted flush button.

Ω Ω Ω

Gus and I met to discuss the evening meal. I told him about my little surprise.

He laughed. "I guess you're more used to chocolates on the pillow."

"It's probably not a good idea to go outside to eat," I said.

"No, it's probably not," said Gus, and I waited for him to ask some really obvious questions like "What the blazes is going on?"

But he said, "We could order in pizza?"

"We could," I said, but the thought of eating a Meatlover in this place made me feel really queasy.

"There's that Japanese we passed," I said. "It's pretty close."

Gus seemed very happy with my compromise, so that's where we ended up.

When the waitress came over Gus said something to her in what sounded like Japanese.

"Sorry, I'm from Korea," she said.

"You speak Japanese?" I asked him after she'd taken our order.

He shrugged. "A bit."

"Where were you all that time?" I said. "When you were supposed to be dead?"

Another shrug.

"Jail?" I said.

"Not jail," said Gus.

Well, if he was telling the truth, and I was pretty sure he was, that was the end of Miranda's Gus-as-crim theory.

"But you were overseas?"

"Some of the time."

"Why do you have to be so mysterious about it? You might not be around for too much longer," I said, half smiling.

An oldie but a goldie.

"Hey, I'm bench pressing seventy."

"I thought it was seventy-five."

"What's five kilos between a kid and his granddad?"

"So why did you come back, anyway?" I said.

"Your dad came and got me," said Gus, and there was no joking in his tone now. "He made me an offer I couldn't refuse."

"Which was?"

"That I would get to see my grandkids growing up."

When our miso soup came Gus cupped the bowl in his hand and brought it up to his face.

"You're allowed to do that when you're having Japanese, right?"

"Absolutely," said Gus. "It's actually bad manners not to slurp."

Great.

I brought my bowl to my face. I slurped.

Gus slurped.

I slurped some more.

It was a total slurp-fest.

When we'd finished, Gus said, "Do you know

what a Herculean task is?"

"Now you're sounding like Dr. Chakrabarty."

"Who's that?"

"This wacky classics teacher at my school," I said. "Okay, let me think. A Herculean task is one that takes a heck of a lot of grunt."

"That's one way of putting it," said Gus. "Okay, what about a Sisyphean task?"

Dr. Chakrabarty hadn't told me about this, but Mr. McFarlane had. "It's one that goes on and on, but you don't really get anywhere. Like digging a hole, filling it up again, digging a hole, and so on."

"Two out of two," said Gus.

The waitress came with the sushi and I watched as Gus expertly mixed the wasabi into the soy sauce with the tip of his chopstick.

I picked up a sushi roll with my chopsticks, dipped it into the mixture and popped it into my mouth.

"Pretty good," I said, as the wasabi blasted my nostrils.

Gus did the same.

"Not too bad at all," he said. "According to the classics there is one more type of task – do you know what it is?"

"No," I said, and I actually felt a bit cheated – why hadn't Dr. C. or Mr. Mac told me about this other one?

"Do you know who Prometheus was?" said Gus.

"The film?" I said. "I downloaded it, but I haven't seen it yet."

"Before the film," said Gus, "Prometheus was a Titan, from Greek mythology. He stole fire for man and as punishment was chained to a rock where his liver was eaten by an eagle every night."

I looked at the sushi that was in transit between the plate and my mouth; fortunately nothing in it resembled liver.

Gus continued. "During the day the liver grew back again."

"He sounds way cool," I said. "But what's he got to do with tasks?"

"Well, the third type of task is a Promethean one. One that is courageous, creative, original."

Was Gus hinting at what I already sort of knew: that I should be out there finding Yamashita's Gold?

"So what are you saying?" I said, chewing on the last of the sushi.

Gus shifted in his seat.

"Do you know why I lost my leg?" he said. "It was because I didn't do that; I didn't take what was Sisyphean, what was Herculean, and make it Promethean."

It seemed like my grandfather was telling me everything and nothing.

"So you're saying I should let a freaking eagle eat my liver?" I said.

"Yes," he said.

Now that that was over, and we'd ordered even more sushi, he said, "Can you show me how to use the map thing on my phone?"

Again Gus's mono-pedalism or his septuagenarianism didn't seem much of an impediment, and he was soon GPS-ing like a pro.

As he went to put his phone away, something occurred to me. "Can I just borrow this for a minute?"

"Of course," he said with a wave of his chopstick.

I brought up Google on both phones and entered exactly the same string *E. Lee Marx* into both.

I hit enter at the same time.

And got very different results.

E. Lee Marx in Australia? was the first hit on Gus's phone, while mine was the same old stale story I always got.

I was shocked – somebody had de-googled my Google!

But who?

And why?

Ω   Ω   Ω

After I'd said good night to Gus, I went back to my room.

If Gus can sleep anywhere, so can I, I thought.

But I thought wrong.

Brought up on Egyptian cotton, on 720-thread-counts, I was never going to drop off on a bed that sagged like a hammock, on a sheet that had the five major continents mapped on it plus another two that nobody knew about.

I tried watching television, but in every program it was snowing. *Priscilla, Queen of the Desert*. Snowing. *Lawrence of Arabia*. Snowing.

And I kept thinking of that turd. Maybe it would return; maybe like wild salmon it would work its way back upstream until it came to the place of its birth.

I felt so grossed out, I had to get out of there.

Can I risk a walk? I asked myself.

No stars, no moon; it was very dark outside. *Yes, I can risk it,* I decided. Cloak of darkness, and all that. I made my way towards the waterfront.

It's like looking for a needle in a haystack, people say. And yes, needles can be very small, and yes, haystacks can be very big, but at least you know what it is you're looking for. Me, I wasn't sure.

There was only person on the wharf: a fisherman sitting on a tackle box, illuminated by a streetlight.

I stayed in the shadows.

Within a minute, he packed up his gear and took off.

Suddenly a van pulled up with a screech of tires, *Reverie Security Service* written on the side. A door swung open and a man got out and walked to the edge of the wharf, peering out to sea. After a little while he got back into the van and it took off again.

It was just me now. Me and my racing heart. Water sloshed around under the wharf. Pylons creaked. There was a faint whiff of fish in the air. I wouldn't say it was a spooky place, but it wasn't unspooky either. I was just about to head back again, back to my sheets and my potential salmon, when I noticed something out at sea.

A light; it seemed to flicker on and off, on and off. But after a few minutes of my watching it, it stayed on, getting brighter.

I assumed it was a boat and it was headed for the wharf. I decided to get further out of view, and retreat behind a rickety pile of wooden pallets. Eventually the boat slid up to the wharf, its only light one on top of the cabin. I'm no expert on seafaring vessels, but it looked like a fishing boat, a trawler, something like that.

Nobody got off it, though.

And the wharf, not unspooky before, had now become really spooky.

There was the sound of a car engine and the Reverie Security van pulled up again, even screechier than last time. The same man got out, but with him was another man. Though he walked with a very pronounced limp, he seemed to have no trouble lugging a large waterproof diving bag to the boat.

The man with the bag got on board and the boat quickly moved off again, heading back out to sea.

I waited for a while before I set off back to the motel with its non-Egyptian-cotton sheets.

As I passed the office, I heard voices from inside. The door was open, and I could see Gus inside with Bob, the owner.

"Those sure were the days," I heard the owner say.

But Gus didn't seem so enthusiastic. "It was nice to catch up, but it's time for me to hit the sack."

"We've got half a bottle left!" said Bob.

"Good night," said Gus.

I hurried away before he could see me.

THE PROCESS

Since The Debt, I'd had nightmares so nightmarish, they'd practically shredded my subconscious. I'd dreamt of amputated limbs, twitching stumps. I'd dreamt of testicles turned to cinders. But those were nothing compared to this.

Chains held me to a rock, while an eagle, enormous wings outstretched, its talons gripping my abdomen, its beak dripping gore, feasted on my liver.

Why had Gus ever told me about this stupid myth?

I woke to somebody bashing my door in.

That's what it sounded like, anyway, but when I said, "Who is it?" it was Gus who answered.

"It's me, Dom."

When I got out of bed I couldn't help running a hand over my torso – my liver was where it belonged. I hurried over and opened the door and it practically fell off its hinges.

So it was the door, not Gus's knocking, that was at fault.

"Rise and shine!" said Gus.

"What is the time?"

"Nearly nine."

Had I really managed to sleep in while on top of those thread-deficient sheets, on that bed?

Obviously, yes.

"The boat's leaving at nine-thirty," I said.

I had considered losing the diving trip and using that time to look for whatever it was I was looking for. But diving was my alibi, and already in my brief career as a minor criminal I'd learned that having a watertight alibi really was an excellent thing.

We headed down to the wharf.

Now, thronging with people, boats leaving and arriving, it was very different from the sinister place of last night. The *Hispaniola* was tied up in its usual place and, if possible, it looked even more battered than the last time I was aboard.

Maxine greeted me like a long-lost relative.

My star pupil, she called me, which was pretty embarrassing because the other diver who was coming out today looked like a real pro, like somebody who would grace the front cover of a scuba diving magazine.

Gus said good-bye – he intended to spend the day reading – and we were off.

I was right about Brett, the other diver. Soon he was talking to Maxine about all these amazing places he'd been to: Great Blue Hole, Sistema Dos Ojos, Aliwal Shoal. It was pretty intimidating, except he was actually really friendly. He asked me how long I'd been diving. When I said I'd only started last week, he threw Maxine a look.

"Star pupil," she said.

"Okay," he said, and I wondered what was going on – was he reluctant to go diving with a newbie like me?

After a while I went inside to talk to the skipper.

"The kid with the questions," he said.

Okay, now I had a problem: how not to be the kid with the questions, while at the same time asking a truckload more questions?

"We're headed somewhere else today," I said, downward inflexion, making sure it was a statement, not a question.

"This mob want somewhere a bit more exciting," he said. "The wreck of the *Meryl*."

"That does sound exciting," I agreed.

The skipper proceeded to give me some of the history of the *Meryl*.

A cargo ship, in 1954 it was en route from Jakarta to the Philippines when something happened to it. Nobody quite knew what. But the crew died, and it drifted aimlessly, sighted from time to time, until it sunk off Reverie Island.

"But how did it end up here?" I said.

"That's a very good question," said the skipper. "One I've actually given a bit of thought to."

He proceeded to pull out a map – sorry, a chart – and spread it out on the chart table.

"We're here," he said, pointing to a spot northwest of Reverie. "And flowing along here is the mighty East Australian Current," he said, thumb tracing the current on the map. "That pumps warm water all the way down into the Tasman. You've heard of the East Australian Current?"

I professed my total ignorance.

"Well, the boffins reckon it starts in Antarctica because of ozone depletion, and this gets something they like to call the South Pacific Gyre going, which in turn feeds into the East Australian Current."

I thought of the *Meryl*, manless, rudderless, drifting down the coast, a ghost ship.

"What it doesn't explain is how the ship ended up this far east. That's got me stumped."

Ω Ω Ω

Half an hour later, the anchor was down and we were ready to dive. Maxine said she wasn't diving today, so it was just me and Brett. As I was getting ready she strapped a dive computer around my wrist, taking a lot of care to make sure it was firmly secured.

"I don't dive without one these days," she said.

I looked at her and smiled, but there was something in her face that I hadn't seen before. Was it concern? Had she remembered the incident with Joyless Joy? Surely it wasn't that; I was her star pupil, after all.

As soon as I hit the water I knew I was going to learn more by observing Brett than I ever would on a thousand courses. Everything he did seemed so smooth, so unflustered. He really did look like a creature that lived in the ocean, not one that only entered it occasionally and even then with the help of some serious technology.

The wreck wasn't deep, only about twelve meters down, and not half as scary as I'd thought it'd be. Encrusted with coral, shaggy with weed, there were schools of iridescent fish swimming in and out of it.

I was transfixed.

Brett kept pointing things out to me: an evil-looking eel in its hole, a manta ray gliding majestically past.

Remembering my training, I again checked my air.

Still a hundred to go – I was fine.

But, suddenly, when I was eyeballing a huge wrasse, my air ran out.

I checked my gauge – the needle was on ninety. But I definitely had no air.

Don't panic, I told myself, looking around for Brett.

He was nowhere to be seen.

Remember your training.

Another controlled emergency swimming ascent was needed. I started kicking upwards, exhaling as I did so.

Again, I remembered what Maxine had said: *You won't run out of air, because your lungs will expand as you rise.*

Finally I broke the surface.

I felt quite proud – I'd successfully done two CESAs now – but it was still pretty weird. Even weirder when I looked around and there was no boat in sight.

And where was my dive buddy?

But I could see it now: a Zodiac headed straight for me. It wasn't the *Hispaniola*, but it was still a boat; it would do.

"Over here!" I yelled, waving one hand as high as I could over my head.

Definitely not drowning, definitely waving.

I needn't have bothered, as the Zodiac had me firmly in its sights. It pulled up next to me and two big strong arms reached over and yanked me aboard.

When I say yanked, I really mean yanked.

"Water!" I said, pulling my mask down so that it hung around my neck. "I need to drink some water."

A bottle of water was passed to me.

After I'd gulped that down, I wiped the salt out of my eyes.

It took a while for them to focus, and when they did I sort of wished they'd remained unfocused.

There were two men in the boat: the man with the big strong arms who had yanked me aboard, and another man, also with big strong arms, who was operating the outboard. Both men were wearing balaclavas, their faces covered except for eyes and mouth. I couldn't imagine any scenario where men in balaclavas was good news.

This was no exception.

This was bad, bad news.

"What's going on?" I said, but the balaclavas weren't in a talkative mood.

Now I noticed where the boat was headed: away from Reverie Island and straight out to sea.

I wondered if they were from The Debt, a thought that was weirdly thrilling. Because if they were, they were just men, just flesh and blood, like I was.

Logically, I'd already come to this conclusion: *they were just plain old money-grubbers*.

But here was the physical proof – there was absolutely nothing supernatural about them, they weren't shape-shifters.

I thought of the two tough kids on the bus that time, how I'd bluffed the bejesus out of them. Maybe I could try a bit of that here, I thought. But I knew I was kidding myself.

There was no way out except overboard.

My fins were hurting my feet, so I kicked them off, made myself as comfortable as I could given that I was currently being kidnapped, and I waited.

As I looked back I could see a hazy Reverie Island recede in the distance.

Until it was a speck.

And then nothing.

The two balaclavas stayed where they were. Motionless, impassive.

A little while later the Zodiac slowed.

And the balaclava who wasn't steering moved forward, grabbed hold of me and tied something to me. Then he hoisted me overboard.

It happened so quickly, so unexpectedly, I didn't quite understand what was going on. Not even when I was in the water, surrounded by water, did I get it.

But as I started descending rapidly my brain moved into action.

I had a number of problems.

The first was air.

I had none, and I was going to the bottom.

I would die.

But why did I have none, when according to my gauge I'd had plenty?

I reached behind, felt the valve. It was off!

There was only one explanation: Brett, my dive buddy – buddy? – had turned my air off without me realizing it!

I turned it back on, grabbed my regulator, purged it and put it into my mouth. Air, beautiful sweet air, flowed into my lungs.

That was one problem solved.

Now for the next one.

My mask was still hanging around my neck. I positioned it onto my face and stretched the strap around my head. Head back, I exhaled through my nose, clearing the water.

Now I could see – second problem solved.

Third problem: I was plummeting to the bottom, and the bottom seemed a very long way down.

I knew ascending too quickly was a problem; it's how you get the bends. But descending too quickly? I looked down; now I could see why I was sinking so fast. The balaclava had tied a rope to me, with something very heavy at the end.

It has to be an anchor.

Okay, easily fixed – just untie it.

But feeling around behind my back, behind my neck, I couldn't find where on my BCD it had been tied off.

Down, down, down I kept going.

I had to get out of my BCD. Chest clip first. Then stomach clip. Stomach Velcro. My left arm out of the harness, I reached across and grabbed the right harness.

I took a quick glance at my depth gauge – fifty meters was way too deep to do a CESA.

I slipped my right shoulder out, and now I was holding the BCD with only my left hand. The regulator ripped from my mouth.

I was going to lose it!

I hooked my arm through, so that the harness was secure in the crook of my elbow. Got the regulator back in my mouth.

Now I could see where he'd tied it off – just below the valve on the tank.

I tried to untie it with one hand, but it was no good, it was too tight.

Should I just ride with it all the way to the bottom?

No.

I relaxed my elbow a bit, so that I could use my hand to grab the rope and take off some of the pressure. With my left hand, I started working the rope loose little by little.

Only a little bit more – and it was free. The rope trailed off, and I was no longer on the downward elevator. I put the BCD back on.

Now for the ascent. I checked my depth – I was seventy meters down.

According to the PADI system, it would take me numerous dives until I was allowed to dive at this depth. But I knew that the golden rule was to ascend no faster than ten meters per minute.

Keeping an eye on my depth gauge, my watch, I swam slowly up.

And, when I was five meters below the surface, I stopped for five minutes.

When I broke the surface, I punched the air.

I'd done it!

But the exhilaration I felt at being alive didn't last long.

Because when I looked around I was in the middle of the ocean with nothing – not a boat, not land, nothing in sight.

I'd just been killed by two men in balaclavas.

No, I hadn't been shot.

I hadn't had my throat cut.

I hadn't been disemboweled.

But it was the same thing, because the result was identical. I was going to drown. Or die of exposure. Or get eaten by sharks.

But just when this despair was spiraling out of control, I saw a glimpse of something on the horizon.

A flash of gray.

The boat heading back to Reverie? The sun, also, seemed to be headed that way. So that was the direction I needed to swim, towards the west.

But was it?

How far away was Reverie Island?

I knew that the *Meryl* was around ten kilometers off the island. I figured the trip in the Zodiac had been at least twenty minutes and that we'd been going roughly twenty kilometers an hour.

So what did that make it in total?

Sixteen or seventeen?

Maybe even more.

But if my mental map was correct, then the mainland was closer, a lot closer. Not only that, that was the direction of the wind and the waves.

But what if I was wrong, what if the map I'd constructed in my head was wrong? Then I would keep swimming, and swimming, and swimming, and never ever reach land.

I had a decision to make.

Towards Reverie, in the direction the sun was heading? Or keep the sun on my left and head towards the mainland?

I guess there was some degree of certainty in the former – I was fairly sure that Reverie was in that direction. But I was less certain of the latter option, because for that I had to rely on memory. And then another option presented itself – if they were The Debt, would they really let me drown?

I mean, seriously?

So was I better off just staying here, treading water, expending the minimum amount of energy, until eventually they came to their senses and picked me up?

But what if they weren't The Debt? And the more I thought about it, the more likely this seemed.

They're just plain old money-grubbers. If this was true, and I just knew that it was, then what would they possibly gain by doing this to me?

No, it wasn't The Debt; I couldn't just tread water, wait for them to pick me up.

Some seagulls flying overhead came down for a closer look. They squawked at me a few times before they took off again. I imagined them when I got weaker, swooping down, pecking at my eyeballs.

I had to start moving.

Reverie? Mainland?

Again I brought up that map on the LCD screen of my mind.

Again it showed the coast doglegging.

It had to be the mainland, I told myself. I had to let the winds and the waves help me.

The first thing to do was lose any extraneous material. I unclipped the tank, and let it sink to the bottom with its attached regulator.

I adjusted the mask.

I blew some air into the BCD, so it had what I thought was just the right amount of buoyancy – not too much that it made swimming difficult, not too little that I had to work to stay afloat.

For some reason I had five kays in my head as the distance I needed to swim.

But you don't want to have that in your head, because five kays is, well, crazy.

So what I decided to do was break it down into manageable portions, portions I could actually get my head around. A process.

Five hundred meters wasn't that far, only ten laps of an Olympic-sized pool; it was twenty-five laps of our pool at home, and I'd done lots of those lately.

But how was I going to measure five hundred meters?

Well, I knew it took me around twelve strokes for one lap of our twenty-meter pool.

I knew that because Tristan kept telling me I had to get this down to under ten or I'd never be competitive. Dude.

So five hundred meters was approximately, very approximately, three hundred strokes.

So this is what I decided to do: I would swim freestyle nonstop for three hundred strokes and then I would stop and have a rest, reassess my position. After I'd done this ten times I'd be there; I'd have reached the mainland.

It was an excellent plan – logical, considered, and for a moment I got very excited by it.

Hey, this is going to be easy, I told myself. *Not even really a challenge for somebody with my considerable capabilities.*

And then I actually started swimming.

And it was total misery.

For a start, I'd already done a fair bit of diving, so it wasn't as if I was fresh or anything.

Everything ached, especially my arms and shoulders. Okay, I'd drunk some water, but I hadn't eaten anything since breakfast. And even then it was only some crappy white bread and a coffee.

It was total misery, but I had a plan, a good plan, and I knew if I didn't stick to it, I was in huge trouble.

One stroke. Two strokes.

Usually I swim bilaterally, breathing every third stroke on alternating sides of my body, but knowing how important it was to keep the sun to my left, I decided to breathe on my left side only, so that I could keep an eye on it.

Three hundred strokes.

Rest.

One down, nine to go.

Ω   Ω   Ω

Two hundred and ninety-nine strokes.

Three hundred strokes.

I stopped, treading water.

Only three more sets to go, I told myself.

I wanted to ignore the thirst, and my cracked lips.

I wanted to ignore the hunger. Cinemascope-sized images of food were screening in my head. Hamburgers were talking to me. Pizzas were cracking jokes.

I wanted to ignore the pain. There was so much of it now, it was hard to find a source. Pain from arms, from elbows, from shoulders. And from other places you wouldn't expect. My neck. My ankles. Just one great raging pain that was eating me up.

I wanted to ignore all of that and concentrate on process, The Process, on the next set of three hundred strokes.

Let's go, I told myself. *Three hundred more strokes, that's all.*

Two more sets and The Process was almost finished.

One more set to go.

Two hundred and ninety-eight strokes.

Two hundred and ninety-nine strokes.

Last stroke, and that was it – The Process was finished.

I'd done it!

Treading water, I looked ahead. To where there should be land. But all I could see was water, water and more water.

But The Process! There had to be land!

Water. Water. And more water.

No land.

The Process had failed me. The Process was wrong.

And I was going to die.

Because The Process had failed, I had to die. I couldn't swim any further, I had nothing left.

I would just let the sea take me. I lay on my back, letting the waves buffet me this way and that, and took in the immensity of the sky.

I guessed there were worse ways to go. This was a peaceful way to die.

Death by ocean. Death by sea.

The waves buffeting me this way and that.

I'm not sure what I noticed first: that the water was a different color, or the change in smell.

Or the birds in the sky.

Okay, The Process needed remodeling. A slight tweaking. Not ten sets, eleven sets.

The chafing under my arms from where the BCD had been rubbing was unbearable; I decided that it had to go.

As far as surviving the night in the water, it was a crazy thing to do. As far as swimming another three hundred strokes, it was the only thing to do.

I slipped out of the BCD, let it float away.

The relief was instantaneous, and intense; I powered through the first fifty strokes. But then my body reminded me just how sore it was, just how tired it was.

I concentrated on form. *Dude, you've got to roll. Dude, elbows up higher. Dude, you got to push that water behind you.*

Only five strokes to go.

Four. Three. Two.

I stopped, treading water, and there was land.

Land so close I could almost reach out and touch it. The Process hadn't failed me at all; I'd almost failed it.

I swam on until my feet touched sand. I dragged myself up onto the empty beach. There was something I hadn't allowed myself to think about: there was land and there was land. I remembered that this coastline wasn't populated.

But it couldn't be as bad as the ocean.

At least on land I could lie down and rest.

At least on land I could find water, maybe even food.

And I was a runner, I was a land creature.

I staggered up the beach, my legs like two pieces of kelp. Beyond the beach I could see thick bush. But no sign of life.

Okay, this isn't fair.

It's just not fair.

And that's when I saw the smoke, twirling upwards over the trees.

I made for it, covering a couple of hundred meters across the sand before I saw a narrow path that led through the scrub.

Where there's smoke, there's fire. Where there's fire, there's people.

I staggered along the path. After about a hundred meters it opened out and I was at a clearing.

A fire crackled.

People were standing around it.

I knew them, but didn't know them.

They were clapping.

Through my fatigue, my pain, it took me a while to realize that they were clapping for me!

One of them, a girl in glasses, said, "Nice work, Dom!"

Another one, tall, his voice incongruously high, said, "Great swim, buddy!" He turned to an older man with a battered face, saying, "Told you he had the right stuff."

Then it all became too much: I dropped onto the ground and lost consciousness.

SHIVER ME TIMBERS

When I came to, there was a second, and that's all it was, where I felt rested, my mind as clear as the water had been when we'd dived on the *Meryl* earlier.

I was in a tent, on top of a sleeping bag. Somebody had stripped my wet suit off and I was wearing only my bathing suit. My backpack, the one I'd taken on the *Hispaniola*, was by my side.

The light filtering through the material fell on my body, bathing me in the most exquisite warmth.

I'd come through an aquatic certain death and I was alive.

I was alive!

Alive!

But now all those thoughts that had been waiting patiently in the SMS center of my head began flooding in, fighting among themselves, clamoring for my attention.

How could they have possibly been waiting for me?

Had I really seen the Zolt?

Who was the older man?

As I got to my feet, my body started to remind me how I had treated it. My arms and shoulders were the worst. I tentatively swung my arms, trying to work some of the stiffness out. But as I did, I could feel just how raw my armpits were, like hamburger meat – the sort with all the gristle in it that Mom never buys. And other pain was coming into focus: the back of my neck was sunburned, and my throat was sore from all the saltwater that had trickled down it.

Another thought: Gus didn't know where I was!

I hurried out of the tent.

What time was it?

"Dominic, you woke up."

I'd been right: it was Zoe.

"I have to let Gus know I'm okay," I said.

"Dom, it's okay," she said, her voice surprisingly calm and reassuring for somebody so young and so, well, Zolton-Banderesque. "He knows already."

"No, he doesn't," I insisted. "I have to talk to him."

Zoe had her phone out, and was already hitting redial. She handed it to me.

"Gus?"

"They told me you're okay," he said, a note of uncharacteristic panic in his voice. "You're okay. Aren't you?"

No, I'm not okay. I've had my air supply cut. I've been dragged to the bottom of the ocean. I just swam about twenty kilometers.

Of course I'm not okay.

I took a couple of deep breaths. "I'm fine, Gus."

"Do what you have to do," he said, back to his usual panic-free self. And then reception dropped out.

But I'd heard enough. Gus and his liver-eating eagle – forget that! What I *had* to do was get out of here. That's what I *had* to do.

I followed Zoe to another tent, this one more like a marquee, open on two sides.

Inside was a table, charts spread over it. And on another table was some pretty impressive-looking electronic gear. Sitting in front of it was the Zolt.

I wasn't sure where the surge of happiness I felt came from – he'd really only ever meant trouble for me. But I guess there was no use denying that I was glad to see him, glad that he was alive, even if I'd never bought into the Zolt-is-dead theory.

He stood up, a huge smile on his face.

Okay, I hadn't seen him for six or so months but – wow! – had he grown up? He wasn't any taller –

I didn't think that was possible – but he definitely looked more buff, and he was older in the face. There was something else about him, too. He had this sort of presence that I hadn't noticed before.

"Mate, you were awesome," he said.

Awesome? What did he mean?

"I'd like you to meet somebody," he said.

I hadn't noticed, but the older man, the one with the battered, scarred face, was sitting in another chair, a chart spread across his knees.

He looked up at me and he seemed vaguely familiar.

"This is my father," said Otto. "Dane Zolton."

Now I knew why he looked familiar: a much younger, less wrecked, version of him was with Cameron Jamison in that photo in the dive shop.

"Everybody calls me Bones," he said. His voice, like his face, seemed damaged somehow.

"I heard you were dead," I said and, remembering what he'd just said, I added, "Bones."

"So do a lot of people," he said. "And let me give you a tip, being dead has its advantages. The dead don't pay taxes for a start. But, as you can see, I'm pretty much alive. You did good today, son. The kids said you had what it takes, but to tell the truth, I didn't believe them. Well, I do now."

Now, I totally got it: they'd just put me through some sort of insane qualification test.

"I could've died!" I said. "You could've killed me!"

"Don't worry, we had your back," said Zoe.

"No, you didn't. I was out there, in the middle of the ocean, all by myself."

Zoe took the laptop from her half brother, and held it up so that I could see the screen. On it was a map, with a red dot glowing in the middle of it.

"Wave your left hand around," she said.

I did, and the red dot wobbled slightly. Now I understood: the dive computer that Maxine had given me contained some sort of tracking device.

They'd tracked my progress as I swam towards shore, and were there to meet me when I eventually stumbled onto the beach. After I'd dropped with exhaustion, they'd carted me here.

How far that was, I wouldn't have a clue.

Which is also why she'd gone to so much trouble to make sure it was secure. But that meant she was in on it, too! Maxine!

So they were right: they did have my back. In a way.

"But I still could've drowned," I said.

"A fellow like you?" said Bones Zolton, putting his hand on my shoulder. "I don't think so."

It was more of Mr. McFarlane's "he flatters to deceive," but it was pretty effective. Besides, I didn't have time to be angry, because something else was rapidly becoming evident to me.

Why had they just put me through what they'd just put me through?

Because they *were* on the hunt for Yamashita's Gold, and they needed to see if I had what it took to join them.

And that realization was so huge, so exciting, it made everything else that had occurred today seem a little puny.

I didn't need The Debt – in fact, they could go and get a Brazilian – because I was going on the mother of all treasure hunts anyway.

"Maybe an explanation is in order," said Bones Zolton, the man who had been dead for the last ten years.

"Not such a bad idea," said Otto Zolton-Bander, his son, who had only been dead for about the last six months.

"Let's eat first," said Zoe, who, as far as I knew, hadn't been dead at all.

Though the light was now fading, I was able to have a good look around Camp Yamashita, as they called it. I had to give it to the Zoltons, they sure knew how to do good hideaway. First Gunbolt Bay, and now here.

"Found this place when I was an abalone diver," said Bones.

I still wasn't quite used to hearing words come out of a dead man's mouth.

As we sat down on folding chairs to eat, he continued his explanation. "There's no land access; in fact, the country behind is pretty much impenetrable. And because it's at the end of a narrow L-shaped bay, it's not visible from the water either. There's a spring, so there's your water supply. And the waters around here are teeming with sea life, so there's always plenty to eat."

They still must have had to get supplies from town, I figured, storing that particular factoid away in my head, perhaps for future use.

The food we were eating – a sort of seafood stew – was delicious.

"Is this where you've been all this time?" I said.

"Good God, no!" he said, and I could tell he was pretty outraged by that idea. "Some of the time, but not all of it."

"But why did you disappear?" I asked.

As I said this, there was the sound of an outboard approaching.

The Zodiac that pulled up onto the beach I recognized immediately – it was the one that had dropped me into the middle of the Pacific Ocean. On it was Maxine, Brett and a man with big arms who had to be one of the balaclavas.

Maxine and Brett greeted me as if it was the most normal thing in the world for me to be sitting there. Eating fish stew.

"Here he is, my star pupil," said Maxine.

"What about the fangs on that moray eel we saw today?" said Brett.

That would've been just before you turned my air supply off!

I glared at Balaclava – *nice trick with the anchor* – but he returned my glare with the friendliest of smiles.

The newcomers then helped themselves to the stew and joined us.

I'd fallen down quite a few rabbit holes into quite a few Wonderlands during the time of The Debt, but this was by far the most wondrous. The White Rabbit, the Mad Hatter, Tweedle Dee and Tweedle Dum – they were all as normal as actuaries compared to this lot.

I only had to remind myself of one thing for this to pale into insignificance, however: they were searching for Yamashita's Gold.

"Skip?" Bones asked Maxine.

"You know how hard it is to get him off the *Hispaniola*," she said. "He loves that tub."

"And Dogger?"

"They've got a card game they need to finish, apparently."

Now I got it: they used the Zodiac to go back and forth from the boat. That way they didn't have to return to port every night, where all those eyes would be watching them. And Dogger, I assumed, was the other Balaclava.

"Anyway, I was just telling Dominic here how I found this place in the old days, when I was diving on abalone for a living. My God, that was a good business when it first started. We were getting, what, two hundred bucks a kilo from the Japanese. Then we had that mercury scare and things got really tough – so tough I had to get that job working out at the airport. But I was always itching to get back to the water."

Sitting there, with the sound of the waves lapping up on the beach, the taste of seafood on my lips, it was like it wasn't Bones but the sea itself that was telling this story.

"Since I was a little tacker I always loved stories of treasure. *Treasure Island*, I must've read that book a hundred times."

I looked over at Zoe and Otto – both looked pretty bored, and I had the feeling they'd heard this yarn quite a few times before.

"Yo ho ho and a bottle of rum!" said Bones suddenly, and loudly, and for an instant I saw Long John Silver himself sitting there, a parrot on his shoulder.

"So of course I knew about the legend of Yamashita's Gold. Though I didn't believe it could have gotten this far down the coast." Bones gouged at his teeth with a toothpick. After he'd spat something onto the sand, he continued. "I saw something on the news one night, about the Jonestown massacre, where all those people in that cult died. And I had this, what do you call it, this revelation? Just because I didn't believe the treasure could be around here didn't mean other people wouldn't. I mean, it's all about faith, isn't it? People who have faith are the most determined people in the world. And the more you question that faith, the more determined they become."

He gouged at his teeth a bit more. "So I started dropping hints. Down the pub I mentioned that maybe, just maybe, Yamashita's Gold had made it this far south. And shiver me timbers, the next week somebody's telling me the same story. So I know it's got legs, this thing."

Shiver me timbers? Maybe Bones really did think he was a parrot-less Long John Silver?

He paused, looked around, eyebrows slightly raised.

"Beer, Bones?" said Otto.

"Man's not a camel," said Bones.

Otto returned with a can and tossed it to his dad.

You could tell from the way he opened it, the way he gulped it, the satisfied smack of his lips he gave afterwards, that it probably wasn't the first one he'd had in his life.

"So I thought, why not set myself up as an expert? Open a business helping people look for Yamashita's Gold."

I didn't like the way this story was developing – Yamashita's Gold was a hoax, was that what he was saying? But if that was the case, what were we all doing here? Especially me, what was I doing here?

"That went pretty well, too. It wasn't making me rich, but it sure beat working for a living."

Another gulp of his beer.

I was getting impatient.

"But what happened?" I blurted.

"What happened?" said Bones Zolton, finishing the can and tossing it onto the sand. "What happened, what destroyed my business?"

He paused here for dramatic effect, and it worked, because when he said, "I actually found Yamashita's Gold," I was gobsmacked.

And as you can imagine, I was finding it pretty difficult to get my head around this. "You found the real treasure?"

"I was out one day with these smart alecks from Sydney who thought they knew everything. Well, truth be known, they were pretty cluey, especially about ocean currents. Usually I took my clients off the north end of the island. Pretty safe there, water's not too deep and the diving's real pretty, so even if you don't find no treasure, you've got some nice memories to take home. But these guys, they insist we dive in the trench. Look, I've been diving my whole life, but two hundred feet's my limit. Anything deeper than that and I start to get a bit edgy. We spend a week at this place and I've stopped diving. Just kicking back in the boat while they take the dinghy out. Well, this one morning they come back and something's happened, I can see it in their faces. They're keeping mum, though. But when they decide to pull up the pick and head back I know they've found something –"

Again I couldn't help butting in. "But why didn't they tell you?"

Bones laughed. "You don't know much about treasure hunting, because if you did you'd know that really it's about one thing: greed. The contract I always had my customers sign said that we'd share the treasure fifty-fifty."

I felt a bit stupid asking him the question. I'd read enough about treasure hunting, watched enough movies, to know how powerful greed was.

"Well, they, like pretty much all people, got greedy. They figured that if they didn't say anything, they could come back in their own time, with their own boat, and take the lot."

Again, Otto got up to fetch his dad a beer.

"So what happened to them?" I said.

"They met an untimely end," said Bones. "Car accident on the way back to Sydney, car incinerated, everything went up in flames."

There was something ominous in the way he said this and the thought flashed through my mind that Bones was involved in the accident somehow. But that didn't make sense. Why would he do away with them when they were the only ones who knew where the treasure was?

"Still, I know roughly where the treasure is, within a twenty-kilometer radius. And I figure, if I keep looking, eventually I'll find it."

That seemed like a reasonable proposition to me, too.

"Every day I go out there, weather permitting, and I look. Spend hours and hours diving in all that water. It's all I think of, night and day." As he said this, he looked over at his son.

I guess what he was saying was that his family life wasn't a big factor.

"In the end, I just stay here, live off the land. Only go back to Reverie to get fuel and supplies. I don't take any customers out – why bother, I know where the treasure is. And of course, over the years, I've begun to question whether those Sydney smart alecks really did find Yamashita's Gold."

Again, he finished his drink and tossed it onto the sand alongside the other one.

"What you've got to understand," he said, "is that treasure does things to people – they change, become different."

"But what happened?" I said.

"I got sick," he said. "Back then, we didn't know what we know now about decompression, about ascent times. In fact, I didn't really take much notice of that stuff. I started having ear problems. Then chest problems. It got so I couldn't dive deep anymore. In fact, the doctor said that diving would kill me. But as Long John used to say, 'doctors is all swabs!' I went out again. And I found Yamashita's Gold. Well, some of it anyway."

"The Double Eagle?" I said.

Bones threw a crooked smile towards Otto and Zoe. "You kids told me he was smart, but not this smart!"

I might've even blushed.

Bones continued, "I was scouring this piece of reef, but feeling terrible. Headache like you wouldn't believe. And then I saw it. It was encrusted in coral, but I knew it was a coin. I kept looking for other treasure. Stayed down too long. And I must've blacked out. Only for a second or two. But that was enough. Somehow I managed to get to the surface. Then back on the boat, into shore. Six weeks in the hospital. I knew I couldn't dive again."

"But you had the coin, now. Why didn't you find a partner to work with?" I said.

"Greed," said Bones.

The way he said it was so matter-of-fact, like it wasn't a bad thing, or an evil thing, it was just what it was.

"I wasn't going to share my treasure with anybody. But more to the point, I couldn't trust anybody. Well, I could, but he wasn't old enough, yet."

He shot a look at his son.

Now this story, far-fetched as it was, and if you fetched it any further it would become fantasy, was starting to have the smell of truth.

"You had to wait until Otto was old enough?"

Bones nodded.

"So you staged your own death?"

"Well, that was more accident than design – my dinghy got loose one night, somebody found it, and suddenly I'm dead. But it suited my purposes to be off the scene, to have the whole Yamashita's Gold thing go off the boil for a while."

"But why did you take so long to come back?"

"I had my own issues," he said. "Who hasn't? But that's water under the bridge, because what we've got here is a crack team. Especially now you're on board, Dom."

Again, it was flattering. Again, I couldn't help but

feel a flush of pride. But, again, there was doubt – what could I bring to this enterprise?

I had no knowledge of where the treasure was. I wasn't a crack diver.

I was just a pretty resourceful kid, that was all.

But then I remembered something Zoe had said about me a long time ago.

When I was around, stuff seemed to happen.

Was that it? Something as wishy-washy as that?

After that, there was a general discussion about the search for the treasure, everybody chipping in.

In the beginning it was obviously for my benefit, so that I could get up to speed. But as the night wore on, as my eyelids grew heavier and heavier, and the number of empty beer cans on the sand increased, it became obvious that it was more about where the search was headed.

Even in my half-asleep state I realized that there actually didn't seem to be a master plan.

Still, I couldn't quite believe that I was part of this – it was only this morning that I'd been setting out to go on my fourth-ever open water dive.

Apparently, we would be getting up at four in the morning.

I couldn't concentrate anymore; I just had to go to bed.

So when Brett said, "Time for some shut-eye," and the others agreed, I breathed a weary sigh of relief.

221

As we left, Bones opened yet another beer.

"I don't know when the old buccaneer ever sleeps," said Brett as we made our way to the tent we were sharing.

As soon as I crawled inside, and into my sleeping bag, I was ready for sleep.

But, remembering the call Zoe had made to Gus, I had one more thought. I rummaged in my bag until I found my iPhone.

It was off.

I tried to turn it on.

The battery was dead. That didn't make sense – it had been fully charged when I'd left this morning.

There was only one explanation – somebody had deliberately sucked the juice out of it.

I wasn't sure how you did this, but there was no doubt that's what had happened.

But my brain refused to go any further with this line of questioning.

My brain demanded sleep.

YOU GOTTA HAVE FAITH

I woke. Brett was gently shaking me, the light from his headlamp in my eyes.

"The quest continues," he said in a sort of mock heroic tone.

"Oh, my arms," I moaned.

But now that the complaints line was open, there were other disgruntled customers. *I hurt*, complained my throat. *We also hurt*, complained my legs. *We hurt even more*, complained my armpits.

Brett handed me another headlamp. "We use these a lot around here."

I didn't need any more prompting; putting the headlamp on, I was quickly out of bed – or sleeping bag – and into the rest of my clothes.

I hurt, complained my throat.

There was only one thing to do – I closed down the complaints line. *Deal with it, body parts, we're hunting for treasure!*

Something occurred to me.

"Who used to sleep here?" I asked Brett.

"Dive bum by the name of Gunn," said Brett. "He got sacked, he quit – not sure. Had a few cycle through here already."

"But what stops them from blabbing about the treasure?" I said.

"For a start, I don't think a lot of them actually believe in it. As George Michael once sang, 'You gotta have faith!' And don't underestimate our Bones. He may look like a bit of a fool, but he's got a dark side, a real dark side. You wait until he starts on some of his stories."

I thought again of the "car accident," the one that had killed the two Sydney smart alecks who had, supposedly, found the treasure.

Something else occurred to me.

"What does he look like, this Gunn fellow?" I said.

"Gunny?" said Brett. "Pretty normal-looking guy, but he had an argument with a shark in the Bahamas a few years ago and lost half his foot, so he doesn't walk so great anymore. In the water, he's a fish, but on land …"

The Zodiac was already afloat, and I could see the marks in the sand where they'd dragged it down. We got on board; Maxine, Bones on one side, Brett and me on the other, Otto steering.

Zoe stayed behind with Balaclava to man the communications.

"Headlamps off," said Maxine, in her divemaster voice. "We're already using too much battery power."

Not for the first time, I wondered how somebody as nice as Maxine had gotten involved with this lot.

But I already knew the answer to this, because I was feeling it. All the doubts I'd had earlier had been replaced by this amazing sense of shared endeavor – we were all after one thing: the treasure – and excitement: we could very well find it today!

As we left the protection of the bay and moved into the open water, the Zodiac started bouncing around and I could feel the wind, fresh on my cheek.

"Weather's pretty ugly," said Maxine, and it wasn't difficult to detect the concern in her voice.

"Nothing to worry about, girlie," said Bones.

Maxine said nothing in reply, but I could see the tension around her jaw.

In front of us the sun was coming up, the eastern horizon slashed with pink and red. Now that I could see the waves I understood Maxine's concern – they were quite big. Out further I could see whitecaps.

If these were the conditions at dawn, what would they be like later?

As we tied up to the *Hispaniola* I could smell bacon.

Sure enough, breakfast was ready for us – the

afore-smelled bacon, and scrambled eggs, and sausages. There was even plunger coffee. Nobody said much as they hoed in, but when we'd finished Maxine said, "What's the latest weather report, Skip?"

Skip looked at Bones before he said, "Might get a bit bumpy, but not enough to be too worried about."

Dogger, the other Balaclava, pulled up the anchor and we were off.

A bit bumpy?

I was soon wishing I hadn't eaten so much breakfast, especially all that dead pig.

Otto was in the wheelhouse, at the chart table, poring over a chart, so I decided to join him.

To the uninitiated, which I guess I was, it looked like some kid had scribbled all over the paper, maybe even a couple of kids. There were all sorts of weird hieroglyphics everywhere. Immediately I was reminded of the map I'd found in the cave, the one with *Dane G. Zolton* written on the back.

"You understand this?" I said to Otto.

"More or less," he said. He stabbed at the map with his forefinger. "I reckon we should check out this area today."

"You reckon?" I said, remembering a phrase from all the reading I'd done about treasure hunting. "Is that what your search algorithm is telling you?"

"Search algorithm?" said Zolt, pronouncing it like it was something that was leaving a dirty taste in his mouth. "No, I've just got a hunch about this place, and Bones does too."

A hunch?

Brett joined us at the chart table then. His presence was reassuring; I'd dived with him, I knew what an absolute pro he was.

"So what sort of sensing equipment are you using?" I said.

"State-of-the-art," said Otto, and I breathed a sigh of relief, because even to my inexperienced eyes they were starting to look like a pretty questionable outfit.

He quickly added, "Two Pulse Fours."

"Otto, we need you out here," said Bones, through the door that led onto the stern area.

When Otto had gone, Brett said, "Did I really hear him say state-of-the-art?"

I nodded.

"Let me tell you, Pulse Fours are not state-of-the-art, not even close. Even when they were state-of-the-art they weren't really, because they always had issues with false readings that no number of software upgrades were able to rectify," said Brett.

I couldn't help but think of Cerberus, or the re-architectured Cerberus, supposedly the new paradigm in marine-sensing devices.

How right now it was probably being used at Diablo Bay.

Where the only metals it would detect would be old fishing hooks. Rusty anchors. And beer cans.

"Okay, we're here," said Skip. And then, to nobody in particular, "Let's get that pick down."

Nobody moved.

I knew nothing about dropping anchors – except that if you're tied to one you descend very quickly – but I figured this was as good a time as any to learn.

I moved out onto the deck, a deck that was moving around a bit too much for my liking, or my safety for that matter. I skirted around the wheelhouse until I got to the bow.

I undid the pin, and the anchor dropped, the chain rattling behind it. More chain and more chain and more chain – I knew it was deep here, but not this deep.

After what seemed like ages the chain finally stopped and I put the pin back into place.

"Good job!" said Skip, as I hurried back into the wheelhouse.

"Skip, we need you out here!" came Bones's voice from the stern deck.

Skip swore, and stomped off in that direction, giving me an ideal opportunity.

Firstly, I scanned the echo sounder, but I couldn't see what I was after there.

I was starting to realize just how naked I felt without my iPhone.

My eyes moved to the next instrument, a Garmin GPS Marine.

Perfect!

There it was, in neon blue: the latitude and the longitude.

There was a pen on the chart table. I used it to scribble these coordinates on a scrap of paper I – shh, don't tell anybody – tore off the corner of a chart. With the paper in my pocket, I hurried out on the stern deck to join all the divers.

"Okay, let's get in there!" said Bones, who seemed to have snapped into command mode.

Otto already had his wet suit on and Brett had started donning his.

"Maxine?" said Bones.

"I'm not diving in that slop," she said. "Vis will be zero."

Once again I wondered what she was doing here, but then it occurred to me that there was a very simple way to counter that question: what was a fifteen-year-old private-school boy doing here?

Bones muttered something under his breath that sounded like, "Arrr, females." He turned to his other divers. "Dogger?"

"I'm in."

"Brett?"

"Let's see what it's like down there," Brett said, but just then a wave hit the boat side-on. The boat pitched and Brett went sprawling. He quickly picked himself up again, though.

Bones turned his attention to me. "What about you, Dom? You don't seem the timid type."

I looked across at Maxine.

Her eyes said it all – *Don't go!*

I looked across at Brett – his face was neutral.

"Dom's buddying up with me," said Otto. "We're getting the band back together."

I got the *Blue Brothers* reference, of course. Even though it was a pretty retro film, I didn't know anybody who hadn't seen it. Several times.

And I got what he was saying, too.

That time we'd had together, stealing the plane, flying the plane, landing the plane, although not long – only a couple of hours – had been intense. INTENSE.

Obviously, Otto felt the same way as I did.

He was Jake. I was Elwood. We had to get the band back together. But go diving in these crap conditions? Maybe we weren't on a mission from God exactly, but we on a mission nonetheless.

As I got changed into a wet suit Maxine appeared at my side.

"Dom, one day you're going to be a great diver. But right now you've only got four shallow water dives under your belt. My advice is: don't do this."

"And one rocket to the bottom," I said.

"That was never my idea," she said. "Don't do this."

In retrospect, it was great advice, but I was too busy getting the band back together to take it.

"I'm going to dive," I said.

Maxine sighed, and said, "In that case, make sure you wear this." She handed me a dive knife in its sheath. "And listen very carefully as I take you through your times."

As I strapped the knife to my leg, I listened very carefully.

Then I asked her to tell me again.

Again, I listened very carefully.

"It's all on your computer," she said, indicating the watch/tracking device that was still strapped to my wrist.

And then we were ready to dive.

Riding the anchor, the boat pitched and reared in a much more unpredictable way than before.

Even walking across the deck was hard work.

Eventually I got to the stern.

Brett was first into the water, then Otto, each of them holding one of the yellow Pulse Four metal detectors. Then it was my turn.

"Let's do it," I said, and I jumped.

As soon as I hit the water I knew Maxine was right: I was a very inexperienced diver, and this was a very bad idea. The band could wait, there was plenty of time to get it back together.

The water was soupy, and swirly, and even underwater I was getting smacked about.

Through the muck I could see Brett give the descend sign.

As for Otto, it soon became obvious that signs weren't really his thing, but I guessed he'd done as many PADI courses as he'd done flying courses. None.

Despite this, he, like Brett, was a very smooth diver – not a wasted movement or gesture.

I concentrated on following them, keeping one eye on Brett, one eye on Otto.

Through the soup, through the swirl. Towards the bottom.

Even reading my depth gauge wasn't easy: I had to bring it all the way up to my mask in order to make out the numbers.

Thirty meters now.

Although I wasn't getting quite as buffeted down here, there was something really eerie about the water.

I went deeper.

Forty meters.

I was starting to freak out now, thinking of all that water above me, all that water pressing down on me.

Get it together, Dom.

Maxine had been so right: I was too young, too inexperienced to dive in these conditions.

It's so easy to sit on the deck and mouth some slogan you've picked up from a sporting-goods manufacturer, but the reality is always very different.

And then we were there, on the bottom.

Or what I could see of the bottom.

My plan to keep within eye contact of both my fellow divers soon went awry – Otto sped off in one direction, Brett in the other.

Buddies? Who needed them?

I followed after Otto. But it didn't much feel like we were getting the band back together.

I wasn't even sure whether Otto realized I was there. If he did, he certainly gave no indication of it.

Last night, listening to Bones's, story, I'd wondered why he hadn't found the treasure – I mean, he knew the general area, didn't he? It couldn't be that difficult, could it?

But now I so got it.

It seemed to me there was even more reason to approach it methodically, scientifically, not randomly.

Because if there was any method to Otto's technique, I couldn't see it.

The bottom was very, very silty, but occasionally there would be some sort of feature: a small weedy outcrop of rock, a colony of coral.

Otto seemed to concentrate solely on these, swimming from one to the next, running the Pulse Four over them.

But what about those areas between the features? There was nothing to say the treasure wasn't under the silt.

Remembering Maxine's words, I kept track of my time at this depth on the dive computer.

When I reached the time limit I managed to get Otto's attention – *it's time to ascend*.

He didn't bother using any of the signs I'd learned – just held up his hand, fingers outstretched – *five more minutes*.

I showed him my computer.

This time he did respond with a gesture, but it wasn't one you'd find in any dive manual.

He could stay down here if he wanted – I was going to ascend. But as I went to head up, something caught my eye. It was just a piece of reef sticking out from the silt, but there was something about it that looked unusual.

I figured I could afford to give it a minute of my time, so I finned quickly towards it. As I did I could feel the current, a current I hadn't felt before, flowing strongly against me.

Just one minute, I told myself, checking my watch.

I reached the reef, holding on to it to avoid being swept away.

I was right about it being unusual!

I could make out an engine. Old and encrusted,

it had almost become part of the reef itself. I didn't think it was very significant as far as Yamashita's Gold went, but I couldn't help feeling proud of my eye.

But wait – there was something else – just the tip of it visible above the silt. Was it an anchor? Or something much more valuable?

I felt down with my other hand.

I could feel a straight edge.

If only I could see it, if only all the silt wasn't there.

I had an idea: I'd read about this technique they used in marine archaeology where a downward blast of air is used to blow the silt away.

Couldn't I do something similar with my fin?

I took one off, and holding it with both hands, I brought it down quickly.

It worked – the silt dissipated and I could see that the object was indeed only an anchor. The disappointment I felt was really intense.

But then something else caught my eye.

Something embedded in the rock.

No, it couldn't be.

I brought my face as close to it as possible – yes, it could be. A coin. Encrusted. It was roughly the same size as the Double Eagle.

The disappointment turned into elation, an elation that was turbocharged. *Welcome to the world of treasure hunting, Dom.*

I looked around for Otto.

Where are you, Jake?

Where are you, Jake?

But then through all that emotion, I had a thought. And when I say "thought," that's exactly what I mean: this came straight from my neocortex.

And this thought said: *Jake does not need to know.*

And immediately I knew this thought was the right thought.

So much for getting the band back together.

I checked my computer – I had thirty seconds left at the bottom.

I unsheathed my knife, and started hacking at the coral around the coin.

It was much harder than it looked.

I checked my computer – it was time to ascend.

I kept hacking.

The water around me was becoming cloudy again, visibility was becoming a problem. I attacked the coral with renewed vigor, stabbing at it like Bob, the *Psycho* dude. I could hardly see at all now.

Finally, a chunk of coral with the coin embedded broke away. I put it into the pocket of my BCD.

I went to put my fin back on, so I could get out of there as quickly as possible. I dropped it.

I thought of what Dr. Chakrabarty had said about the god Pan, how he'd created panic in order to help the Greeks win the battle of Marathon.

Stay calm, I ordered myself.

My first calm thought: *you don't need the fin.*

My second: *you need to move.*

I was having trouble orientating now – where was up, where was down?

Of course, my air bubbles! I checked which way they were headed, and swam in that direction.

It didn't take long to get clear of the turbid water, but the current had increased and I was getting dragged along at an incredible rate.

Stay calm, I ordered myself.

I checked my dive computer.

I was supposed to stop for five minutes at this depth.

But the current was ripping me along at such a rate I was worried I would be taken too far away from the boat.

But then I remembered what Maxine had taught us about decompression sickness: the headaches, muscular weakness or paralysis and, in some cases, breathing difficulties, unconsciousness and death.

I stopped, letting the current rip me along like the scariest ride at Dreamworld. When the five minutes were over and I came up, the boat was a spot in the distance. But Maxine, true to her word, was already in the Zodiac, already on her way to pick me up.

Her first words to me as I pulled myself on board were, "So you did your decompression stop?"

"Of course," I said.

Star Pupil couldn't let his teacher down.

"What happened to your fin?" she said.

"I lost it," I said.

A what-the? look crossed her face and then she said, "Where in the blazes is Otto?"

"Still down there," I said. "He wouldn't come up."

"What?" she said. "Brett's been up for five minutes already. Let's get you back to the boat."

Back on the boat, I was conscious of the big lump in the pocket of my BCD. The first thing I did was to put the coral with its encrusted coin into my dive bag.

"Didn't stick with your buddy?" Bones said when he saw me, in a tone that was half joking, half accusing.

"If he's not coming up now, he's a taking a big risk," said Maxine.

Bones waved away her concerns. "You guys, always by the book."

It was a pretty weird thing for somebody with his health problems, all supposedly a result of diving, to say.

"I could go down and get him," said Maxine.

"No chance of finding him," said Brett. "Not with that current ripping the way it is."

"Hey, what's the problem?" came a voice from behind us.

None of us had noticed that Otto had climbed up the ladder at the stern.

Bones smiled a crooked smile – *I told you so*.

Maxine fumed.

Brett said nothing.

By now the boat was rearing and bucking at its anchor. Skip appeared at the door at the back of the wheelhouse.

"We've got to get out of this," he said, and Bones gave a reluctant nod of his head.

"Pull the anchor."

Again this was directed to nobody in particular, again nobody in particular made a move, so I took it upon myself to go up to the bow. Here the bucking was even more exaggerated, and it wasn't easy to keep my feet.

First, I had to work out how this was done. I'd been too embarrassed to ask anybody.

But then I saw the switch – great, the winch was electric.

I looped the chain around, hit the button and the chain started winding in. All I had to do was feed it into the chain locker while the boat bounced around like one of those crazy bulls you see at the rodeo. Eventually the anchor appeared and I pinned it into place so we could head back.

It was a scary ride. The boat disappeared into the troughs, and then, when it came up over the next wave, it gathered a frightening amount of speed as it surfed back down into the trough.

The others had disappeared to various places on the boat, but I stayed with Skip.

I was intrigued, amazed, as to how he managed to keep control of the *Hispaniola*.

Or maybe I was concentrating on being intrigued and amazed just to stop being plain old worried.

He affectionately referred to the boat as "she" and "her" and "lady" and even occasionally "the missus."

As in, "She always pulls to the port a bit when the waves come in from that angle," and, "The missus will be glad to drop anchor and rest her bones."

When I asked Skip if he was married, he gave exactly the answer I expected: "Married to this old girl."

"I'm going to anchor her here," he eventually said, pointing to a bay on the sonar. "Not as much protection as I would like, but it will have to do."

"So the camp's here?" I said, pointing to another point on the map.

"Exactly," he said. "You've got some good map sense."

"And Reverie's around that headland?" I said, pointing to another area.

"Yeah, about fifteen nautical miles away."

This time when he said, "Drop the pick," I knew exactly what to do.

I retrieved my coin from its hiding place.

From our anchorage we boarded the Zodiac and made for Camp Y.

Again the helmsman – Otto this time – showed considerable skill in negotiating the whitecaps, but great sheets of spray still flew in the air.

By the time we bumped into the sand, we were all soaking wet, but there were no injuries.

I helped Otto and Brett and Maxine drag the Zodiac up onto the sand, well above the high tide mark. Even then, Otto made sure it was tied off on a tree.

As for the key, I watched, elated, as he left it in the outboard.

Because I realized I'd already made my decision: I was going to get out of this place. And Otto Zolton-Bander aka The Facebook Bandit aka the Zolt had just made it a whole lot easier for me.

SIGN OF THE ZODIAC

At dinner – you guessed it, fish stew – the conversation was about one thing and one thing only: the treasure. The urge to say something – *Hey, guess what I found, you guys?* – was enormous and a few times I had to bite my tongue, and bite it hard. I felt guilty, because I hadn't told them, and sort of cheated, because if I did then for sure I would be the total rock star in Camp Y. But my neocortex had spoken, and I knew I had to listen to it.

After such an early start, everybody was pretty tired, and after dinner they quickly made their excuses and headed for their various tents.

Finally there were only three of us left – Bones, Otto and me, sitting on folding chairs, facing the dying fire.

By that time Bones had drunk five beers. Not that I was counting or anything. Okay, I was counting or anything. Because I'd figured the more he drank, the drunker he'd become, and the sooner he'd go to bed.

Though it had occurred to me, and a terrible thought it was, that Bones never slept, that he was one of those insomniacs who stayed awake all night.

"Well, I'm going to hit the sack, too," said Otto as Bones started on his sixth beer.

"Yeah, well, sweet dreams," said Bones, and then he added the words that, to use a Bones term, pretty much shivered my timbers. "So where did you put the keys to the Zodiac, son?"

"Um, they're in it," he said.

"In it!" thundered Bones. "How many bloody times have I told you?"

"It's not as if anybody's going to steal it out here," he said.

"Never leave the keys in an outboard," said Bones. "Go and get them now!"

Otto hesitated, and I didn't blame him. Just because Bones was his dad, that didn't mean he was the boss of him. That sort of stuff, you have to earn it. But Otto went and got the keys and tossed them to his father, who put them in the grimy pocket of his grimy shorts. Otto then took himself off to bed.

"So do you need another beer?" I asked Bones.

"Man's not a camel," said Bones.

I fetched him another can.

"Did I tell you about the time me and a mate started up this bar in Angeles City in the Philippines?" he said.

"No, but I'd love to hear it," I said as enthusiastically as I could, because I figured that the more stories he told, the more beer he would drink and the more chance I would have of getting those keys.

Bones's mate's name was Ferret, and the bar was called Dingo's Breakfast or something like that, and the story wasn't really a story at all. Just all this stuff about all the beer they'd drunk and all the girlfriends they'd had, though I'm not sure "girlfriends" is the right word.

It actually made me feel a bit dirty listening to it.

But I kept smiling, and laughing, and saying stuff like "Wow!" and "Really?" and "That's wild!"

Bones drank three more beers.

When he'd finished the story, I wanted, more than anything, to have a long hot shower and go to bed. Okay, there were no showers, and no beds in Camp Y, but you know what I mean.

But instead I said, through somewhat gritted teeth, "Wow, that was so informative. You got any more stories? And can I get you another beer?"

"I'm going to tell you about how me and Ferret smuggled a surfboard full of hash into Indonesia. And sure, man's not a camel."

I actually thought this story was going to be better, and it actually did start off better, but it soon degenerated into a less coherent version of the previous story. Beer they'd drunk. Girlfriends they'd had. But Bones drank another three beers.

"So you got any more?" I said.

"Kid, you're a real stayer, I'll give you that," he slurred, because the alcohol, at last, was having an effect on him. "You're gunna like this one for sure, it's how me and Ferret cleaned out the casino in Macau."

"Man's not a camel?" I suggested.

"Too right," he said.

I don't know much about casinos or gambling, but that's probably not the reason I didn't understand this story – he was almost speaking in tongues now, really drunk ones.

"Another beer, Bones?" I said brightly when he'd finished.

"Shiver me shimbers," he slurred, looking at me, before he toppled slowly off his chair and onto the sand.

"Bones?" I said.

He didn't stir.

"Bones?" I said, even louder.

No movement at all.

I knelt down on the sand next to him. I steadied my hand. And I slid my finger into the pocket that had the key.

The tip of my finger touched metal.

"Ferret!" mumbled Bones, and I couldn't imagine what sort of dreams he was having.

I hooked the tip of my finger around the key ring and slowly, slowly, slowly pulled until it was free of the pocket, and free of Bones.

I have to admit, as I took the headlamp out of my backpack and put it on, and made for the Zodiac, I was perhaps feeling a wee bit full of myself.

Once there, I put my backpack, with its coin, in the bow and I stuck the key in the ignition – no problem, it was the right one.

Another pat on my own back.

I checked the fuel – it was about half full, but there was another full tank.

Back. Pat.

Now all I had to do was drag the Zodiac down to the water, and I'd already noticed that the water was a long way away; the tide must've gone right out.

I untied the rope and tossed it into the boat. I grabbed the stern of the Zodiac and pulled. It hardly budged.

Surely it hadn't been this hard last time?

But last time had been with other people, and I knew that Otto and Brett and Maxine were much stronger than they looked.

I used the rope to drag the boat around so that the bow was facing towards the water.

Now it would be easier, I reasoned.

It was, but not easy enough: there was no way I could drag the Zodiac all the way to the water by myself.

If I'd been full of myself before, I was pretty much empty of myself now.

Dom, you're an idiot.

A fool.

But then I remembered something I'd seen once, I couldn't recall where, but it was a man rolling a boat up a beach on two big squishy rollers. As the boat spat one roller out the back, he'd stop, go and get it, and feed it into the front.

Okay, even a science dud like me could get the physics: he was decreasing the friction. So where could I get two big squishy rollers so I, too, could decrease the friction?

Camp Y seemed somewhat deficient in the big squishy roller department, but what it did have was an abundance of much smaller, much less squishier, rollers.

I went back to where Bones was sprawled out on the sand. Making as little noise as possible, I filled a bucket with empty beer cans, carrying this back to the Zodiac.

I carefully arranged these cans side-on at the front of the Zodiac, making a sort of track for it to follow.

And then, facing the front of the boat, feet on either side of this track, I wrapped the rope tightly around both hands and pulled with all my might.

The Zodiac rolled forward!

I'm not sure that man on the beach would ever want to swap his big squishy rollers for my smaller, less squishy versions, but it worked. I just had to make sure I didn't run out of beer cans to slide over. So I was forever stopping, going around the back and gathering the cans the Zodiac had already slid over, and arranging them in the front.

It took about an hour until, finally, the Zodiac was afloat, and I was aboard.

I lowered the outboard, started it, and I was away.

The sea, so bumpy during the day, had calmed right down. There was a three-quarter moon, and no shortage of stars.

With the map in my head, I made my way towards Reverie Island, keeping about fifty meters off the darkened coast.

Despite my – so far – successful getaway, I was feeling really anxious.

What if they were already after me?

What if they were waiting for me?

What if?

What if?

What if?

Anxiety bred more anxiety; my heart was

thumping, my palms sweaty. So I turned off the outboard. The outboard ticked for a while, but then there was nothing but absolute silence.

The moon mooned, the stars twinkled, the sea said nothing.

The anxiety evaporated.

Instead, I had this how-good-is-this? feeling, this how-lucky-am-I? feeling. Take away all the noise, and the world was such a beautiful place.

I floated for a while longer, maybe fifteen or twenty minutes, before I started the outboard up again, and continued my journey.

An hour later and I was tying the Zodiac off at the deserted wharf.

As I made my way up to the motel I couldn't help thinking how remarkably straightforward my escape had been.

The Debt just wasn't like this.

Nobody chasing me.

No getting shot at.

Just a rather lovely ride in a Zodiac.

Then I saw the WRX, parked opposite the entrance to the HarbourView Motel.

Hoping they hadn't seen me, I retraced my steps, and took the back way into the motel; i.e. I scrambled over a fence.

I checked the time – it was just past four – and knocked softly on Gus's door. It opened straightaway.

And as soon as he saw me, Gus wrapped his sinewy arms around me.

"You're okay," he said.

Eventually he let go of me and I noticed that he was fully dressed. Not only that, I could see that his bags were packed.

"You were leaving?" I said.

He nodded. "On the early ferry."

"You were going to leave me behind?" I said, shocked.

"I thought you were in good hands," said Gus.

"But why?" I said.

"I have to get back home," he said, and I knew I wouldn't get any more out of him than this. Gus could out-stubborn a mule any day.

Besides, I needed to get back to the Gold Coast as quickly as possible, too. So there wasn't really much to argue about.

"We've got some company," I said.

"Yes, they've been keeping an eye on me," he said. "They see you come in?"

"I don't think so."

Gus readjusted his prosthetic, scratched at his chin. Then he took a piece of paper and a pen and wrote a note which he left on the bed.

"Let's go," he said.

We lugged our bags outside, and towards the

truck. But when I went to throw mine in the back he said, "Keep walking."

I kept walking.

When we reached the HarbourView Motel vehicle, a Toyota pickup, Gus took a quick look around before he brought something out of his pocket. He used that something to open the door of the Toyota. He slid into the driver's seat, and opened the passenger's door.

By the time I got inside, Gus had already yanked some wires out. Soon, he had the engine started.

Wow, I thought. *He's out-Zolted the Zolt here.*

"Get right down," he said.

I did as he asked, sinking as low as I could in the seat.

Gus backed the truck out, and then swung out of the driveway.

After a few minutes he said, "You can get up now."

I looked behind – there was no unwelcome WRX.

"Bob?" I said.

"He'll be understanding," said Gus. "He's that sort of bloke."

As we rolled onto the ferry, I suddenly realized something: I was still wearing Maxine's dive watch/ tracking device!

As the ferry moved off, the sun peeking over the horizon, I got out of the Toyota. I went into the bathroom, and took the lid off the cistern. Then I put the watch inside, and the lid back on again.

When I returned to the Toyota Gus said, "What's so funny?"

"It's not easy to explain," I said, thinking of that red dot on that computer at Camp Y, going back and forth, back and forth, between the island and the mainland.

INTERNATIONAL DAY OF NOT ANSWERING YOUR PHONE

All the way back to the Gold Coast, Gus driving uncharacteristically quickly, I could only think of one thing: I had to talk to them, I had to contact them, show them the coin, tell them that they were looking in the wrong place.

But it had always been one-way traffic – The Debt talking to me, telling me what to do.

Maybe Dad could help me.

I called his phone – no answer.

And again, no answer.

And again, no answer.

What was this: International Day of Not Answering Your Phone?

I couldn't call Mom because she was still in Beijing, so I called Miranda instead.

Maybe it wasn't International Day of Not Answering Your Phone, because she answered.

"How was the diving?" she said.

"Nice," I said. "Do you know where Dad is?"

"At work, I presume," she said. "At his office."

Again, I tried his phone.

Back to International Day of Not Answering Your Phone.

When we finally arrived at Halcyon Grove, Gus pulled up at the curb near the front gates.

"You're not going inside?" I said.

"I have to go somewhere," he said.

"But aren't you looking after us?"

"I have to go somewhere."

Almost before I was out of the door Gus the Mysterious had taken off again.

Back home, I decided I would have to just wait until Dad a) answered his phone or b) came home.

But waiting was probably the one skill I hadn't really developed during the time of The Debt.

So I made the decision to go to Dad's office.

I called a taxi, and as I got in I thought about the last time I'd been there.

I had some sort of vague memory of a secretary and a big desk, but it was very, very vague and I wondered if it was a memory at all or something my imagination had conjured.

Secretary, big desk: it was pretty generic stuff.

There was an obvious question to be asked; why hadn't I been to my dad's office? Because he hadn't invited me? Tick to that. Because I hadn't wanted to go, because I thought he was just a boring businessman? Tick to that, too. But, still?

"The Voss Building, please," I told the driver.

He grunted and took off.

I tried Dad's number again as we drove, but again with no luck.

We arrived and I paid the driver and entered the lobby.

Silvagni Enterprises, it said on the directory, *18th floor.*

I got into the elevator, pressed that button, but it wouldn't light up.

Did everything have to be so difficult? So Herculean?

A woman got into the elevator and swiped her security pass.

As she did, I pressed the button again. It still didn't light up.

The woman pressed *17.*

Fine, I'd get off at the seventeenth and find a way up to the eighteenth floor. The elevator flew swiftly upwards, my stomach only catching up when we reached our destination.

The woman stepped out and I followed her. She threw me a suspicious look, but I took off in the opposite direction so she didn't have a chance to say, or do, anything.

There were lots of offices here, but eventually I found what I was looking for: the fire escape.

This fire escape is alarmed, said the sign.

Poor thing, I thought.

How to deactivate the alarm?

There was no how, or if there was, it was too complicated for somebody with limited alarm-deactivation skills such as myself.

So I did it the dumb way – I yanked open the door and let the alarm ring its little heart out.

And then another alarm.

And another alarm.

A Metallica of alarmed alarms.

I ran up the stairs until I came to the eighteenth floor.

The same deal there; I had to crack open the door, which caused even more alarms to join the Metallica.

At least I was here now, and Dad, or his secretary, could deal with the fallout.

What Dad?

What secretary?

The floor was silent, the lights were off; there were no people.

I ran from room to room.

Some of them were furnished – a dusty desk with a single matchbox on it, an empty filing cabinet –

but most were not, and it was obvious that nobody had used this place for years. Even the cobwebs had cobwebs.

Dad the businessman. Dad the tycoon. Dad the fraud. Once again.

They were coming after me now, too, footsteps echoing all over the place.

I guessed I had two choices.

Explain what had happened, in which case I'd probably have to talk to the cops, and they'd have to check my story out with Dad, if they could actually find him on this International Day of Not Answering Your Phone. That would take at least one, maybe even two hours.

Two hours I couldn't afford, not if Salacia was telling the truth and E. Lee Marx was going to leave Australian waters "as soon as possible."

So really my other choice was my only choice: I had to get out of here.

Doors opening. Voices. Footsteps.

But how to make my escape?

Think, Dom!

The answer came to me as a single word, a neon sign flashing brightly in my head: *chaos*.

Sirens, footsteps, voices now – I'd created a bit, but now I needed to create even more.

I remembered on one of the desks there'd been a matchbox. I ran back, grabbed it.

Took the wastepaper basket, threw some random paper into it.

Found a smoke detector – even if the office was derelict I figured that the regulations would ensure that they had to keep the smoke detectors up-to-date.

Using a match, I set fire to the paper, and put it under the smoke detector.

The detector did its job: another blaring sound joined the Metallica.

Not enough!

I needed more chaos, more Metallica.

The radio? Perfect.

It worked – even more perfect. I turned the volume to full.

A door opened, and I threw myself under a desk.

Feet running past me. Chaos begetting chaos.

Go, Dom!

I got to my feet and made a run for the open door. Into the corridor, along the corridor, to the elevators. I pressed the button – thank heavens, it stayed illuminated.

Ding!

The elevator stopped, the doors jawed open. And I stepped inside, joining two IT types.

"Any idea what's happening?" one of them asked me.

"Chaos," I said.

The two IT types exchanged looks.

"Lot and lots of chaos," I added, in case they didn't know what I was getting at.

The elevator reached the ground floor, the doors opened, and I got out of there. As I hurried along the street, a fire engine, lights flashing, pulled up, and then another one.

Who else? I thought, because I wasn't going to give up now. In fact, that little adventure had made me even more determined. Who else was involved with The Debt?

Seb?

But how could I contact him? I didn't even have a number for him.

That was it, I'd run out of leads.

Or wait, had I?

That day at Preacher's Forest, when I'd helped rescue Brandon, I'd been woken up by the Preacher himself. His paint-stripper breath right in my face.

So must thou bear witness also at Rome! he had said.

But how had he known that?

There could only be one explanation: he was hooked into The Debt somehow.

It was a crazy thought, that the mad old man, he of the biblical ranting, was somehow involved in an organization as secretive as The Debt.

But I didn't have any other leads.

It only took me twenty minutes to get there: a bus, and some rapid walking.

Past the lake where a dad and his son were operating remote control boats, and towards the Preacher's campsite.

The sky was black, and getting blacker.

And, out towards the sea, thunder rumbled.

Apart from that, there were no other noises.

Into the clearing, and the Preacher wasn't there. His campfire was dead. I stirred it with my foot – not even any embers.

So where was he?

I remembered PJ saying that when the weather got bad he slept in the drain.

I set off in that direction.

The rain that had been threatening threatened no more; it started bucketing down. Instantly, I was soaked. Maybe not to the bone – that always seemed like a bit of an exaggeration to me – but definitely to the skin.

Up ahead, through the trees, I could see the end of the storm water drain poking out.

I increased my pace, my feet slipping and sliding in what was now mud.

If it had been bucketing down before, I'm not sure what you would call it now – you almost needed scuba gear to get through this.

So when I got into the drain, I felt instant relief.

And it took me a while – well, it seemed a while but it was probably only a few seconds – to take in the scene.

And even when I had, my brain refused to acknowledge it.

PJ and Brandon were there, something I'd half-expected; it was one of the places they slept in, after all.

And the Preacher was there, which was what I'd hoped.

Though I'd hoped for a Preacher who was vertical, and conscious.

Not a Preacher like this, who was stretched out on the concrete, covered with a tattered blanket, his eyes closed.

But what I didn't expect, what my brain wouldn't acknowledge, was Gus's presence.

What was my paternal grandfather doing here?

Why was he next to the Preacher, wiping his forehead with a white cloth which, every now and then, he dipped into a bowl of water?

"Gus!" I said.

Gus looked at me, and there was surprise in his face, but not that much.

"Dominic," he said, picking up the bowl. "Can you get me some more water?"

"Where?" I said.

Brandon snickered in that winning way he had, and it took me a second to realize why.

Outside, water was pretty much all there was. I headed back down the tunnel a bit, and held the bowl out at arm's length and it filled up in no time at all.

After I'd passed it to Gus he said, "How did you find out I was here?"

"I didn't," I said.

He said nothing, but all over his face was a big old *huh?*

Welcome to my world, Gus, the world of *huh?*

He continued wiping the Preacher's face.

"Is he sick?" I asked PJ.

She nodded.

"On the way out, I reckon," said Brandon.

"We found him by the fire," said PJ. "I wanted to call an ambulance, but he insisted no. Asked me to call this number instead."

Gus's number.

The Preacher stirred; pushing himself up on his elbows, he opened his eyes.

He may have been sick, maybe even dying, but his eyes still had that same burning intensity.

Although he took us in one at a time, his eyes seemed to linger on me.

"The Debt," I said to him. "I need to talk to them."

Now it was Brandon and PJ who had the *huh?* look.

"Not now!" snapped Gus. "Now is not the time!"

"What about what's-his-name?" I snapped back. "The dude with the liver that eagle kept eating?"

"Epic!" said an appreciative Brandon.

Gus ignored me, returning to his patient, wiping his face.

I'd come to a dead end.

I sat down.

Took a few deep breaths.

And I realized how crazy I'd been. Crazy bordering on the insane. Maybe not even bordering. *Having crossed the border, receiving the obligatory stamp in his passport, Dominic entered into the country commonly known as Insanity.*

This wasn't The Debt, this wasn't an installment. I wasn't in danger of losing my leg, not over this. Yet I'd been skittering madly from one place to another.

So what if the useless Bones crew were looking in more or less the right place.

So what if the extremely organized E. Lee Marx crew had been looking in totally the wrong place. And were probably on their way home right now.

That wasn't my responsibility, wasn't my fault.

The Preacher moaned, and I wondered how close to death he was, because I figured that was what was happening here: he was dying.

"You need some more water?" I asked Gus.

He nodded, handing me the bowl.

I held the bowl out in the rain again, and as I did so I saw some birds waddling past.

They were too big to be ducks.

Geese? I wondered.

Geese. Goose. Loose as a goose on the juice.

Again I realized how reckless I'd been, running from one place to another in order to contact The Debt.

It had been under my nose all the time.

I took out my phone and called a number, hoping International Day of Not Answering Your Phone was officially over.

"How about this rain?" said Miranda.

"Do you have Seb's number?"

There was a pause, and immediately I knew this wasn't going to be as straightforward as I'd hoped.

"What makes you think I've got it?" she said.

"Well, usually when people exchange saliva, they exchange phone numbers."

In spite of herself, Miranda laughed. "Not sure we got that far before mumsy-wumsy stuck her big nose in. Still, it's a pretty funny thing to say."

"Thanks," I said.

"Have you got somebody writing your gags these days, because I've noticed you've suddenly gotten a whole lot more amusing."

A whole lot funnier or a whole lot more desperate – who knows?

"So do you know where he lives?" I said.

Another one of those pauses, and I knew I was in trouble again.

"He's a pretty mysterious sort of guy, isn't he?" said Miranda. "I mean, I've never been to his house, never met his family, and when he used to call me his number never showed up."

She seemed to mull on this for a while before she added, "He's hot, though."

"So when are you going to see him again?" I said.

Now that I had this rep as a bit of a funny guy the pressure was on, so I added, "You know, for a bit more of the old saliva exchange."

"I'm not," she said. "Mom put her foot down, remember?" And then she added, "But he will be cleaning our pool at eight tomorrow morning."

"Thanks, sis," I said, and I hung up.

Tomorrow morning was too late for me, but she had given me a great lead.

But how was I supposed to follow it?

When you think about it, all the action types have a pretty nifty way to get around.

Superman can fly.

Batman's got the Batmobile.

James Bond's got his cars and his boats and his helicopters.

Me, I've got a grumpy old Brazilian taxi driver, and that's about it.

"Excuse me, Gus," I said.

"Yes?"

"Is there, like, anything you need?" I said.

It was a pretty flimsy pretext but fortunately Gus said, "Yes," and then proceeded to give me some very explicit directions as to what, exactly, he needed.

"Is there a car key in the pocket of his coat?" I said.

"A car key?" said Gus, whose mind, I guess, was on other things.

A hearse key, actually.

"I know where it is," said PJ.

"Okay, where is it?" I said.

"You think you can handle that beast by yourself?" she said.

"I drove a bulldozer once," I said.

"Awesome," said PJ. "Was that, like, on a date?"

Another comedian.

"I don't do dates," I said.

PJ gave me a funny look, followed by a *let's go* gesture.

I followed her out of the drain. The rain was still heavy, and by the time we reached the hearse, we were both soaked to the … yes, bone.

I watched as PJ knelt down and felt underneath a back tire. Eventually she held up a key.

"So where we headed?" she said as she unlocked the door.

"Home," I said.

"Great," she said. "I always wanted to see where you live."

As PJ drove she told me what she knew about the Preacher. It didn't take long, because she really didn't know any more than I did.

"I will miss him, though," she said, the sadness in her voice genuine.

I recalled what she'd once told me: *Us outcasts, we watch each other's backs.*

I'd already decided that it probably wasn't the greatest idea to enter Halcyon Grove in a hearse with a sixteen year old driving, so I directed PJ to park in Chirp Street.

"You want to stay here in the car?" I said. "I mean the hearse?"

"No way," she said, taking the key out of the ignition. "I'm so going to check out how the other half lives."

"You need ID to get through the front gate," I said.

PJ reached into her pocket and brought out a handful of ID cards.

"Pick a card, any card," she said, in one of those magician's voices.

The rain had stopped, and outside had that after-rain smell. We got through security without a problem and then hurried towards Gus's house.

"Dominic," came a voice, a voice from up high.

I looked up. Imogen was at her window.

Her hair out, she looked Rapunzelesque, like somebody out of a fairy tale.

"Hi, Imogen," I said, wondering how I should introduce PJ.

"Hi, Imogen," said PJ. "My name's PJ."

"Hi," said Imogen, and then to me, "I really need to tell you something."

"I've just got to get this thing for Gus," I said.

Imogen's hair shifted in the breeze.

Rapunzel! Rapunzel!

"I've got all this info about what happened to my father," she said.

"Seriously, Imogen?"

PJ gave me a sideways glance.

"That woman, Joy Wheeler, for some reason she's now my best friend and she's been sending me a whole lot of stuff."

"Can it wait?" I said, and straightaway realized that I'd said absolutely the wrong thing: of course it couldn't wait! "I'll be back in a few hours, I promise."

I felt bad, more than bad, I felt like a traitor, but what choice did I have?

"Wow, she's probably the most beautiful person I've ever seen in my life," said PJ as we neared my house.

I nodded.

"What happened to her father?"

"He was this politician who disappeared."

"Havilland," she said.

I looked at her, shocked.

"You know him?"

She shrugged and said, "I heard the name somewhere."

By this time we'd gotten to Gus's house.

I followed his directions: the fourth drawer in his desk, the manila envelope.

Now that I had that, it was time to hit our house.

"Okay, so this is how the other half lives," said PJ as we went inside.

But that was about all she said.

My mother is nothing if not organized. She is one of those a-place-for-everything-and-everything-in-its-place people.

Like you'll buy something at the shop – say a bouncy ball that looks like a huge testicle – and within ten minutes you're bored with it so you just throw it in any old drawer. And within ten minutes, guaranteed, she'll say, "But that's not where the bouncy balls that look like huge testicles live. You of all people should know that, Dominic!"

So I as soon as I opened her filing cabinet I knew it would be straightforward: I would find a receipt, with a phone number. I would then call that phone number and find a way to get them to give me the number of one of their employees: Sebastian Baresi.

I looked under *K* for Komang Pool Cleaning.

It wasn't there.

P for pool.

Not there either.

C for cleaners.

Not there either.

I just couldn't find it.

I took my phone out and googled *Komang Pool Cleaning*.

It didn't exist.

I even resorted to analog, looking it up in a tattered copy of the Yellow Pages that was on the shelf.

It wasn't in there either.

Dad's office, now this: was the whole Gold Coast one great big façade?

But then I had another thought.

"Where we going now?" said PJ, as I hurried out through the front door.

For a second I'd forgotten she was with me, and I wondered whether my explanation for all this – that I wanted to contact a long-lost relative of Gus's – was looking a little flimsy.

But if she thought so, she didn't say. I guess when you're a street kid, craziness is pretty much your life.

"We're going to talk to the security guard," I said.

"The one with the nice smile?" she said.

I nodded.

"You record the license plate number of every car that comes in here, right?" I asked Samsoni.

"That's right," he said.

"Even the pool cleaners, those sort of people?"

"Everybody."

"Do you mind if I have a look at the register?"

"I'm not supposed to let anybody look at it, Master Silvagni."

What to do? I really needed to see that register but I didn't want to compromise Samsoni at all.

PJ grabbed something from the desk and made a dash for it.

Samsoni took after her.

I hurried over to the desk, opened the register. Quickly scanned the pages.

Komang Pool Cleaning.

I took out my iPhone, snapped off a photo, put the register back where I'd found it.

I was back in my place when Samsoni returned, a Maglite flashlight in his hand.

"She dropped it and disappeared," he said, giving me an I'm-confused look and I couldn't blame him.

I wondered if he had any idea what I'd done.

"She's pretty loco," I said. "Always doing stuff like that."

"Maybe not the sort of person to bring back to your home," suggested Samsoni gently.

I agreed: she wasn't the sort of person to bring back to your home.

The sort of person you don't bring back to your home was waiting in the hearse.

"You're amazing," I said.

"I've been around," she said. "Where to now?"

"I don't know," I said, because my thinking hadn't taken me much beyond this point.

I had the license plate number, but so what? You can't call a license plate number, you can't drop around to somebody's license plate number to watch the game

"Dead end?" said PJ.

"Pretty much."

"Tell me about it," she said.

I told her about it.

"Why didn't you say?" she said, smiling, taking out her phone, calling a number.

"Hi, Sticks," she said. "Can you run a license plate for me?"

Something from Sticks.

"Yes, I know. But I'm always good for it, aren't I? Come on, you going to be one of the good guys or one of the bad guys? Your choice."

More from Sticks.

"That's my boy!" said PJ, and she read out the license plate number from the photo on my iPhone.

Then she hung up.

"Huh?" I said.

"He'll send a text," she said, and sure enough, less than a minute later her phone beeped.

She showed me the address.

It was in Chevron Heights.

I plugged it into Google Maps and we took off, me reading out the directions.

It was actually very close to my house, only ten minutes away – an ordinary suburban house in an ordinary suburban street.

But, parked in the driveway, was the Komang Pool Cleaning van.

I knocked on the ordinary suburban door.

A girl answered, holding an iPad; she looked like she was around Toby's age and I had the feeling that I'd seen her somewhere before.

"Is Seb here?" I said, my voice louder and more strident than I intended; it'd been a long day.

I could see the alarm in her face.

"Is Sebastian around?" I said.

She said something over her shoulder in a language I recognized from Italy. A man answered in the same language and the girl slammed the door shut.

Well, not quite shut, because I managed to put my foot in the way. I pushed the door open. For a while there was resistance, but then I put my whole shoulder behind it and shoved as hard as I could.

The door swung open and I was inside, hurtling down a corridor.

"Seb!" I yelled, my voice bouncing off the walls. "You there, Seb? You there?"

People were coming at me from the other end, their figures silhouetted.

I admit, I was sort of half deranged by now. Blood was thumping at my temples. And I was feeling completely reckless. I didn't care what happened to me. I just needed to say something to Seb.

Voices. One? Two? More?

A mixture of languages.

Somebody trying to pin me against the wall.

But I struggled free.

And I ducked under another set of arms.

And I pushed somebody else away.

And there was Seb, sitting at the table.

"Seb!"

I wanted to hug him.

But the look on his face was one of pure hostility.

"You have to tell them –" I started, before another set of arms grabbed me from behind.

I swung my elbow back and high, and collected whoever it was hard on the chin. A *crack!* and whoever it was let go of me.

Seb was standing, ready to get away from this madman.

But I wasn't going to let that happen. I launched myself at him, my legs two pistons.

Caught him in the midriff. We tumbled to the floor. I had him now, and he couldn't escape. I spat the words directly into his ear. "You have to tell them they're looking for Yamashita's Gold in the wrong place."

Hands had me and they were dragging me off.

"The map they've got is a phony."

Seb's eyes were burning, his face a mask of disgust.

"I know where the real treasure is," I said.

"You do not tell me anything," he said, and it was seriously like he was channeling *The Exorcist*.

"You are a debtor!" he said, or the devil that resided in him said.

I dragged the piece of coral with the coin out of my pocket. And I thrust it at him before I was dragged down the corridor and through the doorway and literally tossed out onto the road. But before I was, I managed to steal a look at the three men who had manhandled me out of the house.

Two of them I didn't know, but the third one I knew well: it was Roberto, our head gardener.

PJ helped me back onto my feet and into the hearse.

"Are you okay?" she said.

"Nothing broken," I said.

No bones, nothing like that, but I was still reeling from what Seb had said.

It was like every word had been double-dipped in hate and disgust. *You are a debtor.*

Like I was black in a world of white supremacists.

Like I was gay at a homophobic convention.

Jewish at a Nazi rally.

"Are you okay?" said PJ.

The same Seb who had helped me over the Colosseum wall, who had pulled off the great heavy metal diversion.

What had happened to him?

"I have never been hated before, not like that," I said.

"Hmmm," was all she said.

She started up the hearse, drove back up the ordinary suburban street, away from the ordinary suburban house, with its very unordinary prejudices.

"There was this one day when Brandon and I were asking for money outside that really posh place in Surfers."

"Palazzo Versace?"

"Yeah, that joint. Anyway, this old bag comes along and she's dripping in jewelry. Absolutely loaded. So I try the usual line: 'Can you spare me the bus fare to get home and see my parents?' She looks me right in the eye, and she spits in my face. Then she keeps walking like it was the most normal thing in the world. Goes inside to have her lobster or her caviar or whatever those rich old bags eat."

I tried to imagine what it would be like to have somebody else's spit running down your face.

Maybe *You are a debtor* wasn't so bad after all.

But I only thought that for a second, for as long as it took the spit to fade from my mind.

We pulled up at Preacher's, and it was actually a relief to turn my mind to other things.

I had intended to have a sneak preview of what was inside the envelope, but I hadn't had a chance and it was too late now.

Now that the rain had ceased there was a rich smell rising up from the wet earth, the sort of chunky smell you could probably grow tomatoes in.

The three people, Gus, Brandon, the Preacher, were in pretty much the same position as we'd left them.

"Everything okay?" said Gus. "You were gone for a while."

"Fine," I lied, holding out the envelope. "Is this what you wanted?"

"Lovely," said Gus, taking it from me.

Now I really wished I'd had a look at what was inside when I'd had the chance, because Gus made no move to open it.

We sat there for maybe ten minutes, nobody saying anything.

If not for the almost imperceptible rise and fall of his chest, I would've thought that the Preacher had died.

In that time I received two texts that I didn't open, both from Imogen.

Eventually the Preacher opened his eyes; there was no fire or brimstone – whatever that was – in them now. But his face seemed more relaxed, all the wrinkles ironed out.

Gus slid his hand into the envelope and pulled out a photo.

I moved closer; I wanted to see.

"Here we are," said Gus, his voice barely above a whisper. "You and Alessandro, and me."

I inched closer; I still didn't have a great view.

"You were twelve here and I must've been fourteen."

I moved closer and closer until I could see the photo clearly.

Gus had said *must've been fourteen* because he still had his leg in the photo.

I'd seen Gus's mother and father, my great-grandmother and great-grandfather, before, in that other photo I'd seen in the drawer.

The mother, old and worn.

The father with that fierce look.

"Look at Alessandro," said the Preacher, and I think that was the only time I'd ever heard him say anything that wasn't biblical. "My twin was an angel."

Gus agreed. "An angel."

My phone beeped again. *Please, not now, Im.* I looked down.

It wasn't from Imogen.

It was from an "unknown sender."

And it said, *Be at Warner's Wharf at 6 am – you are going for gold.*

Punching the air with my fist, I screamed "Yessssssssss!"

And that was the last thing my great-uncle heard before he died.

THE ARGO

Okay, I wouldn't say I've got the biggest vocabulary on the planet, but I'm pretty sure the English language does not possess the word that could adequately describe the state I was in as I stood at that empty wharf at six the next morning.

I don't think French, Portuguese or Bahasa Indonesia do either.

"Excited" did not come close.

Even a phrase like "jumping out of my skin" didn't get near it.

So I'm going to say that, as I stood at the empty wharf waiting to be picked up, I was !@#$%^&*, and let you fill in the rest.

I checked my watch – two minutes to go – but when I looked out to sea I saw no sign of a boat, or a ship, or any sort of seafaring vessel.

Another feeling was finding a way through all the

excitement – sorry, the !@#$%^&* – a feeling of apprehension.

Had I been tricked somehow? Set up?

But that didn't make sense.

Then the silence was broken by the whir of blades from up above.

A helicopter!

Swinging around, it hovered directly above me.

I wanted to run, but I knew not to.

I'd expected a boat, so of course they'd sent a chopper – I should've known not to second-guess The Debt.

The chopper landed, and I ran over and climbed on board.

The pilot held out his hand, introduced himself, but over the roar of the engine I didn't get his name. Tanned, with a square chin and blue eyes, he looked like a Chuck or a Biff or a Wow.

Once I'd strapped myself in, and put on the headset that Chuck/Biff/Wow handed me, he took off. We followed the line of the coast, the sequined ocean to our left, the coast with its high-rises to our right. Every now and then, something else would nibble, ratlike, at the very edge of my excitement – sorry, !@#$%^&*.

The Preacher dying.

Imogen on the trail of her missing father.

The fact that this was my fifth, my penultimate, installment.

But only for a fleeting second, before the !@#$%^&* took over again.

Chuck/Biff/Wow was on the radio.

"Copy that!" he said, punching some numbers into the flight deck.

As he worked the controls and we swung away from the land, heading out to the sea, something pretty basic occurred to me.

"How do I get on board?"

"We land, of course," he said.

Obviously we were talking about a very different type of vessel from the *Hispaniola*.

Clouds were starting to invade the blue morning sky and down below I could see the scuds of white.

"Though this might make it interesting," said Chuck/Biff/Wow.

After twenty minutes he was on the radio again.

"Got a visual on the *Argo*," he said.

He nudged me and pointed to his left.

Following the line of his finger I could see the *Argo*, all thirty gleaming meters of it, plowing majestically through the water, spray flying up over its bow, the vee of its wake messed up by the waves.

A very different type of vessel from the *Hispaniola*!

More talking on the radio, the gist of it being that it was too rough to land the chopper on the boat.

The excitement – the !@#$%^&* – became its opposite, became *&^%$#@!.

I wouldn't be boarding.

"So what do we do now?" I said.

"If they're serious about having you on board, which they seem to be, then I guess they will have to go into port," he said. "Which will take them eight hours at least."

The *&^%$#@! must've been written all over my face, because he added, "Unless you've done some abseiling?"

I nodded, though the abseiling I'd done had been pretty limited, and in the gym.

"I hover above the deck," said Chuck/Biff/Wow. "We drop the rope, and you abseil down. I've done it hundreds of times."

"I'm up for it," I said.

"You sure?"

"I'm sure," I said.

Chuck/Biff/Wow smiled his Chuck/Biff/Wow smile and showed me where I could find the gear: the rope, the harness, the helmet, the gloves, the life jacket. After he'd finished explaining the gear, and the procedure to me, he said, "So what do you think?"

"Let's go," I said.

It was the same technique we'd learned in the gym. Except in this case I'd be dangling over a heaving, shark-infested ocean from a helicopter.

He got back on the radio, and told them what was happening.

I put on the life jacket, the helmet, the gloves, and slipped my legs through the harness.

After Chuck/Biff/Wow had ensured that the rope was securely tied to the chopper, he showed me how to thread it through the descender. And then attach the descender to my harness.

"You still good?" he said.

I nodded. "Still good."

Chuck/Biff/Wow got back on the radio – we were ready to go.

As the *Argo* slowed down, we swooped in closer, and lower, until we were hovering about twenty meters above the deck. I could see figures in yellow spray jackets down below.

"Rope over!" said Chuck/Biff/Wow.

I threw the coil of rope out and over the helicopter's skid, and watched as it unwound, the last couple of meters landing on the *Argo*'s deck.

"No tangles?" said the pilot.

"None."

"Okay, get out there!"

Guiding with my left hand, letting the rope out with the right, I stepped onto the skid.

"Ready?"

I positioned myself on the balls of my feet, knees flexed.

"Go!" he said.

Every atom in my body told me one thing: *don't jump!* Ignoring them, I jumped out, letting the rope flow through both gloved hands.

And then I was falling down, faster and faster.

I brought my right hand up slightly. The rope bit, and I slowed.

From then on, it was pretty easy – left hand guiding, right hand braking. It was really no different from what we'd done in the air-conditioned climbing gym.

Soon eager hands reached out to grab me, to unclick the harness.

I'd done it!

I looked up and waved to Chuck/Biff/Wow. He responded with a wobble of the chopper's tail.

"Bloody Kevin, showing off again," somebody said.

Kevin?

A quick glance around the boat was enough to show that the *Argo* was indeed a very different vessel from the *Hispaniola*.

The *Hispaniola* was old. This was pretty new.

The *Hispaniola* was dirty. This was spotless.

The *Hispaniola* was disorganized. This was a boat my mum would've totally approved of: a place for everything, everything in its place.

"How was your trip, Dominic?" said a voice I recognized as belonging to the world's most successful treasure hunter.

I wanted to say !@#$%^&* but didn't quite know how to pronounce it, so went with "Way cool" instead.

E. Lee Marx looked about twenty years younger than when I'd last seen him, the light in his eyes shining brightly.

He put his arm around my shoulder and said, "It's great to have you on board, son."

He was Indiana Jones, he was Jacques Cousteau, he was Hans Solo, and he had his arm around my shoulder.

"Let's have a bite to eat and a chat."

As the boat lurched into a wave, spray flew into the air and the deck was awash with water.

"Below decks!" he added, smiling.

The people who had helped me aboard had disappeared and there was nobody around.

It was a bit strange; I'd imagined a dedicated treasure-hunting ship as a place that was always bustling with activity. But as I followed him below decks and into a cabin, we didn't see anybody at all.

There was a single bed, a fixed table and chairs, a large flat screen TV, a little bathroom with a shower and toilet, and a window or a porthole or whatever it's called with a view of the sea.

Again, I was totally surprised – I guess I'd been expecting hammocks not something that was like a pretty generic hotel room.

We sat down, but immediately there was a knock on the door and E. Lee Marx got up, returning with a tray of food: two amazing-looking ham and cheese baguettes and a chocolate milkshake.

I was pretty hungry, so I wasted no time in demolishing it all.

"I'd forgotten how much a growing boy can eat," said E. Lee Marx, looking at me admiringly. "So why don't you tell me everything? Nice and slow, there's no rush and I ain't as quick on the uptake as I used to be."

I didn't tell him everything, of course. But I told him as much of everything as I thought he needed to know. But as I did, I wondered whether, if you took The Debt out of my life, the things I'd done lately actually made any sense. Because let's face it, for most of it The Debt was the number-one motivation.

"But why were you so keen to catch this Zolt character?"

The Debt. But I couldn't say that.

"But why were you so keen to get me here?"

The Debt. But I couldn't say that. And I wondered how much E. Lee Marx knew about his employers.

"So do you, like, see much of your boss?" I said.

He gave me an odd look and said, "Funny you should ask that, because when we started out there seemed to be about three levels of management between me and them. Look, I'm not saying this is necessarily a bad thing. I've done jobs where the boss has been breathing down my neck every second of the way and you don't want that. But one of my stipulations if this search was going to continue was that I had somebody on board who had some authority, who could give a direct yes or no. So, yes, we've got our man, now."

He seemed lost in thought for a while.

"Treasure hunting's a strange business, full of strange types. Maybe that's why I've been doing it for so long. But this job, well, it's been stranger than most," he said, his hand delving into his pocket.

"If it wasn't for this," he said, his voice brighter, holding out his hand, the Double Eagle sitting on its palm, "we would've gone home long ago."

"Lucky you didn't," I said, my voice as bright as the coin he was holding.

"So let me get this right: you've actually dived in this area?"

"That's right," I said, remembering how scary it had been.

"So what can you tell me about it?"

"It was sixty meters deep," I said.

"They were diving on sixty meters?" he said incredulously.

"Sure," I said, wondering how else you were supposed to discover underwater treasure if you didn't dive on it.

"So they obviously don't have an ROV?"

"A remote-operated underwater vehicle?" I said.

"Yes, we have two of them on board, state-of-the-art, a Castor and a Pollux," he said. "I would never risk my people diving at those sorts of depths. Way too dangerous."

Wow, so I'd either been really brave or really stupid.

"And what was the bottom like?" he said.

"The visibility, I mean the vis, was really bad," I said. "It was pretty silty. And there were these wicked currents."

Okay, I'd been really stupid.

"And you wouldn't have an approximate position for me, would you?" said the world's most famous treasure hunter, a real-life Indiana Jones.

This was, without doubt, my proudest moment.

Or what I thought was going to be my proudest moment. I took out the scrap of paper, the bit I'd torn off Skip's chart and read out the latitude and longitude. E. Lee Marx referred to a piece of paper in front of him but didn't write anything down.

It was almost as if he knew already what the figures would be.

We talked a bit more until E. Lee Marx said, "Well, we've got six hours of steaming, so you may as well rest up."

Rest up?

"Plenty of DVDs to watch," he said, pointing at the plasma.

He left the room.

E. Lee Marx was right, there were plenty of DVDs.

Which was great because what I really wanted to do, more than anything in the world, while I was on the most exciting adventure of my life, was to watch DVD after DVD. Then after that, perhaps I could catch up on all the math homework I hadn't done for the last ten or so years. And then get stuck into some contextualizing actuarial solutions.

I checked my phone; no further messages from Imogen, from anybody – no signal. I chucked it on the bed. Bored, I actually did start watching the first Indiana Jones movie. I got all the way to the cave scene before I realized what a dumb choice I'd made. If you're going to be stuck in a cabin by yourself you should watch the film version of *Waiting for Godot* or some uber-mushy chick flick, something that makes being stuck in a cabin by yourself seem quite exciting.

I turned Indiana Jones off mid-exciting adventure, having decided that I deserved a little look around the ship.

I went to open the door – it was locked.

Surely not! He couldn't have locked me in. I turned the handle, pushing harder this time, but it didn't budge.

He, or somebody, had locked me in.

And the cabin instantly seemed to get smaller, shrinking to about the half the size it had been before.

I began searching my brain, trying to find some justification for this.

In the end all I could come up with was that this ship was a finely tuned mechanism and they couldn't have just anybody wandering around.

But as soon as I'd thought of that I came up with several reasons why it was crap. I wasn't just anybody, I was the reason this ship was now headed to where the treasure actually was. And if they hadn't wanted me to wander around, why hadn't they just asked me to stay in my cabin?

But there wasn't much I could do about it except watch DVDs.

I finished the first Indiana Jones movie.

And I'd just reached that part in the second when they jump off the pilotless plane in a blow-up raft when I decided that enough was enough.

The door was locked, but the window or the porthole or whatever it was called was definitely unlocked.

I pushed it wide-open and poked my head outside.

The sea, three or so meters below, looked gray and uninviting. Certainly wouldn't want to take a dip in there.

I twisted my head around to look up. The guard rail, or whatever it's called, wasn't within reach, but a life buoy that was attached to the guard rail definitely was. A plan was formulating in my head: I could squeeze through the window, hoist myself up using the life buoy, and scramble onto the deck. It actually looked pretty straightforward.

Why would you want to do a stupid thing like that, Dominic? said my internal Nanna. *Obviously they don't want you around.*

That, internal Nanna, is exactly the reason I am going to do it, to show them they can't bully me, lock me in my room like a naughty five year old.

I pulled myself through the window or porthole or whatever you call it so that I was sitting on the ledge, my body outside, legs inside.

This wasn't a particularly difficult maneuver, and if I'd been at home, with spongy lawn beneath the window, I wouldn't think twice about what I was doing. But this wasn't lawn, this was water. If I fell I would probably have a softer landing, but I'd never heard of sharks living in lawn, or any other potentially life-ending predator.

I'd also never heard of anybody being lost at lawn, or drowning at lawn.

I was starting to seriously question what I was doing.

Despite this, my right hand reached up and grabbed hold of the rope at the bottom of the life buoy. My left hand did the same.

I was now able to carefully hoist myself to my feet, my toes balanced on the edge of the window.

The next move was the trickiest: I had to pull my whole weight up and use this momentum to swing my leg over the guard rail.

But it really wasn't that difficult, I'd done stuff like this many times before.

On the count of three, I ordered myself. *One. Two. Three!*

I clenched hard, swung myself out and pulled myself upwards.

Too easy, I thought, because already I knew I had enough momentum to carry me over the guard rail.

When I was about halfway there, the life buoy came off the guard rail and, instead of going up, I went down, dropping into the ocean.

I reckon in all times of disaster there is always a second of excitement, when you're thinking: *Wow, this certainly is a spiffing adventure with a capital A!*

It was only a second, however, maybe not even that, as I plunged into the sea, the taste of salt a shock.

My first thought, as the engine's throb sent tremors reverberating through me, was: *Propellers!*

So I swam, arms thrashing furiously, away from the ship.

And when I could no longer feel the engine, I stopped.

The ship, which had seemed to be going so slowly before, was now a speedboat, something out of a James Bond film, flying away from me, disappearing in and out of view as it was obscured by the toppling waves.

I screamed at it, though I knew it was no use.

I screamed.

And I screamed.

And when I finished screaming I started crying.

Salty tears into salty ocean.

Because I knew I was dead, that I had just killed myself.

Whoever it was who had locked me in the cabin wouldn't be checking on me for hours, maybe.

Even if it wasn't hours, even if it was only minutes, I knew it would be next to impossible to find somebody in a sea as lumpy as this.

I screamed some more.

And I cried some more.

And screamed some more.

And cried some more.

As the ocean played catch with me, throwing me from one foam-crested wave to the other.

The second Indiana Jones isn't even such a bad movie, I told myself. *In fact, in some ways it's better than the first. It has that kid in it, and he's pretty cool.*

And I actually laughed at my own pathetic joke.

A sound.

What could that be?

A sound getting louder.

As I rose up on the crest of a wave, I could see it, the *Argo* heading straight for me. They were coming to get me!

I was dead no more.

It wasn't until the elation had subsided that I asked myself the obvious question: *but how?*

I remembered how E. Lee Marx had seemed to know the position before I'd told him.

I remembered what Zoe had told me once: *You are so owned.*

I realized now that she was absolutely right – I was so owned.

But how was I so owned?

I traveled back to the morning of my fifteenth birthday, the day The Debt had come into my life.

Those missing minutes, the small raised lump on my hand.

Some sort of chip had been inserted into my body.

That's how I was owned.

Thank God I was!

The *Argo* stopped about a hundred meters away and a Zodiac slid down some rails and off the stern of the ship.

As it neared me I could see E. Lee Marx on board.

He pulled me over the side.

"What the blazes were you doing?" he said, wrapping me in his arms.

It was then I noticed the man behind him.

I knew him. Not by name, but I knew him.

I'd seen him three times before. Twice in the flesh.

The first time had been at Nimbin – he was the other man who had been walking with my dad, Ron Gatto and Rocco Taverniti, talking in Calabrian. One of the Nimbin Four, as I liked to think of them.

The second time had been when Seb had been picked up on the street – I'd caught a glimpse of the driver through the open door. It was the same man.

And the third time, the not-in-the-flesh time, had been when I'd been snooping on Imogen's computer and seen a photo of her father just after he'd won an election.

The man who had been holding up her father's hand was this man. Yes, a much younger version, but it was him all right.

Suddenly three separate beings became this one man.

"If it wasn't for Art here," said E. Lee Marx, releasing me from his bear hug, "we wouldn't even have known that you were gone."

THE COVE

"So you reckon you know where this treasure is?" said Sal, in that direct manner she had.

"Well, put it this way – I'm pretty sure it isn't where you were looking," I said.

Sal chewed her bottom lip, and gave me what almost seemed like a look of gratitude.

"So you're not angry with me anymore?" I said.

"Not as angry," she conceded.

"And your mum?"

"She's okay," she said. "She flew back to Italy."

"And now you're supposed to be my minder or something?" I said.

"Why did you jump into the ocean like that?"

"I didn't jump, you idiot!"

"That's not a considerate thing to call another human being."

Salacia was right, it wasn't a considerate thing to call another human being, especially not one who was supposedly the Goddess of the Sea.

We were in her cabin, which looked exactly the same as the cabin I had been in, except for the pictures everywhere. ·

Pictures of dolphins, dolphins and – you guessed it – dolphins.

She was in one chair, I was in the other.

"Okay, I take it back," I said. "But I didn't jump, I was just leaving my room and I slipped."

Again Sal chewed some lip for a while, which, I soon realized, was what she did when she was giving something serious thought.

"The thing is," she said, "you just can't wander anywhere you like on the *Argo*."

"So I've noticed," I said.

"Some parts, I've never even been to," she said. "And it's my dad's ship."

"Do they lock you in, too?" I said.

"You heard – Dad said that was an accident."

I wasn't sure how you could accidentally lock a door, but I also didn't think it was E. Lee Marx who had done it. Either that, or he was a very good actor, because he had seemed genuinely shocked when I'd told him.

"So you just sit in your room and watch DVDs?" I said.

"And I write in my journal. And I do drawings," she said. "Do you want to see some?"

"Let me guess," I said. "They're of dolphins?"

I was right, they were of dolphins, but they were really good drawings and I couldn't help but be impressed.

"Have you ever seen *The Cove*?" she said.

"Has it got Indiana Jones in it?"

"I doubt it, it's a documentary."

I checked my watch: we had five more hours of steaming until we reached the area of Reverie, at which time, E. Lee Marx had promised me, I would be able to be part of the action.

So why not watch *The Cove*, the Indiana-Jones-less documentary, while we waited?

We actually watched it three times; well, two and a half because I feel asleep during the third screening.

I have to admit, the first time I was more fascinated by how they managed to film at the Cove; it was a sort of dummy's guide for gung-ho ecological activism.

But the second time I watched, it was all about the dolphins, and by the end I had tears splashing down my cheeks.

The third time, it was a bit of both.

But I must've nodded off, because I was woken by somebody shaking me gently.

I blinked my eyes open, and it was Imogen, saying, "Wake up, we're there."

"Imogen?" I said.

But as soon as I said her name the spell broke and Imogen's face became Sal's face.

I felt a stab of longing: I wanted Imogen to be here; and an even bigger stab of guilt: I hadn't even replied to her texts.

But the here and now asserted itself – we were there, back in the world of sunken treasure, the world of untold !@#$%^&*.

Even though I knew about the ROVs, I was still imagining a ship where the decks were bustling with activity, with divers wet-suiting up, even with Castor and Pollux getting readied for extreme underwater action.

"Dad says we can go up to the control room," Sal said.

Control room!

This was more like it!

Excitedly I followed her down a corridor, up some stairs, and into a room. One whole wall was a bank of flickering screens.

On one I could see the now-familiar contours of the Reverie Island coastline, and a shiver, no, a tremor, passed through me.

Yamashita's Treasure was down there somewhere!

E. Lee Marx was sitting on a swivel chair, a microphone on a stalk at the level of his mouth, and another man, who was obviously the tech guy, was sitting in front of an enormous console, like something out of an airplane on steroids.

It was seriously sci-fi, and so far removed from the last time I'd been in these waters that I had trouble getting my head around it.

"Welcome to the nerve center," said E. Lee Marx proudly, with a sweep of his hand. "This is Felipe, number one treasure hunter."

Felipe, with his V-neck cashmere sweater, and his comb-over, and his paunch, looked so different from my, admittedly Indiana-Jones-influenced, idea of a treasure hunter that I had to stifle a laugh.

I stood there for a while.

Screens flickered.

Felipe tapped at the keyboard a couple of times.

E. Lee Marx said some stuff into the microphone, stuff like, "Okay, we're drifting a bit to the left."

After what seemed like quite a while, but was probably only a few minutes, I said, "So when do you send down the ROVs?"

E. Lee Marx and Felipe exchanged smiles, and immediately I knew I'd said something so stupid it would probably go viral on Facebook in about five minutes.

"Not for a while yet," said E. Lee Marx and then launched into an explanation of what we were doing.

Apparently the *Argo* was presently towing something called a towfish, which was bouncing a series of acoustic pulses off the sea bottom. The resulting sonogram showed any difference in texture or material of the seafloor.

E. Lee Marx pointed to one of the many screens and said, "That's pretty much what's under us now."

The screen was a sort of uniform metallic gray.

"So there's nothing exciting there?" I said.

"Silt, I would say," said E. Lee Marx. "And a lot of it. Pretty much an archaeologist's worst nightmare."

He then told me that the *Argo* was following a searching algorithm based on the coordinates I'd given him, and when it was finished all the sonograms would be stitched together to make a map of the sea bottom in this area.

"Once we have that," he said, "all the experts knock heads together and see what we've got. If there's anything we think warrants further investigation, we drop the towfish deeper, get a more detailed sonogram. And then if it still looks promising we might go in with the ROVs."

"How long does all this take?" I said.

"Felipe?"

Felipe checked the screen in front of him.

"Well, we're about 0.24 at the moment, so that would be approximately another thirty hours for the first map."

Now I totally got all the DVDs.

And wondered why they didn't have Xboxes, PlayStations and Nintendos as well.

We stayed in the nerve center for half an hour more and Sal said, "I'm going back to the room."

"I might stay a bit longer," I said.

That bit longer became a lot longer, because it was sort of captivating watching the continually changing sonogram of the sea bottom. Mostly it was that same sort of uniform metallic gray, but occasionally there would be another feature.

"Is that something?" I would say excitedly, but neither E. Lee Marx nor Felipe would get too excited.

"Probably a bit of rubble," they would say.

"Or just a small reef."

This went on for another half hour or so.

"Do you ever miss the old days?" I eventually asked E. Lee Marx.

It was a pretty rude sort of question, but he took it in his stride.

"Of course, all old men like me miss the old days. But that's not what you're asking, is it? Do I miss the old way we used to hunt for treasure?"

I nodded, because I was sure he was going to say yes.

"Not at all," he said. "The old ways were too dangerous, too many good people died. Yes, this is a bit boring, but it is much, much safer."

Now I felt like a complete tool.

When E. Lee Marx left the room I took the opportunity to bother Felipe with further questions.

Despite the V-neck cashmere sweater, he was a pretty cool sort of guy.

"So what's that screen there?" I said.

"That's a magnometer readout," he said. "It measures ferrous metals and we use it if we find something interesting on the sonogram."

"What about the one next to it?" I said, pointing to a screen that looked as if it had been more recently installed than the others. There didn't appear to be any output on it, though, just a single unwavering line across its center.

"Okay, that's a bit hush-hush and I probably shouldn't be talking about it, but put it this way: it could revolutionize the whole science of marine remote sensing."

"It could?" I said, keeping my voice low, buying into both his enthusiasm and his sense of secrecy.

It worked, too, because he kept going.

"We're going to be trialing a new sort of transducer, one that can transmit both acoustic waves and electromagnetic currents simultaneously."

"Wow!" I said.

It wasn't much, but it was enough to keep him going.

"And apparently if we get the calibration right it will exclude lower-density sedimentary material from the final image."

Again I went with an all-purpose "Wow!"

"What really spins me out," he said, "is that this transducer was supposedly adapted from some sort of high-end telecommunication device that never even hit the market."

"Cerberus," I said, the oh-so-familiar word slipping from my lips.

It was now Felipe's turn to be surprised. "How did you know that?"

It was a question I didn't really have an answer to, not one that didn't involve a lot of explanation, so I borrowed a technique from every slippery politician I'd ever heard interviewed on TV and asked a question instead.

"So when's it coming online?" I said.

It worked, too.

"The hardware boys keep running into compatibility issues."

"Ah yes, compatibility issues," I said knowingly.

Suddenly, it was if the adapted Cerberus transducer was privy to our conversation and, ashamed of its compatibility issues, decided to do something proactive about it.

The screen flickered to life, and for the briefest of seconds there was what looked like an incredibly clear photo-like picture of the ocean floor, what it looked like under all that silt.

But then it was gone.

"See what I mean, compatibility issues," repeated Felipe.

E. Lee Marx came back into the room then to tell me it was dinnertime.

I thought this would be my opportunity to meet the rest of the crew: the salty skipper, the hardware boys, the gung-ho divers, the engineers in their oily overalls.

I was wrong.

E. Lee Marx, Sal and I ate in Sal's cabin.

The food was amazing: lasagna and a salad with this really tangy dressing. As we were eating dessert, my phone went crazy, downloading about twenty messages.

"We must've just gotten a signal," I said.

"Happens like that when you're at sea," said E. Lee Marx.

I gobbled down my dessert, excused myself and went to check my messages. There were a couple from Mom saying what a great time she was having in Beijing. How she missed all us kids. No "make sure you brush your teeth." No "make sure you change your undies."

So I guessed that Dad hadn't told her anything about my little cruise.

There was one from Dad: *keep me posted!*

There was one from Imogen: *dom, I really need to talk to you about this thing.*

There was one from my carrier.

And there was one from Zoe Zolton-Bander.

you dog

Zoe, I knew, was actually a lover of dogs, but I knew that was not exactly what she meant.

Dog, as in traitor, as in snitch.

On the one hand I didn't care what she said – I'd done the right thing, the right thing for me, Dominic Silvagni, and the right thing as far as finding Yamashita's Gold went; those incompetents were never going to bring it to the surface.

But on the other hand I knew she was absolutely right: I was about as dog as a dog could get.

Because Zoe and her brother and his father had done all the hard work as far as keeping the treasure hunt alive, turning the myth into a reality once again.

"You up for another movie?" said the Goddess of the Sea.

"Why not?" I said, thinking of the thirty agonizing hours that were needed for the search pattern to finish.

First, though, I had to send a text to Imogen. It failed – no signal. So much for the marvels of modern communication.

307

"This movie's about sharks," said Sal.

What you have to understand about Sal was that when she said "movie" she actually meant "documentary." Yes, generally it was a movie-length documentary, but it was a documentary nonetheless.

We watched the one about sharks, which actually made me feel sorry for them, especially when fisherman cut off their fins – to be used in shark fin soup – before letting them go again.

Afterwards I said good night to Sal and went to my own cabin.

But this time I did a thorough inspection of the lock on the door and then felt really embarrassed that I'd resorted to climbing through the window, because there was really nothing to it – I could've picked it in no time.

I'd never spent the night on a boat before, and I thought I would have trouble going to sleep.

The opposite was true.

As soon as I put my head on the pillow and felt the rocking of the boat, the distant thrum of the motor, I knew I was going to have no trouble getting to the wonderful land of Nod.

THE NERD CENTER

I was back in the water, the anchor tied to my gear.

Plummeting deeper and deeper.

But I couldn't untie it; the more I tried, the tighter the knot seemed to get.

Deeper and deeper I went.

My gauge said empty.

I sucked, but nothing came.

Deeper and deeper.

And no air to breathe.

Deeper …

I woke with a yell. "No!"

And it took me a while to remember where I was.

When I checked the time on my iPhone I noticed that I also had two more messages from Imogen.

when can we talk??? said the first one. *i really need to talk to you*, said the second.

Again, I tried to send her one back. Again it failed.

Feeling claustrophobic, I had to get out of the cabin. I tried the door; it was unlocked.

The corridor was well lit, and I couldn't see anybody. I followed it until I came to the door of the room I'd been in earlier, the nerve center or "nerd center," as I'd renamed it in my mind.

I knocked.

No answer, so I pushed it open.

It was exactly the same as before, with that bank of flickering screens, except there was nobody here, and on one of the screens was the familiar shape of Reverie Island.

That's weird, I thought. But then I realized it wasn't so weird at all.

The *Argo* was following a search algorithm, the towfish was sending out waves, the results were being recorded somewhere.

As E. Lee Marx himself had admitted, an operator wasn't needed for any of that.

I sat in the same chair that the world's most famous treasure hunter had sat in, and watched the sonogram.

It was the same featureless metallic gray.

Firstly making sure the microphone was definitely turned off, I gave some commands in a mock English voice.

"Move a little to the left, please, old chap.

"I say, there appears to be a rather large treasure down there. Shall we stop?

"U-boat! U-boat. U-boat on the starboard bow! Prepare the depth charges!"

But then I noticed something: the top monitor, the one that supposedly showed the output from the reconfigured Cerberus, had started working.

Not only was it working, the image it was showing was extraordinarily detailed and clear.

It was actually like looking at a video of the ocean floor. I could see every rock, every crevice.

I remembered what Felipe had said, that this would revolutionize marine remote sensing, how it would exclude lower-density sedimentary material.

I sat in the swivel chair, entranced.

It didn't seem possible that between me and what I was seeing on the monitor was more than sixty meters of saltwater. A meter or so of silt.

And then I saw it, a fleeting image on the screen.

No, it can't be!

I searched the console for some sort of rewind, some sort of recall button, but there wasn't one. Not one I could recognize, anyway.

Maybe you imagined it, I told myself.

No, you saw it.

I turned the microphone on and spoke clearly into it.

"This is Dominic Silvagni in the nerd … sorry … nerve center and I've just seen Yamashita's Gold!"

YAMASHITA'S GOLD

A man barged into the room or cabin, or whatever you call it, two minutes later.

He wasn't E. Lee Marx.

He wasn't Felipe.

He was Art Tabori.

The man who had, in a weird sort of way, saved my life.

He was older than my dad but younger than Gus. Mid-fifties, maybe – who knows with old guys?

He had silver hair, and lots of it.

Nice watch.

Rings.

Polished was the word that came to mind; he was a polished sort of man. Maybe once there had been some rough edges, but they had been dealt with and what was left was smooth and shiny. Like a gem.

"Dom," he said, his voice, like his appearance,

smooth. "I don't believe we've met, properly. My name is Arturo. Arturo Tabori."

Tabori, like the crypt in the cemetery.

I've spent some time with your relatives, the dead ones, I didn't say.

"There are some Taboris at my school," I said. "They play cello."

"No relation," he said, but then he quickly qualified that, "though all us Taboris come from the same area in Calabria."

Four successful installments, and I'd learned a little about the information game: generally you withhold, but occasionally it works just to let them know you aren't a fool.

"From San Luca?" I said.

If he was surprised by this, his impassive face gave no indication.

"San Luca," he repeated, though with the right stresses on the right syllables.

"So what's your position on the boat?" I said, though I was already pretty certain what his position was.

If Art Tabori wasn't The Debt, he was as close as you could get.

He didn't have an opportunity to answer my question, because suddenly the cabin was full of people: E. Lee Marx, Felipe, another man, and a woman.

"Kid, you better not be playing some sort of trick, because –" said the man, who had a distinct whiff of the sea about him.

The skipper, maybe. Or the divemaster. The person in charge of Castor and Pollux.

E. Lee Marx cut him off. "Dom, tell us what you saw," he said.

Had I imagined it, after all?

No, I had to have faith in what my eyes had told me.

"It was on that screen there," I said, pointing to the top one.

Unfortunately those compatibility issues had reasserted themselves, and the top screen was displaying nothing but that unwavering line again, and I couldn't really blame the man for letting out a *pffft!* of disbelief.

"Felipe, can we see what's on the disk?" said E. Lee Marx.

"Already on it," said Felipe, showing Miranda-esque dexterity with the keyboard and mouse.

"It was around three fifty-two," I said. "If that's any help to you."

Felipe threw me a grateful smile and hammered the keyboard some more.

"Okay, I've got something," he said eventually.

Pointing to a blank screen, he said, "We're looking at this monitor, folks."

All eyes were now on the screen.

Had I just imagined it? Was it a combination of the nightmare I'd just awoken from, the strange surroundings I was in, the accumulated stress of repaying The Debt? Maybe I had post-traumatic stress disorder? I'd read about that; soldiers and ambulance officers get it, people who have seen terrible things, and it plays tricks with their minds.

Is that what had happened to me?

The screen was still blank.

Another *pffft!* of skepticism from the man.

But then the first flicker: the bottom of the sea, just as I had seen it. Relief, I hadn't imagined that.

The rocks, and the fish.

A patch of sand.

The tension was unbearable. You could've sliced it with a knife. Eaten it with wasabi.

Had I imagined it? Did I have some sort of PTSD?

I heard it before I saw it.

"Oh, my living —!" said the skeptic.

"Stop it there!" said E. Lee Marx.

The frozen screen, clear as the clearest photo, showed hundreds and hundreds of bars of gold bullion strewn along the bottom.

"What do you think, Dr. Muldoon?" E. Lee Marx asked the woman.

"What do I think?" she answered, her voice tremulous. "We're looking right at Yamashita's Gold."

I didn't think anybody here could quite believe it.

"Are you sure?" said Art Tabori.

"No, I'm not sure. But what else could it be? Those bars look to be about the right size."

"Mr. Marx?" Art said, turning to the world's greatest treasure hunter.

"Dr. Muldoon's right to be cautious, but every bone in my body's telling me that this is the mother lode."

"So we start bringing it up?" said Art Tabori.

E. Lee Marx and Dr. Muldoon exchanged looks.

"We'll have to do an archaeological survey – map the area thoroughly before we disturb anything."

"No, I'm not sure you heard me properly," said Art Tabori, the smooth in his voice turning to something much more menacing. "We start bringing it up. Right now."

"I wouldn't be so sure about that," said Felipe.

All eyes immediately swung to him.

He pointed to the radar, to a blip just to our right.

"It looks like we might have us some company."

"The *Hispaniola*," I said.

THE WAITING GAME

I sat on the stern of the *Argo*, my feet dangling in the water, and looked across the mirror-calm surface towards the *Hispaniola*.

It was, at the most, fifty meters away.

Occasionally a figure would appear on its deck.

Oh, that's Bones, I would tell myself.

Or *That's Otto*.

Or *Zoe*.

Every now and then I'd hear snatches of conversation; the acoustics, far out at sea like this, played some strange tricks with voices.

I even thought I heard one of them yell something out.

"Dom, you dog!"

The waiting game, E. Lee Marx called it.

"They don't know where the gold is, but we do," he'd explained. "But we can't let them know that we know. We can't put anything in the water, not even a toe."

Guiltily I'd raised up my legs, but I knew he'd been talking figuratively: we couldn't put a ROV or a diver into the water, because they would follow them to the treasure.

I'd lowered my feet back into the deliciously cool water.

"So we play the waiting game," he'd said. "Though it's not really a game, because they've got no chance of winning. We have enough food on this boat for three months, and that's without taking into account what we can take from the sea. We have enough fresh water in the tanks for a month. But that's irrelevant because we have a desalination unit. So really we have enough water to last us forever. I reckon they've got a week in them, ten days at the most. There is a chance they could be resupplied at sea, but from what you've told me, Dom, I doubt it: their resources are already stretched. Ours haven't even been touched."

I didn't think I was very good at the waiting game, crazy with impatience as I was.

Yamashita's Gold was just sitting there on the bottom of the ocean and we were up here, twiddling our thumbs.

Or cooling our feet.

Or whatever the appropriate analogy was.

"Watch out for the sharks," said Sal from behind me.

Despite this warning she sat down next to me and did exactly what I was doing, immersing her feet into the sea.

"It's so hot," she said.

Her words really didn't give any indication of how hot it was. It was stinking. And there was absolutely no wind.

Even the seagulls perched on the rigging looked like they were over it.

There were footsteps on the deck, and E. Lee Marx was standing behind us.

"'Day after day, day after day, we stuck, nor breath nor motion,'" he said. "'As idle as a painted ship upon a painted ocean.'"

"Did you just come up with that?" I said.

He laughed. "No, not quite. It's Samuel Taylor Coleridge, *The Rime of the Ancient Mariner*."

"Do the scary bit, Dad," said Sal.

Her father didn't need any more prompting than that.

"'Water, water everywhere and all the boards did shrink; water water everywhere nor any drop to drink. The very deep did rot; O Christ! That this should ever be! Yea, slimy things did crawl with legs upon the slimy sea!'"

"Wow," I said, pulling my legs out of the slimy water with its slimy things.

"Speaking of which," said E. Lee Marx, bringing a pair of binoculars up to his face, "looks like we have some movement on yonder vessel."

Even without the binoculars I could see the gangly figure on the deck of the *Hispaniola*; it had to be Otto.

"Charming," E. Lee Marx said, putting the binoculars down.

"What is it?" I said.

He handed me the binoculars and I focused them on Otto Zolton-Bander, aka The Zolt aka the Facebook Bandit, and I sort of wished I hadn't. He'd pulled his pants down and was shaking his very bare, very white bum in our direction.

The waiting game, I thought as I moved away from Otto's bum and scanned the horizon.

I wasn't looking for anything in particular, but right on the western horizon I saw what looked like a smudge of gray.

"Is that something out there?" I said, handing the binoculars back to E. Lee Marx.

He focused on the horizon for a while.

"Maybe the waiting game won't go on for that long," he said.

"Why's that?" I said.

"Well, we've been monitoring a storm that's been flirting around this area for a while, looks pretty sizeable on the satellite. Seems like it might be headed towards us."

My first thought was: *We'll have to make a run for it.*

I was just about to say this, too, but I gave it some more consideration instead. We were a ship, a hundred meters of hi-tech maritime engineering. We didn't have to run anywhere.

The *Hispaniola* was a tough old boat, but that's all it was – a boat. They would be the ones hightailing for the coast, not us.

Now I understood the smile playing on E. Lee Marx's lips; if the storm kept coming, the waiting game was pretty much over.

Mother Nature had seen to that.

E. Lee Marx disappeared below decks and it was just Sal and me again.

The smudge on the horizon was getting darker, and the water had changed color; it was a sort of weird bronze.

If it had been still before, it was stiller than still now.

I looked over at the *Hispaniola*.

So idle.

So painted.

But why wasn't it moving?

Surely they knew about the approaching storm.

E. Lee Marx appeared again, but this time Art Tabori was by his side. Half the sky was black, swirling with clouds.

"Time to get below decks," said E. Lee Marx. "The weather bureau has just upgraded its warning."

"To what?" I said.

"Looks like we've got ourselves a cyclone," said Art Tabori, looking over at the *Hispaniola*, a smile on his face.

"Category one," added E. Lee Marx.

He must've seen the alarm on my face, because he quickly added, "That's the weakest grading, winds only up to eighty-eight kays."

Only eighty-eight kays?

Again I looked over at the *Hispaniola*, the painted ship on the painted sea.

I thought of Zoe, and Otto, and Maxine and Brett and Skip and even Bones.

"But what about them?" I said.

Art Tabori turned to me, and suddenly, again, his voice didn't sound so silky smooth. "We all make our decisions in this world," he said. "And we live with the consequences."

"If they need help, then we'll offer it, of course," said E. Lee Marx. "But I'm afraid you can't make somebody accept your assistance."

I thought about what Tabori had said; but what if Otto or Zoe hadn't made that decision? What if it had been made for them?

And I also thought about what E. Lee Marx had said.

Maybe, in special circumstances like these, you actually had to force your help on people.

"Okay, let's get below decks," said E. Lee Marx. "Nerve center is as good a place as any."

CYCLONE

In the nerve center, all eyes were on one screen and one screen only: the radar, with its approaching cyclone, an angry white swirl.

The *Argo*, apparently, had all the latest in hi-tech stabilizing equipment.

Still, when the cyclone hit, I sure felt it. The ship lurched this way, and that way, and for a second I thought we would be the ones who needed help.

But then all that hi-tech hardware kicked in and the ship became much more stable.

E. Lee Marx got on the mike. "Skipper, can you patch me to the *Hispaniola*'s radio?"

A few seconds later the reply came: "You're good to go."

"*Argo* to *Hispaniola*, do you copy me?" said E. Lee Marx.

Silence from the other end.

"*Argo* to *Hispaniola*, do you copy me?"

Not a sound.

"Maybe they sunk already," I blurted.

Felipe pointed to the radar, to a white spot in the middle of the swirling storm.

"I'm pretty sure that's them," he said.

I knew that the *Hispaniola* was a tough ship, but was she this tough?

E. Lee Marx tried again, but all he got was silence.

Twenty minutes later Felipe said, "They've just upgraded to a cat two."

Again E. Lee Marx got on the radio.

"*Argo* to *Hispaniola*, do you copy me? Do you need any help? I repeat, do you need any assistance?"

Why bother? I thought, but just as I did there was a crackle from the other end and a voice, barely audible, said, "*Hispaniola* to *Argo*, yes, we require assistance."

Thank God, I thought.

"You can kiss my hairy butt," said Bones Zolton in that broken voice of his.

And the line dropped out.

E. Lee Marx threw down the handset in disgust – the first time I'd seen him lose his temper.

I stayed there for half an hour more, a cyclone of anger brewing inside me. I so hated adults and all their rules and their protocols and their regulations.

"I have to use the head," I said, thinking that using the proper term would make it more authentic.

I actually did use the head, but afterwards, instead of returning to the nerve center, I went up the stairs. The door that led out onto the deck was shut tight and for a second I thought I wouldn't be able to open it. But, using all my might, I managed to wrench it open.

Immediately I knew why it was shut so tightly. The wind was so strong, it almost blew my teeth into the back of my head. The deck was awash with water, like some sort of crazy physics experiment – what happens when waves from every possible direction meet, over and over again.

I stepped outside. Hooking one arm around the door handle, I brought the binoculars to my eyes with the other.

If the deck was a physics experiment, the ocean was a perfect lesson in chaos.

A seascape of troughs and peaks, the air full of wind-whipped spray.

Despite this, I found it almost straightaway, like it wanted me to know where it was.

Unlike the *Argo*, which sat low and let the sea wash over it, the *Hispaniola* was getting tossed from wave to wave, like some sort of plaything.

I couldn't imagine what it would be like to be on board, to be below decks, to be continually smashed from side to side.

The very thought sent an arctic chill right through me.

I was about to put the binoculars down when I saw it: flapping from one of the portholes was a white sheet.

So what? I thought.

But I knew there was nothing so-what about this, because people don't randomly hang sheets out of portholes.

And it wasn't exactly the time or place to dry your bed linen.

I had no doubt that it was a cry for help.

And I knew who it was from, too.

There was a nudge in my ribs.

Sal was standing behind me. She brought her mouth to my ear and said, "What are you doing?"

I, likewise, brought my mouth to her ear and explained what I'd seen.

"But who did it?" she said.

"Otto and Zoe," I said.

She looked at me blankly.

"These two kids," I explained, thinking again of all the adult rules and protocols and regulations. "I'm going to get them."

"But Dad said –" she started, but I didn't let her finish.

"I'm going to get them."

Immediately her bottom lip disappeared into her mouth. Until it eventually reappeared, I held grave fear as to whether it would still be whole.

It was, though.

"Okay," said Sal. "Let's go get those kids."

She walked onto the heaving deck, leaning into the wind. I followed her every step, her every motion. When we reached the Zodiac, she motioned for me to get into the front.

I pulled myself in.

She got into the back, getting as low as she could on the floor. She turned on the ignition and the outboard coughed into life. She pointed at the bow, to where the Zodiac was tied up.

I released the ratchet, let out some rope and unclicked the karabiner.

Theoretically we were supposed to now slide down the rails and off the stern and into the water.

Theoretically, because we stayed exactly where we were.

But then the *Argo*'s bow rose up, and the Zodiac began sliding, gathering speed as it flew down the rails. It happened so quickly – one second we were on the deck and the next the *Argo*'s stern was five meters away.

On my knees, I grabbed the rope that was tied to the bow, wrapping it around one hand like a bronco rider.

Sal gave some throttle and the Zodiac started to move.

But then we slid down a trough, and all around us were these huge walls of water.

We're goners, I thought.

But then, somehow, we were lifted out of this, and we were now on the crest of a huge misshapen wave.

From here I could see the *Hispaniola*, about fifty meters away. I pointed to my right, but Sal had seen it too, because she'd altered course. I'm not sure if "course" was the right word, because it seemed to me that we were completely at the mercy of the sea, trough then peak, trough then peak, the same terrifying pattern.

Even though I knew from my trip to Italy that Salacia, Goddess of the Sea, was pretty handy with an inflatable boat, I didn't realize how handy.

In a word, she was incredible.

In two words: really incredible.

How she negotiated through that chaos, I'll never know.

Just when it seemed we were going to get swamped by a toppling wave, she found a way up.

Just when it seemed we were going to get catapulted off a crest, she found a way down.

If ever there was a Zodiac event in the Olympics, she was a cert for the gold medal.

Slowly, ever so slowly, we were getting closer.

But then I saw another problem: how could the *Hispaniola* and the Zodiac, both of them tossed around like crazy, ever get to the same level so that I could attempt to scramble aboard?

They were like two high-speed elevators going in different directions.

Through a series of hand signals Sal indicated that she wanted me to board while she stayed on the Zodiac.

Should I tie the Zodiac to the Hispaniola? I signaled.

No, she signaled.

As we came closer I couldn't see a soul on board the *Hispaniola*. In fact, it had the air of a ghost ship. A very battered ghost ship, because one of its satellite dishes had come loose and there were various ropes dragging in the water.

Sal held off, waiting for the right moment.

Personally, all I could see was a whole lot of wrong moments.

But she twisted the throttle, the propeller bit, and we surged forward, the Zodiac quickly gathering momentum.

The *Hispaniola*, which had been meters above us, was dropping down, dropping down.

We met, more or less at the same level.

I didn't have time to think how she'd done it: I threw myself from the bow of the Zodiac and catapulted over the rail and crashed onto the deck of the *Hispaniola*.

I felt pain, but not of the broken-bone variety.

Now that I was aboard, I actually wasn't sure what to do next.

A real pirate would've burst into the wheelhouse, cutlass swinging, all yo ho ho and a bottle of rum! But that wasn't really my style, especially since I seemed to be somewhat deficient in the cutlass department.

The usual way into the wheelhouse was by the back door, the one that led out onto the deck I was on. The stairs that went to the downstairs cabin were right next to this.

Depending on who was in the wheelhouse, and how alert they were, it would be possible to enter it and get down those stairs without them knowing.

Difficult, but possible.

So that, now, was my plan.

I made my way along the deck – not as easy as it sounds. It was a deck awash with water, water that sometimes surged around my waist and was continually tilting this way and that.

Handhold by handhold, eventually I was at the door.

I pushed the handle. The door was locked from the inside. That was the end of that plan.

Just for a second I allowed myself to despair – why was it always so difficult? Why couldn't it be easy sometimes?

But immediately another plan was forming, pushing the despair right out of the frame.

As far as plans went, it was pretty crazy, so crazy it made pirates look like actuaries.

But I knew I had to go with this plan – there weren't a lot of options left.

Back along the deck I went, until I came to the porthole with the sheet.

Conveniently, there was a rope tangled around the guard rail. I quickly untangled it and tied one end securely around a nearby bollard. The other end I tied around my waist.

I'd already had one swim in the open ocean; I wasn't keen on another.

I waited for the right moment and hit the deck. Literally. And then I shuffled forward on my stomach. From this angle, the up-and-down motion of the boat was even more dramatic. Think of the most sick-inducing ride you have ever been on, multiply it by plenty, and you will get some idea of what I mean.

Tower of Terror? Piece of cake.

Superman Escape? Too easy.

It was like my guts were sloshing around inside my body.

Eventually my eyes were at the level of the porthole.

But of course the boat picked that very moment to roll violently, and I went under the water, just managing to grab a lungful of air before I did.

Deeper and deeper it went, less and less air was in my lungs, and just when it seemed as if it was going to roll all the way around, it started coming back the other way.

Just a little more, I kept telling myself, my lungs burning.

Just a little bit more.

We broke the surface.

Gratefully, I sucked in air and opened my eyes.

And there, at the porthole, loomed a white misshapen face.

A dead person!

The dead person wiped the mist off the glass with her dead-person hand, and it was Zoe.

Well, a version of Zoe, because this Zoe, unlike the usual one, did not have any color at all in her face.

"Dom," she mouthed.

Very perceptive of you, Zoe.

I mouthed something of my own: "Otto?"

She disappeared for a second and when she reappeared it was with Otto.

Otto was green, so green he made Kermit the Frog look anemic.

I pointed at them, and then at the deck, then made a motion with my hand as if I was twisting a throttle.

As far as charades went it was pretty crap; as far as communicating went it worked a treat because they both nodded enthusiastically. *We'll meet you on the deck.*

I shuffled back the way I had come; all I could do now was wait.

There was no use signaling Sal until I was certain that they were coming back with us.

I didn't have to wait long, however. The back door opened and the two of them appeared, holding on to each other.

That was pretty easy, I thought, but not for long because I had to signal Sal.

I waited until she was right up high on the crest of a wave, and then frantically waved at her. She responded with a less frantic wave of her own.

Goddess of the Sea?

Probably.

We were on.

I took Zoe's hand, she took Otto's hand, and we daisy-chained our way across the deck, through the churning water, to the stern.

Sal waited and she waited and she waited.

"Come on," I mouthed, anxiously looking around me, half expecting Bones to come flying through the door.

And a real pirate like him would have a cutlass, or its modern-day equivalent: an Uzi or an AK-47.

But again Sal chose the perfect moment, and the Zodiac and the *Hispaniola* met on the same horizontal plane.

Zoe scrambled on board first, and then Otto, and then it was my turn.

By this time the two boats had separated; there was perhaps a meter between them. In normal circumstances a meter jump is nothing, but, as you may have gathered, there was nothing normal about this. I hesitated – not a great idea, because it was now a meter and a half.

"Go!" yelled Sal.

I sprung up and out.

My knees hit the side of the Zodiac, and I bounced backwards, towards the roiling sea.

But a gangly figure reached out, grabbed a handful of my shirt and jerked me into the Zodiac.

My nose hit the bottom of the boat hard, and blood began gushing from it.

The pain was that sort of pain that makes you instantly angry.

You want to punch whoever did this.

Still, nice catch, Otto.

Sal again performed her miracle act, negotiating the sucking troughs and the towering peaks to get us back to the *Argo*.

Our absence had not gone unnoticed, and there were several yellow-suited figures on the deck waiting for us.

Sal came up behind the stern of the *Argo* and waited until a swell rolled beneath us.

She gunned it, and we rode that swell up and onto the stern, but when it subsided we were sitting on the guard rails, perfectly positioned.

I didn't need any prompting: I clipped the karabiner.

The yellow-suited figures were already securing the Zodiac, dragging us out of it. We were told to get out of our wet clothes, given dry ones to change into. Then there was basic first aid: somebody I had not seen before had a look at my nose.

"You've banged it up pretty good," he said. "But it's not broken."

And then it was repercussion time.

The four of us were in a room and E. Lee Marx and Art Tabori were sitting down in front of us.

"That was a pretty crazy stunt you kids pulled," said E. Lee Marx, but already from the tone of his voice I knew it wasn't going to be that bad.

And it wasn't.

It went on like this for a while, him telling us how crazy it was, how we could've all been killed.

But then he said we could go.

The four of us went to get up, but Art Tabori, who had been strangely quiet, said, "A word with our two guests, if I could."

"I'd like to stay with them," I said.

"You won't be needed, Dom," he said, and I knew there was no use arguing; when old Mr. Smooth As Snot says you're not needed, you're really not needed.

And to tell the truth, I wasn't too upset – those two were big enough and feral enough to look after themselves.

And besides, I was overcome, and "overcome" is the right word, by the need for rest.

I went back to my cabin, and closed the blind, and crawled into bed and entered into a very, very deep sleep.

GEOMETRIC DILUTION OF PRECISION

I woke to a world that seemed way too still.

I pulled up the blind to reveal a sea as flat as our pool at home. Though perhaps not quite as chlorinated.

It didn't seem possible that something so tempestuous had become so not.

I stumbled out of bed and there was breakfast sitting on the table.

There was muesli and fresh fruit and toast and I ate the whole lot of it, even scraping the last of the jam out of the little packets.

And then I went to find somebody.

It didn't take me long – the nerd center was buzzing with activity.

E. Lee Marx and Felipe were in their usual positions and Dr. Muldoon was looking at a photo that had obviously been lifted from the Cerberus output, the bars strewn across the ocean floor like pickup sticks.

"Morning," said E. Lee Marx. "How'd you sleep?"

"Like a pirate," I said, which didn't really make sense, because pirates aren't exactly renowned for their sleeping ability.

E. Lee Marx seemed to get it, though, because he said, "That's my Long John Silver."

"What happened to the cyclone?"

"Apparently it went off to terrorize some poor little Pacific island somewhere."

"And the *Hispaniola*?" I said, my eyes drawn to the radar.

"Out of range," said Felipe, which was a pretty ambiguous statement.

Out of range because they'd drifted away from us? Or – an infinitely more terrible thought – out of range because they'd sunk?

I didn't know whether to feel guilty – why hadn't I saved everybody? Or triumphant – I'd managed to snatch Otto and Zoe from Davy Jones's locker.

"Radar's only got a forty-kay range, so they're probably just hanging off us for a while," said Felipe.

"And Otto and Zoe?" I said. "Have you seen them around?"

E. Lee Marx and Felipe exchanged glances. "They're in good hands."

Again, I wasn't too upset. It was probably better that the troublesome twosome were safely locked away somewhere.

"So what happens now?" I said, envisaging hour after boring hour of towing the dreaded towfish, mapping the bottom, all that archaeological drudgery.

"We go for gold," said the world's greatest treasure hunter.

"Now?"

"As soon as we find the mother lode again."

"We dive on it?" I said, my imagination scampering ahead of me.

"Well, Castor and Pollux do."

Can you really be jealous of a machine? Yes, you can. Bloody Castor and Pollux.

I thought finding the mother lode would be a pretty straightforward procedure; the GPS position was actually printed on the photo that Dr. Muldoon was perusing.

But, of course, marine positioning isn't as easy as that; I soon learned that there is something called atmospheric error and something called signal arrival time error and something called multipath error and even something called geometric dilution of precision.

Phew!

Eventually, we – okay, they – managed to overcome

all these and we – okay, they – got the *Argo* back into roughly the right position.

Now it was up to the sensors.

The side scan sonar was working fine, but the output from the adapted Cerberus was intermittent: those compatibility issues had still not been resolved.

But the side scan sonar was not coming up with anything of interest.

"I just don't get it," said Felipe. "All that metal should be sending the sonar crazy."

I had a terrible thought: somebody had gotten there before us and taken the bars. How this was possible, I wasn't sure, but how else to explain what was happening?

"Why don't you get the other sensor working properly?" I said.

Felipe gave me a look: *Kid, you don't know what you're talking about.*

"Hardware guys have been at it twenty-four seven," said E. Lee Marx, "but they just can't crack it."

"Compatibility issues?" I said.

"You got it."

Ten minutes later, however, and those compatibility issues must've been resolved, temporarily anyway, because the screen flickered to life again.

And again the quality of the image was breathtaking.

E. Lee Marx was spewing words into the microphone, about lines and tangents and algorithms.

I looked at the screen and I said, "He needs to turn right."

"To the starboard?" said E. Lee Marx. "What makes you say that?"

"I don't know, I've just got this hunch," I said.

"Great, a hunch," said Felipe.

But E. Lee Marx wasn't so dismissive. "In the old days, hunches were sometimes all we had. Very occasionally they paid off. Mostly they didn't."

"Of course not," said Felipe.

It was a fair bet he didn't believe in Santa Claus, the Easter Bunny or the Tooth Fairy, either.

Actually, neither did I, but, eyes on the screen, I said, "Now."

E. Lee Marx hesitated, but then he said, "Swing ninety degrees to starboard."

Felipe shook his head as if to say, *So it's kids running the show now.*

Two minutes later and we were back over Yamashita's Gold – on the screen was that breathtaking image, of the gold bars strewn across the ocean's floor.

"I just had a hunch about the kid's hunch," said E Lee Marx, slapping Felipe on the back.

POLLUX AND CASTOR

Lying on my bed, swimming laps of the pool, even sitting on the toilet, I'd recovered Yamashita's Gold hundreds, maybe even thousands, of times in my mind.

The details may have varied, but the plotline was basically the same: me donning scuba gear and entering the water; cut to me descending, fins moving rhythmically; cut to me and the treasure, and I have to admit, the treasure I'd imagined was more your yo-ho-ho-and-a-bottle-of-rum treasure: a chest overflowing with pieces of eight, and diamonds and rubies and … Cut to me ascending, my arms laden with treasure, bursting out of the water and into a world that was now bigger and brighter and much, much more interesting.

Sitting in a nerd center, on a comfy chair, watching two machines wasn't anything like this.

Don't get me wrong, it was exciting, as exciting as all get-out, but it just wasn't what I'd imagined.

I'm not sure what Pollux and Castor reminded me of – giant aquatic cockroaches, perhaps. Something insectoid, anyway.

Down they went, deeper and deeper, the camera on Pollux filming Castor, the camera on Castor filming Pollux.

As they did, their movements became jerkier, more erratic.

"The currents down there are murder," said E. Lee Marx.

And then they reached silt.

It was such an anticlimax, the whole room emitted a collective groan. Including me. Even though we all knew that the image from the adapted Cerberus wasn't "real," that it had taken out the silt the same way an X-ray takes out the flesh.

"Blower time," said Dr. Muldoon.

E. Lee Marx was already talking into his microphone. "Let's engage the blower."

I'd read about using a blower; a technique developed by another famous treasure hunter, Mel Fisher, when he was working on a wreck that was covered in silt.

Basically, it was just a downward blast of water.

I'd even utilized a version of it myself by using my fin.

"We're on it," said the voice at the other end.

A minute or so later the voice said, "Engaging blower!"

The blower blew, the silt disappeared, and underneath was Yamashita's Gold, those magnificent bars of bullion.

Now there was a collective intake of breath.

Followed by cheers and high fives and back slaps.

If not the best moment in my life, it was definitely in the top ten.

I looked across at Art Tabori, and he responded with a nod. If he was The Debt, and I didn't see how he couldn't be, then I'd just repaid the fifth installment.

E. Lee Marx was back on the microphone.

"What are you waiting for, guys? Get in there and tidy up that mess."

More cheers. More high fives. More back slaps.

I'd read that the ROV's two clawed arms were controlled by different people and Felipe confirmed that this was, indeed, the case. You'd think the result would be chaos but the absolute opposite was true. It was amazing how dexterous they were, and I had to admit there was no way divers could pick up so much gold so quickly.

"Okay, guys, let's bring them up," said E. Lee Marx.

As Castor and Pollux began their ungainly ascent, those of us in the room were mesmerized by the screen; no computer game was ever so enthralling.

When there was only twenty meters to the surface, a couple of the people left the room, no doubt wanting to be on the deck when the ROVs surfaced.

I guess they, like me, needed to see the bars, touch the bars, before they could believe they were real.

That it hadn't been some film we'd all been watching.

The rest of us? Still mesmerized.

So when Felipe said, "Where did they come from?" everybody almost jumped out of their skin.

He pointed to a blip on the radar. "We've got company."

"We sure have," said Dr. Muldoon, her eyes on the video feed.

Divers.

Two of them. Three of them. Four of them!

Swimming past Castor and Pollux.

One of them wearing the most outrageous orange fins.

On the way to the bottom and the rest of the treasure.

"Gunn," said E. Lee Marx. "I'd recognize those fins anywhere."

"We need divers down there now!" screamed Art Tabori, pushing E. Lee Marx away from the mike.

"Got a visual on the boat," said a voice over

the loudspeaker. "About twenty meters long. Steel-hulled. And totally black. Not a marking on it."

It was the boat I'd seen pull into the wharf that night. The one that Gunn of the shark-made limp had boarded.

"Where are our divers?" said Tabori. "I want them armed!"

What with, machine guns? I thought, smiling to myself.

E. Lee Marx let Art Tabori scream some more before he said in a level voice, "Nobody on my boat is diving in these waters."

"Are you going to let those pirates plunder our treasure?" Art Tabori said, though with quite a few expletives thrown in there.

E. Lee Marx was back on the mike.

"Can you patch me through to the ship's radio?" he said.

A few seconds later there was a response. "Okay, you're good to go."

"This is *Argo* to unidentified vessel, can you copy me?"

No response, but E. Lee Marx persevered.

"*Argo* to unidentified vessel, can you copy me?"

This time there was a burst of static and a voice came on. "Yes, I copy."

It was a voice I knew, a voice that belonged to Cameron Jamison.

"Sir, this is E. Lee Marx from the *Argo* –" started E. Lee Marx, and I figured only an American would call somebody who was trying to steal their treasure "sir." "I'm not sure who you are and I'm not sure how much you know about diving, but we have a situation here. Those conditions down there are absolutely treacherous, over sixty meters, with silt and currents ripping. The chances of all your divers getting out of there alive aren't great."

I suppose if it was any other person speaking – except perhaps Jacques Cousteau – then Cameron Jamison would've been tempted to think, *Yeah, whatever*.

But this wasn't any other person, this was the most famous treasure hunter in the world.

"We don't all have fancy ROVs," said the voice.

E. Lee Marx sighed, a deep sigh that didn't need radio waves to travel across to that ominous black boat.

"Last year we were working on the Portuguese wreck *Las Cinque Chagas*. Maybe you've heard of it. Eighty meters of water, unstable seafloor like this. Granted, the currents were more vicious, but conditions were not dissimilar. The claim was under dispute, a number of authorities contested it. When we learned that a French naval ship was on its way, our shareholders demanded we get that treasure out, and we get it out quickly. So I sent all my divers down."

E. Lee Marx took a deep breath, and I could see the tears pooling in his eyes.

"One of those divers was my nephew," he said. "And he never came back."

Nothing from the other end, only static.

I looked over at Sal; her face was completely impassive.

E. Lee Marx continued. "I'm sure we can work this out fairly, without resorting to violence and without risking anybody's life."

Again, the only response was static.

"Sir, do you copy?" said E. Lee Marx.

Cameron Jamison's voice came from the other end. "Let's meet, then, Mr. Marx."

I happened to catch sight of Art Tabori.

His jaw was moving, but no words were coming out of his mouth.

For the next six or so hours they negotiated, Zodiacs whizzing back and forth between the two vessels.

Sal and I watched some more movie-length documentaries.

We watched *Bowling for Columbine*.

We watched *Waste Land*.

And we got halfway through the whole series of *Blue Planet* when word got out that the deal was done: Castor and Pollux would retrieve all the treasure safely and then it would be divvied up.

GOLD GOLD GONE

The Zodiac tied up and the men got out.

Cameron Jamison was dressed in a polo shirt and white shorts, like he was ready for a day on the golf course, not a spot of contemporary pirating.

With him were his usual muscle, the moronic Mattners. They both fixed me with a predictably hostile look; I smiled back at them. And there was another man, pudgy but athletic, who actually looked like a golfer. Cameron introduced him as a business associate.

As soon as he opened his mouth, my hackles rose.

It was *him*, the testicular torturer, the other Warnie.

I looked at the bars stacked neatly on the decks.

Even in their present state, encrusted with sponge and coral, they were an extraordinary sight.

E. Lee Marx had banned people from taking photos with their smartphones, because for a while there that's all anybody wanted to do.

"Okay," said Cameron Jamison to the Mattners. "Let's get our share on the boat."

As they moved towards the bars there was another sound, coming from above, the familiar – for me, anyway – *thwocka thwocka thwocka* of a helicopter.

All eyes were on the sky.

All faces showing surprise.

Except, I noticed, Art Tabori's.

The chopper circled, then alighted on the helipad.

Three figures got out, dressed in black, toting serious-looking machine guns.

It was so unexpected, so Hollywood, I had to shake my head to make sure I wasn't watching yet another screen.

No, no screen; it was real life, or hyper-real life.

"Nobody do anything silly," said Art Tabori. "Or you'll end up in Davy Jones's locker."

Despite all that was happening, a smile found its way to my lips. That old expression!

"So what's going to happen is that the gold is going in the helicopter. And don't worry, everybody will be paid according to our agreement – I'm not about to rip anybody off," said Art, back into smoother-than-snot mode. He nodded his head towards Cameron Jamison, who scowled. "Except these bozos."

Two of the men, machine guns slung across their backs, started transferring the bars to the chopper while the other kept guard.

Not that there was much guarding to do. All the crew just sat there. So did Cameron Jamison and his men. Who was going to argue with a machine gun?

I looked across at E. Lee Marx. He just shrugged. *It's a funny business, treasure hunting.*

Eventually I heard one of the men in black say to Art Tabori, "Pilot reckons we've reached the load limit."

"Nonsense," said Tabori. "You don't need to go back with him, you can stay on the boat."

They kept on loading the bars until they were all cleared from the deck.

The pilot climbed on board the chopper, started the engine, but then cut it again. He hurried down to the deck and began an agitated conversation with Art Tabori. I couldn't hear what they were saying, but it was pretty obvious what it was about: the pilot wasn't happy flying with such a heavy payload.

They'd just reached what seemed like an uneasy resolution when the chopper kicked into life again.

How could that be?

All eyes turned towards the helipad.

Who the blazes had started it?

But I already knew the answer.

Really, who did they think they were? Fooling themselves that they could keep Otto Zolton-Bander locked up like that. He was the Zolt, for Pete's sake. The Facebook Bandit. He had 1,232,345 fans. Make that 1,232,346. Make that 1,232,347 ...

And Zoe, she was Robin to his Batman.

The man in black nearest to the helipad raised his machine gun.

Tabori gave the nod: *Take them out.*

But a weight belt came flying through the air and collected the man in black on the side of the head, knocking the gun out of his hands, across the deck and into the water.

When I looked over at E. Lee Marx I could see the Indiana Jones he'd once been.

The helicopter took off.

Well, it sort of took off, lurching drunkenly this way and that, as though it had vodka instead of aviation fuel in its tank.

I thought of that book in the Zolt's lair: *Principles of Helicopter Flight*. How much of it had he read?

"Give it some more right pedal," urged the pilot. "More elevation."

Otto Zolton-Bander must've been on the same wavelength, because the chopper lifted up higher.

"Nice work, kid," said the pilot, despite himself.

And it swung away, headed for the shore. As I watched the chopper getting smaller and smaller before it finally disappeared, I wasn't sure what to think.

Had I repaid the installment? Well, I'd done what they'd asked, I'd gotten Yamashita's Gold. It wasn't my fault that it had been heisted.

If that was the case, then it was mega-cool that a couple of kids had gotten away with all that loot, but I also wondered if they would actually get away with it, if the world would let them.

Art Tabori was already below decks, no doubt on the ship's radio, talking to people, devising ways to track them down.

I kept thinking that I should feel devastated that the treasure I had coveted for so long was now gone.

But I wasn't at all.

In fact, the treasure that had glowed so bright and golden in my mind had now pretty much lost its luster. It was just a chemical element with the symbol AU and atomic number 79.

I don't want to sound too much like some sort of hippie, but I guess it was never about the treasure as money, but about the treasure as treasure. Fifteen men on the dead man's chest, yo ho ho and a bottle of rum! – that sort of thing.

As for E. Lee Marx, he was already talking to Felipe about his next quest: "I've looked at it before, but with this new technology I think we'll have a much better chance."

Soon after, there was that now-familiar sound from above and another chopper landed on the *Argo*.

Art Tabori and his goons climbed aboard and they were gone.

Again, I wondered about Otto and Zoe: were they really going to get away with it?

"Well, we better get you back to port," said E. Lee Marx. "The weather looks good, what say we run you into Reverie in the Zodiac?"

For a second I had the greatest idea I'd ever had: I'd stay on the *Argo*, join the crew, and travel the world in search of treasure.

Become an *Argo*-naut!

But the greatest idea I ever had lasted about a nanosecond.

I had one more installment to pay – one! – and I would then be free from The Debt forever, free to live my own life.

Who knows, one day I might travel the world in search of treasure, but not now.

"That'd be great," I said. "But I'd have to contact somebody to pick me up."

Using the ship's sat-phone, I tried to call Gus, but I couldn't get through to him.

So I got in touch with Dad instead.

"I'll come and fetch you myself," he said.

THE STONE DOLPHIN

I sat in the bow with Sal, while Felipe, who wanted to pick up a couple of things in port, steered the Zodiac.

We didn't talk much.

As Reverie came into sight, a pod of dolphins joined us. It was almost too much, like some cheesy movie: *Salacia, Goddess of the Sea, summons the dolphins to accompany her on her quest.*

"Friends of yours?" I joked.

"*Tursiops truncatus*," she said.

"Sorry, I don't speak Dolphin."

"Scientific name," she said, reaching over, trailing her hand in the water.

After bow-riding for a while, the three dolphins decided to put on a show, taking it in turns leaping out of the water, their blue-green flanks gleaming in the sun.

One of them even managed to pull off a somersault.

As far as shows went, it was pretty cool, and a fair bit cheaper than the one at Sealands. There was no up-selling, either. No T-shirts or lingerie.

As quickly as *Tursiops truncatus* came, they left.

As we neared the wharf, I could see a familiar boat, rust streaking its sides.

Could it be?

Yes, it was the *Hispaniola*! Or what was left of the *Hispaniola* after it had managed to limp back to port.

Relief flooded through me.

What a wreck, though. It was listing dramatically to the right – sorry, starboard – and more of it seemed broken than unbroken, if you know what I mean.

As we neared the wharf, Dad came into view. He was looking so corporate, so the antithesis of anything to do with treasure hunting, even the modern cabin-bound version, it was actually a bit embarrassing.

"That your dad?" said Sal.

"Yes," I mumbled.

We glided in and he did manage to tie us off, though.

"I guess this is it," I said to Sal.

I felt like, after all we'd been through, I should give her a hug or something.

But it didn't happen.

"Yeah," she said, in that garrulous way she had.

Her hand went into her pocket and she handed me something.

It was small stone carving of a dolphin. Not finely done; it was almost like something a child would do.

"From Chile," she said.

"Wild animals should not be kept in captivity?" I said.

"Wild animals should not be kept in captivity," she repeated.

I put the stone dolphin into my pocket and stepped onto the wharf, straight into Dad's arms.

He squeezed me tight.

"You're okay," he said. "I was so worried about you."

"I'm fine," I said, thinking of his deserted offices with their cobwebby cobwebs.

"One to go," he said.

How did he know that? I hadn't said anything on the phone.

But him saying it out loud like that made me realize exactly how colossal that should feel; five down, one to go. I was eighty percent done.

Why was I feeling so bad, then?

Like I was The Debt's little errand boy.

Their lackey.

Another rib-cracking hug from Dad.

"Home?" he said.

"Home," I said.

We got into the Porsche and I sank back into the seat, letting all that luxury envelop me.

I thought of the motel I'd stayed in with Gus, the icky sheets, the turd in the bathroom; I never, ever, wanted to be poor.

And it was Dad who had dragged our family out of the gutter; that was something I needed to keep reminding myself.

I put my now-dead iPhone on the charger. As we pulled into the service station for gas a message downloaded.

Imogen was desperate to meet, to talk to me.

I sent her a text – *let's meet tonight when i get home*.

I felt the stone dolphin in my pocket, and the most outrageous idea came into my head. *Go away, outrageous idea*, I told it.

It didn't.

I took the dolphin out of my pocket, and tossed it from hand to hand.

Wild animals should not be kept in captivity ...

The last few days I'd spent so much time just sitting there, nerd-like, peering at screens. The idea of actually doing something was incredibly exciting, incredibly seductive.

Besides, if the Zolt and Zoe could snatch Yamashita's Gold like that, surely I could do something as outrageous. It's not as if those two were any smarter, or more resourceful, or even more ruthless than I was, was it?

My mind went into full-on planning mode; when could I do it, what did I need?

I thought of *The Cove*.

And in some ways, it was a manual, a Dummy's Guide, for any aspiring ecological saboteur.

"Dad, I've got some bad news," I said as we neared the ferry.

He gave me a searching look.

"We need to go back to the wharf," I said. "I just remembered I forgot something important on the *Hispaniola*."

"No way around it?" he said.

"No way around it. I'll be five minutes. Ten at the most."

"Your seat belt on?" he said.

I nodded.

Dad checked the rearview mirror and the road ahead, and did something incredible with the hand brake and the steering wheel and the accelerator. After wheels spun, and tires smoked, we were heading in the opposite direction.

All of a sudden he wasn't so corporate anymore.

"Wow!" I said.

"Hand brake turn," he said. "I can teach you how one day."

Not for the first time, I had a glimpse of how Dad had managed to pay off all his installments.

Dad parked by the wharf and I told him to wait for me. I hurried across to the boat. It was a relief to see all the scuba gear, safely tied up.

Although a pump was noisily pumping water from the bilge, I still hoped there would be nobody aboard. Especially not Bones. Especially when I remembered what Brett had said about him: *he's got a dark side, a real dark side.* I climbed down the ladder, stepped onto the deck, and Skip popped out of the cabin, a battered double-barreled shotgun in his hands.

"Take one more step," he slurred, "and I'll blow yer brains out!"

Skipper looked as broken as his boat, his face red and splotchy, his clothes as filthy as that motel turd.

And he was drunk – yo ho ho and quite a few bottles of rum – listing from side to side as if the boat was out at sea, being rocked by the waves.

"Skipper, it's me – Dom," I said. "The kid with all the questions."

The shotgun lowered slightly.

"You done the right thing deserting like you did," he said.

The gun dropped to his side. I took this as a sign I could keep walking.

"Come inside, have a drink with me," he said.

If outside was broken, inside was even worse.

"Wow," I said. "Cleaner's day off?"

The joke, if you could call it that, didn't get a laugh from Skipper; he was too busy sloshing Bundaberg rum into two glasses.

Handing one to me, he said, "Get that inter ya."

"I'm a bit too young to drink," I said, looking at the liquid.

"Nonsense," he said. "You think you're too good to drink with me?"

I didn't see I had much choice: I drank it.

Actually, it didn't seem too bad, maybe a bit rough as it gurgled down my throat.

But when it hit my guts, that was a different story.

Basically, there was a nuclear explosion that sent my internal organs flying in all different directions.

"Hit the spot, eh?" said Skipper.

Well, "hit" seemed like the right word.

"Where's Mr. Bones?" I said, for some reason affording him an honorific he really didn't deserve.

At the mention of his name, Skipper pretty much had an apoplectic fit. His face, already red, went even redder.

"He's vamoosed!" he said.

"Where?" I said.

"When we were limping into port, he could see all the coppers on the wharf, so he jumped overboard."

"So he drowned?" I said, thinking how rough the seas had been that day.

Skip shrugged.

"Who knows. But all that money he promised, I haven't seen a red cent. And all those bills he said he'd take care of, I've now found out that he didn't. They're all coming after me now."

And then he launched into a very hard to follow story about what a fool he'd been to believe him anyway.

When he'd finished, I said, "I'm sorry, I have to get my stuff and go now."

"Your stuff?"

"Yeah, I left some diving stuff on the boat," I lied.

"You better have one for the road," he said.

Again, I didn't feel as if I had much choice.

Again, there was that nuclear explosion in my guts.

But this time I felt weirdly uncoordinated.

"I'll latch you cater," I said to Skip. "I mean, I'll catch you later."

"They're all coming after me," he said. "Every last one of them."

I made my way to where the scuba gear was.

That wasn't as straightforward as it sounds, because the deck, so stable before, had become less so. And my legs, normally so trustworthy, had likewise become less so.

Eventually I got there.

I picked out a wet suit, full tank, a regulator, a BCD, fins, mask: a lot of gear. And I don't think you realize how much stuff you need to scuba dive unless, like me, you've had two nuclear devices detonated in your guts, resulting in radiation poisoning to the legs.

I looked around for a bag to put the stuff in – there wasn't one. How to lug it all up the stairs?

Then I had a brain wave: put some of the gear on!

Which is exactly what I did, though not without some – okay, a lot of – difficulty.

My athlete's coordination, which had served me so well on so many occasions, had gone and I had a real insight into what it was like to be one of those unco kids, the sort who are always picked last for any team.

Eventually I did it and, with wet suit and fins in my hand, started climbing the ladder.

A couple of things had happened since I'd come down it: firstly, the tide had dropped so there was much further to go; and secondly, the ladder, so straight on my ascent, was now all bent.

I coached myself up, one step at a time. Until finally, thank heavens, I was standing on the wharf. I took two steps forward and fell flat on my face.

I believe the technical word for this is "slapstick," which sounds sort of funny.

It wasn't: my nose started bleeding again, and the other people on the wharf, people fishing, families out for a walk, couples holding hands, started looking at me, pointing, whispering.

Some of them didn't even bother to whisper. "I believe that boy is quite inebriated," said an old lady.

Dad must've seen what was going on, because he rushed over to help me.

"What the blazes is happening?" he said between clenched teeth.

I giggled, because, let's face it, it must've looked pretty funny: a wobbly kid in full scuba gear being helped by somebody who looked like an actuary.

Dad, I guess, didn't think it was that amusing, because he grabbed me by the arm – clawed me by the arm – and dragged me towards the Porsche.

Once there, we crammed all the stuff in the back and got out of there.

First we stopped at a service station and Dad bought me some black coffee and a big bottle of water.

"I thought this only morked on wovies," I said as we took off again. "I mean, worked on movies."

"Just get it into you," he said.

Which I managed to do.

Once I sobered up enough, I started working the radio tuner, got online on my iPhone. But breaking news: *Zolt Steals Yamashita's Gold!* was nowhere to be seen, nowhere to be heard.

Had the Zolt and Zoe really gotten away with all the treasure and – even more unlikely – gotten away without one mention in the news?

The former seemed barely possible, the latter almost the definition of impossible.

"That's highly annoying," said Dad as I changed radio stations yet again. "What exactly are you looking for?"

"Something by Justin Bieber," I said, laughing uproariously at my own joke.

WILD ANIMALS

When Dad dropped me off at home around five and said he had to head straight out for some work thing, I resisted the temptation to say something smart aleck – *Office party, is it, Dad? You and the broken photocopier?* – because him taking off like that suited me perfectly. Fortunately, there was nobody else home. Mom was still in Beijing and Miranda and Toby were ... actually, I wasn't sure where they were, but they weren't home.

I rushed up to my bedroom and got onto Skype. Making sure I had the "record conversation" option on, I called Sealands.

I could've used my iPhone, but I wanted the call to be as anonymous as possible.

"Hello, I'd like to speak to Saffrron," I said, making sure I pronounced the extra "r."

"Can I ask who's calling?"

"Yes, it's Sebastian Ovett," I said, combining the names of the two English champion runners of the eighties.

"Just a minute, Sebastian."

I was put on hold; whale sounds played.

Then Saffrron's voice. "Hi, it's Saffrron."

Again I made sure "record" was on, but said nothing.

"Hello, is anybody there? It's Saffrron here."

Still nothing from me.

"Is anybody there?" said Saffrron a couple more times, before she eventually hung up.

I copied the resultant mp3 into Audacity, and looped it until I had half an hour of Saffrron talking. Then I transferred this mp3 onto my iPhone.

Next, I checked the weather.

There was a strong wind warning, a high seas warning – perfect for my purposes, because the fewer people around the better. Still, no matter what the weather, it seemed to me that there was always somebody on the beach doing something: surfing, swimming, walking, fishing, something.

I found a large sports bag and crammed in all the gear I'd liberated from the *Hispaniola*. Then I called a taxi, and asked the driver to drop me off at the Mermaid Beach breakwater.

It was risky, but I didn't see any other way of getting there.

Fortunately she wasn't one of those nosy drivers. The only words she said, as she drove me to my destination, then processed my card, were "thank you."

Hoisting the bag over my shoulder, I made for the breakwater where the sun was setting in a sort of eerie haze. The sea was chopped up, a flurry of white. And the sand, whipped up by the wind, stung my face.

No time to be at the beach. But of course there was somebody there. A kid suddenly materialized out of the swirling sand.

He sat huddled on the sand, a hoodie stretched down over his knees.

"Hey," he said as I struggled past with my bag. "Can you please help? I'm really sick."

I kept walking, and the figure became less distinct, almost spectral, as the sand swirled around him.

His disembodied voice followed me, though: "I think I'm going to die right here."

I stopped.

I didn't believe him. Not for one second. He probably told people he was going to die, right here, in that pleading, whining, cajoling voice of his, about a thousand times a day.

But what if he did die, right here? What if he did? I took out my iPhone.

Called triple-0.

Told the operator that there was somebody lying on the beach just south of the Mermaid Beach breakwater. She told me to stay with them. She told me that they'd now logged my number and they would use that to contact me when they arrived.

"Hey, there's somebody coming," I called back to the indistinct figure.

There was no answer from the person. So I retraced my steps. He was gone, though I could just make out the indentation in the sand where he'd been sitting.

"Hey!" I yelled out. "You there?"

But there was no reply, so I called triple-0 again and told them what had happened.

"Prank-calling triple-0 is a very serious offense," said the woman.

"I wasn't prank-calling," I said. "Seriously, there was this sick kid here, but now he's gone."

I wasn't sure if she believed me or not, but again she reminded me that my number had been logged.

The breakwater wasn't really living up to its name; white water chopped and churned around it.

I unzipped the bag.

First I stripped down and put on my wet suit. Clipped on my weight belt. Then the BCD with tank and regulator attached. I put my iPhone in the waterproof pouch and attached it to my belt. Same with the waterproof flashlight. I strapped the knife to my leg. Mask on. Fins on. I piled some rocks on top of the bag, hiding it from view, and I was ready to hit the water.

I knew vis wasn't going to be good – how could it be with all that messed up water? – but I didn't realize how not good it was going to be until I went under.

Basically, there was no vis.

Basically, the sea was soup. And not one of Toby's clear, fragrant consommés, either; this was pumpkin soup, this was lentil soup, this was pea soup.

And there was quite a strong current, headed seawards.

I'd planned to swim in a more or less straight line from here across the bay to Sealands. But that plan wasn't going to work. If the current took me, if I missed Sealands, I'd eventually end up in New Zealand. I'd already been to New Zealand, on a school trip last year, and wasn't keen to return. Especially not without a passport and plenty of spending money.

So I'd have to go the long way round and follow the arc of the coast.

I kept to the bottom, using my depth gauge to make sure I wasn't going too deep, that I wasn't wandering off course. It was hard, exhausting work. And when the light faded and I had to use my flashlight, it became spooky work as well.

Objects suddenly appeared out of the murk. An old motor festooned with weeds. The ribs of a sunken boat. In clear water, during the day, I probably wouldn't take a second look at them, but in this context they became sinister, malevolent.

They were out to get me.

So it was a relief when finally, after about an hour, my flashlight picked out the mesh of the Sealands net. I'd thought that I'd have to cut through the net itself – hence the knife – but now I could see that there was a much simpler way to get on the other side.

The thick rope at the bottom of the net was tied at regular intervals to what looked like lumps of concrete.

I used the knife to saw through one of these anchor points. I was now able to push the net up enough so that I could just squeeze through underneath. There were no sirens. No sounds. I'd made it!

A shape flashed past. And then another one.

They're checking you out, that's all, I told myself.

Another shape. But this one stopped. And looked. It wasn't a dolphin.

It was a shark, a gray nurse, its mouth overcrowded with snaggled teeth.

Immediately I understood what had happened. Despite my precautions, the current had swept me past the dolphin enclosure to the shark enclosure.

Something brushed my leg.

I screamed into my mouthpiece, causing it to pop out. Water started entering my mouth. My mask was filling.

You're going to drown, I told myself.

But I also remembered what Maxine had said: *it's what you do when things go wrong, that's when all that training kicks in.*

Obviously, I was better off with the mouthpiece back in my mouth. Breathing air, not water. So I did that.

And I had no trouble clearing my mask.

I could see again.

See the sharks that were now circling me.

A small shark, less than a meter long, smudges of white on the tips of its fins, swam right up next to me. So close that I could see how horribly black its eyes were.

And it bit me on the arm!

I'm not kidding, it bit me, gave me the sort of half-playful nip that a puppy would give.

And I thought: *I've just been bitten by a shark!*

And nothing has happened. I'm not dead. I'm not bleeding. I'm not on the front page of the Gold Coast Gazette.

And it was almost as if the white-tipped shark was on my side, because the bite sort of released me from the fear that had been paralyzing me.

Dom, you need to get out of here, I told myself, as I quickly assessed my options. This didn't take long, because there weren't very many.

Either I went back out the way I came, or I found the dolphin enclosure.

So I started swimming, with long powerful strokes of my fins, towards what I hoped was the enclosure. And the sharks – there must've been at least ten of them now – swam with me.

Eventually I reached the net, except it wasn't really net, more like mesh. Steel mesh.

My sharks and I looked at the mesh, wondering what we could do next. The mesh seemed to go all the way to the bottom.

I swam down, dug around it a bit. It was buried.

There was no way under there. I could try and pull myself over, but that would mean I'd be exposed.

Or I could retrace my aquatic steps.

"What do you reckon?" I asked my companions.

But then I realized that I no longer had any companions, that all my little sharky mates had disappeared.

That's strange, I thought. *Maybe they know something I don't know.*

And suddenly, from deep within the ancient part of my brain, came this urgent warning: *Get out of here!*

I reached up, grabbed two mesh handholds, and hoisted myself upwards.

Keraang!

A huge gray torpedo smashed into the mesh just below me, where my legs had been a second ago.

Cedric the Great White Shark!

Except now his name didn't seem quite so comical.

I was half in the water, half out of the water. Out of the water, it was stunning; the water, protected here from the wind, was smooth and burnished by the moon's dull light.

Under the water, it was murder. Another *keraang!* as the great white came at me again, smashing into the mesh next to my right hip.

I knew that if I didn't get the rest of my body out, then the shark would claim it.

I'd outdo Gus then. Leg missing? Whatever. Both mine would be gone.

I frantically felt for some more handholds, and when I had them, I heaved one leg up, and over. Now that I had enough purchase, I starting pulling up the other leg.

Keraang!

The water was a swirl of shark, of leg, and fin.

I got my leg free of the water.

The bottom was missing! Bitten away.

But then I realized that it was the fin – not flesh, not blood, just high-grade graphite silicone.

I tumbled over into the other side of the mesh, into the dolphin's enclosure. And the biggest great white shark in captivity gave one last *keraang!* before he disappeared into the darkness.

Relief, and lots of it; I'd made it.

I let my body unwind, uncoil.

But then a dolphin head-butted – or nose-butted – me right in the guts.

It was the second time I'd been pile-drived in the guts. The first time it had been unexpected but not unsurprising – Tristan was a random punch-in-the-guts sort of guy. But this time it was both unexpected and completely surprising.

Dolphins are our friends.

Dolphins rescue drowning fisherman.

They don't nose-butt us humans in the guts.

"Rack off, Flipper," I wheezed.

But again it came at me, so I pushed its nose away and swam off.

As far as I could see there were no guards, no dogs.

Still, as I hoisted myself onto the wharf I half expected a siren to go off, a guard to yell out, but there was nothing, just the rhythmic sound of water lapping. It was exactly as I'd hoped – they hadn't factored in the possibility of a seaborne invasion. I checked my watch. Despite the mix-up with the enclosures, the altercation with Cedric, I was still on time.

I took my iPhone out of its waterproof casing, turned up the volume to full, hit the play button. Putting it back in its casing, I held it under the water.

"Hi, it's Saffrron. Hello, is anybody there? It's Saffrron here. Hi, it's Saffrron. Hello, is anybody there? It's Saffrron here."

A little white fin sliced through the water, making straight towards where I sat on the edge of the wharf.

A little white nose appeared at the wharf.

Putih was soon joined by other, bigger, dolphins. I put my hand in the water and Putih nuzzled her nose against it.

"Over there!" somebody shouted and I was caught in the beam of a powerful spotlight.

An alarm triggered.

All over Sealands lights were switching on.

Had Sealands been a shoot-on-sight sort of place, then I would have been one dead fifteen year old.

Even so, I was dazzled. I couldn't move.

And I could hear people converging from all directions.

"I've got him," somebody said, somebody who sounded a lot like Buzz the Security Guard.

Getting got by Buzz wasn't an option.

I crammed in my mouthpiece and was just about to push off into the water when I got hit.

Buzz was a big unit, maybe even bigger than Tristan, and he hit me hard, driving me face first into the wharf.

And then he basically sat on me.

"I've got him," I could hear him yell triumphantly. "He's all mine."

There was no use mucking around with this: I had to get Buzz off me, and I had to get him off fast, before the others came. My hand reached for the knife on my leg.

My hand unstrapped the knife.

I went to stab him in the foot.

But then I changed my mind, turned the knife upside down, and brought the hilt down as hard as I could on the tip of his boot.

The effect was instantaneous: Buzz screamed, and his bulk was off me.

I rolled off the wharf and into the water, kicking hard with one and a half fins, going down.

Above me, spotlights crisscrossed the surface, but I was too deep now for them to reach me.

Keeping to the bottom, I headed seawards, avoiding the shark enclosure.

I checked the iPhone.

"Hi, it's Saffrron. Hello, is anybody there? It's

Saffrron here. Hi, it's Saffrron. Hello, is anybody there? It's Saffrron here."

It was just as I'd planned, as I'd hoped – the dolphins were following me.

"Let's go," I said.

When I reached the net, I took out the knife and started hacking.

It wasn't easy going; the net was made from thick fibrous material.

Above me was the sound of outboard motors. I kept sawing away.

There was a boat above me, a light on me.

And then dark shapes dropping down – divers.

One final saw with the knife, and the square of net dropped down. I swam through the hole, legs thrashing hard, worried that one of the divers were after me.

It was only when I'd go some distance between me and Sealands that I risked a glance behind.

No divers were following me. But the dolphins were.

I took out the iPhone, still in its pouch, and hit the off button.

Wild animals should not be kept in captivity, I thought as I watched the dolphin shapes disappear.

It's not getting to Everest that kills people, it's getting off. I'd sort of climbed Everest and now I had to find a way off.

The obvious thing to do was to go back the way I'd come, use the flashlight to follow the curve of the coast, and then on to the beach.

But surely after all that hullaballoo at Sealands, I reasoned, they would have people on the beach waiting.

Surely.

New Zealand was not an option. Not without a passport. Not without spending money.

So really I only had one choice: to head the other way, to head north along the rocky headland. And then all the way around the other side. Even though it was pretty much all exposed cliff, there was a place where you could get up; I'd seen surfers use it in certain swells.

Yes, they might have people waiting there too. But I didn't think so.

I adopted the same technique as I had on the way here: keeping to the bottom, using my depth gauge to make sure I didn't get too deep, too far from the shore.

It was much harder going than before, though. I was getting tossed around a lot, and it was obvious that up above there was a lot going on.

I thought of sitting in that comfy chair in the nerd room, sipping a coffee, watching as Castor and Pollux did their thing. I so got E. Lee Marx now.

Still, I made steady progress.

That is, until I ran out of air.

I sucked and nothing came. I sucked harder, but still nothing came.

So I checked the gauge. Empty, it said. Emptier then empty.

But it can't be, I thought. *A tank lasts at least forty minutes!*

Under normal circumstances, a tank lasts forty minutes. Cedric the shark, caught under the cable: these weren't exactly normal circumstances. Pan had had his revenge after all: he'd made me gobble up all my precious air.

I unclipped the tank, unclipped my weights, and I surfaced.

I knew it would be rough.

Rough as guts.

But this was rougher than guts.

But the swell did have distinct troughs and peaks that formed huge waves as they made for shore, huge waves that broke and smashed upon the craggy rocks.

I looked towards the shore; there were lights flashing everywhere on the beach. Going back would certainly mean a world of pain.

I had to keep pushing on, around the headland.

But what had been possible underwater just wasn't possible on the surface. No matter how hard I swam, how hard I kicked, the swell just kept pushing me in one direction, kept pushing me towards the rocks. Really, I had only one option: arrest. And already my mind was busy manufacturing reasons why I was out swimming on such a night, in such weather, reasons that had nothing to do with Sealands or liberated dolphins.

As I did, I noticed something: the waves, as they smashed on the rocky headland, weren't random, they followed a pattern. A lull, followed by two huge waves, and then an enormous wave, and then a smaller wave, and then a lull.

It was the enormous wave that interested me, because this wave surged beyond the craggy rocks and onto the smoother rocks beyond, and sometimes even reached the vegetation, the small gnarled trees that clung stubbornly to the slope.

If I managed to catch one of these, then ...

But that was crazy – if I didn't catch it I was mincemeat.

I looked behind, at the lights flashing on the beach. At, really, my only option. Arrest. World of pain.

A lull. Two huge waves. And then an enormous wave.

A smaller wave.

A lull.

I swam towards the rocks.

A swell passed beneath me, and I could feel its power, its suction grabbing my legs, shaking them in their joints. The wave broke on the headland, water foaming around the rocks.

I swam closer.

Another swell, but this one wanted me, grabbing me, dragging me with it. I swam against it, legs and arms thrashing. And finally it let go.

Two huge waves.

And now an enormous wave.

I could feel the extraordinary suction, the water drawing back. And then building up, and I thought: *No, this is crazy, I can't do this.*

But it was too late. The wave had me, and the wave was taking me with it, and there was no getting off.

I set myself into bodysurfing position, like I'd done thousands of times before on the gentle breakers at Surfers. Body straight, head tucked in, arms straight ahead.

The wave had me, and the wave was taking me, lifting me high into the air as it crested, as plumes of water were whipped away by the wind. Ahead I could just make out the exposed rocks in the moonlight – craggy, jagged. If this wave dumped me on these, if I fell off the face, then I was gone.

The wave was breaking left to right, so I pulled in my left arm, thrust my right arm to the right. It worked; I moved across the face, staying in the wave's muscle as it took me over the rocks.

Keep going, I urged it.

But the wave was losing shape; all around it was collapsing into a tumult of swirling white water.

Ahead I could see the knotty shapes of trees.

Just a bit more, I urged it.

I could almost reach out and grab a branch. And the wave disintegrated, then I was in air, and then I was underwater, bounced against one rock, and then another rock. My arms and legs felt like they were getting ripped out of their sockets.

And then I could feel it sucking back.

Gravity was taking over, ordering all that water back into the ocean where it belonged. I knew that if I let it do this, that if I let it drag me across the rocks, I would be peeled like a banana.

So the next time I was bounced against a rock, I grabbed at it with both hands.

Left hand – nothing. But the right hand found a knob of rock, a handhold.

Both feet were scrabbling now, but it was no good with fins. I kicked one fin off, then the other half fin.

My left foot found a hole, and I jammed it in.

Right hand, left foot – it was the best I could do.

The water was streaming seaward, pushing against my body, trying to dislodge me. But I pushed into the rock, my face flattened across the rock, kissing the rock. And gradually the water's force decreased. I lifted my head up.

Smooth rock ahead, glistening under the moonlight. And beyond that the trees.

Be careful now, I warned myself. *Those rocks will be slippery.*

I pushed myself up on hands and knees, and started crawling.

Behind me, there was a roar as another wave crashed onto the rocks.

The pattern: an enormous wave, then a smaller wave.

But I knew that didn't mean anything, that patterns were made to be broken and this wave might be even bigger.

I waited for the wall of water to hit me, but it didn't. I kept crawling, and then I was grabbing wet branches.

I dragged myself from one tree to another until the branches were no longer wet, and I knew I'd made it. I stopped, my legs straddling a tree trunk. And I had that same feeling I'd had when I'd escaped from the whirling props of the tanker during the second installment.

After such a momentous experience I should be having feelings, emotions, that were equally as momentous. But I wasn't. I felt extraordinarily calm, more calm than I could ever remember feeling before.

And not only that, there weren't all these thoughts bouncing around in my head like there usually were.

It was as if the enormous wave had washed it clean.

So I just sat there, straddling the tree, feeling calm, my head clear. It seemed like hours, but it was probably only a few minutes. And then the weirdest thing happened. All the pieces of information that had been floating around in my head coalesced and became a whole, became a story.

Why hadn't I seen this before? It was so obvious, so obvious.

Zoe and Otto had set me up!

Of course they had, I told myself as yet another wave crashed onto the rocks below me.

Their putting me through the gauntlet, to test if I had the "right stuff" to join their search.

The ease with which I'd managed to escape from Camp Y.

Me "rescuing" them from the *Hispaniola*.

They'd set it all up! Played me like a Casio keyboard, because they knew that I was connected to something more organized, more resourceful than Bones's tin-pot outfit.

How did I know this?

Easy. The first time I had suspicions that they, or Otto, were searching for Yamashita's Gold was when the police arrived at the dive shop to investigate the disappearance of some dive gear; some dive gear that just happened to be extra-large!

Yes, there were some holes in my theory – how did they know for certain I would come and rescue them from the *Hispaniola*? – but I knew it was right.

And I began to laugh, and as I did I realized I hadn't laughed in a pretty long time. Not properly. Not like this. The laugh began deep in my guts, building momentum until it spilled out of my mouth.

Spasm after spasm of laughter.

Just when I thought it had subsided, it started up again.

Another wave, bigger than the others, crashed just below me, sending a cloud of spray into the air.

Enough! I told myself.

Time to get serious. Time to get out of here.

With all those trees, it was relatively easy to pull myself up the side of the slope.

And then I was on a level walking path, one of those National Park ones with little signs everywhere.

It was time to lose the wet suit, so I peeled it off and shoved it into a hollow log.

Barefoot, dressed only in board shorts, I made my way along the path, following the signs that took me to Burleigh Heads.

One of the great things about living on the Gold Coast, where women go supermarket shopping in their bikinis, is that nobody takes any notice of a barefoot kid dressed only in board shorts, even on such an inhospitable night.

Just as I walked onto the street, into a blaze of streetlights, I heard my phone beep.

I'd almost forgotten that it was still around my neck, ensconced in its waterproof pouch.

Like all phone addicts, I couldn't ignore it. Quickly, I checked who it was from. Imogen! Our meeting!

I checked my watch.

The meeting I was supposed to have gone to an hour and a half ago.

I unzipped the pouch, took out the iPhone.

I was about to call her – the apology was already working itself out in my head – when I hesitated. Better to check the message first.

i know my father is dead, it said.

No wonder she needed to talk to me! According to Imogen her father had always "disappeared." Now he was "dead"?

My phone beeped again.

Another message from Imogen

I opened it.

YOUR FATHER KILLED HIM.

I had never been so utterly, terribly alone. Who could I talk to? My parents? Sure. I wasn't even sure who they were anymore. Who could I ask whether killing another human being is ever justified?

Read the chilling conclusion to THE DEBT ...

THE DEBT

PHILLIP GWYNNE

INSTALLMENT ONE

CATCH THE ZOLT

LESSON ONE: DON'T MESS WITH THE DEBT

THE DEBT

PHILLIP GWYNNE

INSTALLMENT TWO

TURN OFF THE LIGHTS

THE DEBT

PHILLIP GWYNNE

INSTALLMENT THREE

BRING BACK CERBERUS

LESSON THREE: YOU NEVER KNOW WHO'S LISTENING

THE DEBT

PHILLIP GWYNNE

INSTALLMENT FOUR

FETCH THE TREASURE HUNTER

LESSON FOUR: SOME RULES CAN'T BE BROKEN

THE DEBT

PHILLIP GWYNNE

INSTALLMENT FIVE

YAMASHITA'S GOLD

LESSON FIVE: ALL THAT GLITTERS ISN'T GOLD

THE DEBT

PHILLIP GWYNNE

INSTALLMENT SIX

TAKE A LIFE

LESSON SIX: HE THAT DIES, PAYS ALL DEBTS